EV BISHOP

Wedding Bands

Book 1 River's Sigh B & B

WEDDING BANDS
Book 1 in the River's Sigh B & B series
Copyright © 2015 Ev Bishop

Print Edition

Published by Winding Path Books

ISBN 978-0-9937617-4-4

Cover image: Kimberly Killion / The Killion Group Inc.

Wedding Bands is a work of fiction. Names, characters, places, and incidents are either the product of the author's imagination or are used fictitiously, and any resemblance to actual persons, living or dead, business establishments, events or locales is entirely coincidental.

Prologue

The Past

JO SAT ON THE CHILLY metal bench under the grimy shelter in front of the bus station for as long as she could, kicking up gravel with the scuffed toes of her sneakers and drawing designs on the fogged up glass. Where was he, where was he, where was he?

She doodled her and Callum's names inside a heart-shaped flourish, then scrawled "True if erased!" beside it.

When she couldn't hold still any longer, Jo hopped to her feet and paced, not wanting to go inside the building because what if he arrived and thought she was the one who hadn't shown up? But it was raining harder now, and cold wind blew sheets of water into the shelter. She could care less if she was soaked to the skin usually, but the long bus ride would be uncomfortable if her jeans were soggy. Plus, she had to pee. Really bad.

She considered the cozy interior of the station—well, cozy by comparison to where she was now anyway—once more. Then looked up the street and down it. Callum's red Honda Civic was still nowhere

1

to be seen. And anyway, he'd said he was going to walk. It was getting darker, but there were streetlights. She could see all too well there was no one walking toward her in any direction. She cracked her knuckles. The movement sparkled under the streetlight, and she looked down at the delicate gold band on her left ring finger. A tiny diamond twinkled up at her. She rubbed it with her thumb and grinned.

"Callum," she whispered. Then she laughed out loud. "Callum, hurry up!"

It boggled her mind that they were doing this. They were really doing this. They were running away to get married!

But at 9:30, Callum still hadn't shown up and the bus was supposed to board at 9:48. Jo's bottom lip had a raw groove in it from her teeth. A slow but steady trickle of people filed past her into the station to buy tickets, ship boxes, and say good-bye to departing family and friends. Jo's bladder moved past discomfort. It was going to burst. And her heart might too.

She headed into the station and beelined to the washroom. The stall was cramped but clean. She relieved herself without finding any real relief at all. Why hadn't he come? Where was he?

She made her way to the payphones on the back wall by the vending machines. Her sister Sam said one day people would have miniature phones they'd carry on them at all times to call people whenever they wanted. Jo always thought that was far-fetched. Who on earth had so many people to call that they couldn't wait till they got home? But tonight, picking up the gummy receiver, she changed her mind. Personal phones weren't a terrible idea. Maybe Sam was onto something.

Jo inserted her quarter and pressed each digit in Callum's phone number with utmost care, like she was performing a ritual or charm that would bring them together—or not.

The phone rang once, rang twice—was answered midway through the third ring by a clipped, impatient voice. "Yes?"

Rats. Mr. Archer. Callum's dad. He hated her.

"Um, hello, Mr. Archer?"

No acknowledgement that yes, it was him. Not even a grunt.

"Is Callum there, please?"

Mr. Archer's voice warmed suddenly. "Is this you Tracey?"

"Um, no—"

"Oh, I'm sorry. Selene?"

"No, I'm—"

A chuckle interrupted her. "Sorry, sorry. You know how it is for an old dad, trying to keep up with a young buck's does."

A young buck's does? Jo traced a crack in the tile with her toe. What a creep.

"It's Jo," she said, "Jo Kendall."

"Oh, sorry, lad—thought you were a girl for a minute. Must be a poor connection."

Jo exhaled. Her knuckles were white on the receiver. "We've met, Mr. Archer. I've been dating Callum all year."

"Oh, *oh* . . ." There was a shuffling sound, then a porcelain clank, like a plate dropped too quickly onto another. "Well, I don't keep track. He took off with someone in a blue Volkswagen about an hour ago. I just assumed the driver was the girl in his life these days. That's not you? Not your car?"

Jo bowed her head and mumbled into the mouthpiece, "No, not me. Thanks anyway. We'll probably all meet up at the same place later." She hoped she didn't sound as miserable as she felt. Who wanted to give the horrible man the satisfaction that she'd been ditched?

She hung the phone back in place, but stayed by the booth a moment, heels of her hands pressed into her eyes. What should she do? There was another bus at 5:30 a.m. Should she try to round Callum up? But on foot in the pouring rain in the growing darkness? She had no idea where to even start to look. Greenridge had a small population, sure, but it was scattered over a huge geographic area. At the very least, she should call Ray. Of course she should! Obviously Callum would've called to say he was held up. He wasn't an asshole.

Breathing easier, she dug for another quarter.

"Yeah-lo," a raspy voice answered.

Jo smiled at the familiar, corny combination of "Yeah and hello" her uncle always used.

"Hey, Uncle Ray. It's Jo. Has Callum called by any chance?"

"He sure did, kiddo. Sounded kinda upset. I took a message. Let me see. . . ."

Jo waited for Ray to rummage through his head for scraps of the conversation, a familiar, confusing mixture of love and irritation swirling in her gut. She prayed he hadn't hit the bottle too heavy already, or who knew what mixed up, incoherent babble he'd pass on.

But Ray didn't sound overly tipsy and wasn't slurring when he said, "Ah, here it is, princess."

Jo rolled her eyes. Her uncle was the only person in the world who looked at her and saw a princess.

"I wrote it down."

"Wow, will wonders never cease?" The words slipped out before she could stop them.

Uncle Ray only laughed. "Wait a minute, I thought you said you were Jo? How come you're sounding like your big sister Sam?"

Jo shifted from one foot to the other. It was 9:39. People streamed out of the small station toward the big Greyhound rumbling outside.

"He said, um . . . " Jo could practically see Ray squinting at his barely legible scrawl. "He's sorry, but it's over. It won't work—repeated that three times, angry-like. 'It won't work—just won't work.' Does that make any sense?"

Jo closed her eyes and squeezed the bridge of her nose. It made no sense. It also made perfect sense. She could hardly speak. "Yeah, yeah, it does. Thanks."

"Call me when you get settled back at your mom's, all right?"

Jo forced a few more words out. "Yes, yes, I will."

"I love you, baby girl."

The words coaxed a blurry-eyed smile. Oh, Uncle Ray. "I love you too." And she did, but like everything in her life, it was so damned complicated. How could you love someone and not really ever be there for them? Never get your shit together? You'd think with her history, Jo would be used to it by now, but she wasn't. Some day she was going to have a home. A real one. A non-temporary, longer than a summer or a school year place to stay. She and Callum both wanted that—or then again, maybe not. Maybe just she did. She alone. Again.

She swallowed hard and stared up at the ceiling, willing the tide of saltwater in her eyes to recede. She pressed a hand to her sickish-feeling stomach. What was she going to do?

A crackly voice came over the P.A. system and announced last call for eastbound travelers.

Her suitcase was already stowed in the belly of the bus, loaded while she'd sat around waiting. It would be hard to change her mind now, even if she wanted to—and did she want to? Did she want to wander around the small town all summer, facing memories of Callum everywhere? Did she want to have some big high-drama face off with him about the how and why of him calling everything off so randomly and so last minute? No, she just couldn't. It was too hard. And Ray's, much as she loved him, wasn't the place for her anymore. Things were going from bad to worse for him—and she'd just turned eighteen, just graduated. She was too young to settle down to take care of her uncle who was drinking himself to death and refused help. Even through the pain, she knew that.

She took a deep breath, hoisted her backpack, then limped outside as if physically injured. It felt like she was. On her way toward the silver-haired bus driver who stood by the bus door collecting tickets, she passed by the shelter. The blurred words "Callum + Jo, forever. True if erased!" jumped off the glass at her. Out of habit, she lifted her hand to rub the words away, then realized how dumb she was. Her hand returned to her queasy stomach. She boarded the bus.

Chapter 1

The Present

THE EVENING AIR WAS CRISP but not yet freezing. Jo stopped in her tracks just to inhale. The comforting scent of cedar smoke from the house's chimney, the salty-sweet smell of smoking salmon, and the earthy fragrance of the changing season thrilled through her. She wanted to pinch herself. It was all really hers—well, *theirs*. Her sister Samantha would see the light eventually. Imagine living here all year round. It would be like a postcard every season. All the work was worth it. How could Samantha want to get rid of this place? Was she crazy?

The first fallen leaves gleamed gold against the dark lawn and crackled under her boots as she continued toward the old house. The porch light glowed a friendly welcome, though its beam created shadows around her that she wouldn't have noticed if there'd been no light at all.

Jo climbed the three steps to the home's wraparound porch, and leaned her trout rod against a wall, well out of the way of the door. She was careful to make sure the pretty—and more importantly, lucky—

wedding band lure, a bright beaded thing encrusted with rhinestones, was safely held in one of the rod's eyes. She tucked her tackle box beside the rod and carried her basket of treasure into the house. Fresh caught Rainbows—even their name was gorgeous. She whispered a prayer of thanks for the beauty and bounty of the area. Her stomach rumbled.

Jo whistled for Hoover, but the dog didn't come. He was probably still by the river, roaming about. She crossed her fingers that he hadn't found something disgusting to roll in—his favorite trick—and whistled again. Still nothing. Used to his selective hearing and even more selective obedience, she happily transitioned to thoughts of side dishes. Asparagus and oven-roasted baby potatoes? Rice pilaf and broccoli rabe? Mmmm.

She kicked off her rubber boots and left them where they fell. Yes, they blocked the door, but wasn't that one of the luxuries of living alone? The time would come soon enough when she had to worry about appearances and keeping everything just so. She imagined a houseful of paying guests and smiled.

She left her old black and red checked flannel jacket on. She'd get the fish frying before she cleaned up.

Halfway down the darkened hall toward the kitchen, Jo's stomach tightened. There was a light on—and she knew she'd turned them all off.

"Hello?" she called, and felt stupid when she realized she'd clutched the buck knife attached to her belt.

What was she going to do? Stab an intruder?

"Hello," she said again, louder.

The voice that answered almost stopped her heart.

"Jo—is that you, finally? I've been waiting all night. Where were you?"

Jo relaxed her grip on the knife handle reluctantly. If there was someone she actually wouldn't mind stabbing it would be—

"Come on, don't you have a kiss for your sis?"

—Yep, her "sis." Samantha.

Jo flipped a switch, and another feeble bulb lit up. It didn't do much to brighten the wood panel hall, but would keep Jo from colliding with Sam—or colliding literally, anyway. That was the first of many things Samantha complained about regarding the cabin they'd inherited from their uncle: its "archaic" lighting.

Samantha's high heels clacked across the hard-wood floor in the living room, then moved into the kitchen. Jo cringed, envisioning the dints she was probably leaving in her wake.

"Good grief, Jo. It's a tomb in here. How do you stand it?"

Had she called it or what? "Every bulb doesn't have to glare. I like soft—"

"What's in the basket?"

How Jo wished she could disappear into one of the bedrooms, any one of them, no matter how cluttered or unfinished. But as she knew from a lifetime of experience, it wouldn't help. Samantha would be there, in her face, until she tired of chewing at whatever she was after this time—and since "this time" involved money, she wouldn't drop the bone till the cash was in hand.

"Trout," Jo admitted miserably, all fantasies of a candlelit dinner for one dashed to hell.

"Gross."

Jo shrugged. If only that opinion meant Samantha was planning to eat elsewhere—but Jo knew better than that. She headed for the counter beneath the big window that had a gorgeous mountain view, and dumped her catch into one of the stainless steel sinks. "Dot's doing Italian specials all week."

"Pasta? Like I'd eat pasta. Goes straight to your belly."

Jo patted her own "belly" with affection, not caring if she got fish slime on her shirt. It was due for a wash. "Well, I'm making potatoes."

Samantha followed her, keeping a safe three-foot distance from any potential food mess. She gave Jo a quick once over and frowned.

"What are you wearing? You stink like fresh air and you look like a lumberjack. And tonight of all nights!"

"What do you mean 'tonight'? What's so special about *tonight*?"

Jo scrubbed her hands and started peeling potatoes. Samantha sighed dramatically. "I was hoping you'd look human when you met my lawyer, but thankfully I've already warned him about you."

"Your *what*? Here, now—*what?*"

Samantha flourished one hand. "Callum, we're ready for you." A shadow moved in the dining room.

Crap.

Jo was so angry she could hardly see.

And then she was so startled she almost sliced her thumb with the potato peeler. She put it down. *Callum*? As in Callum Archer? Her old Callum? No . . . the first name was a coincidence. Had to be. A tall man walked out of the living room and extended his hand.

"Callum Archer," Samantha said and Jo's brain swam. "Josephine—or Jo, as she's sometimes called—my sister."

Jo tried to give the hand gripping hers a firm shake, but as she met his piercing aqua blue eyes— eyes she'd never forget—she started to freak out. An irrational observation hit her: the man, Sam's lawyer, *her old Callum*, had strong sexy-rough hands for a guy working a desk job. Her stomach churned. Breathe, she commanded herself. *Breathe*. It was absolutely no comfort at all that he looked as shocked as she felt.

"Hello Callum," she said, hoping desperately for a dry, casual tone. "It's been a long time." And it had been. Fifteen years, four months. Not that she'd counted. . . .

"*Jo*? I'll be damned." And Callum did look like he'd just been damned. All the blood drained from his already fair skin, making his blue eyes burn even brighter and his black hair seem all the blacker. "You look exactly the same," he said.

"When it's half dark, perhaps," Jo said wryly. "But thanks." So he was still a flatterer. That much hadn't changed.

Samantha's eagle sharp gaze darted to Callum, then speared Jo. "So what—you guys know each other?"

Jo raised her eyebrows and shook her head. "Uh, no. I wouldn't say that really. Used to. A bit. Kind of."

"Kind of," Callum repeated with a bitter note in his voice that Jo didn't understand—and that pissed her off. What the hell did he have to be bitter about?

There was a moment of uneasy silence, then Callum had the nerve to laugh. "Sisters. Wow." Jo hated the sexy, low timber of his voice and his easy confidence. "Here I'd just assumed the Josephine Kendall everyone in town was talking about, and that you went on about, was some aunt or something. I didn't link *Jo* to Josephine at all."

"Well, it's a terrible name, but it's better than *Jo*," Samantha said.

"She doesn't really strike me as the next thing to a bag lady," Callum said, his head tilting as he studied Jo.

The next thing to a bag lady? What on earth had Sam been telling people?

Samantha sounded as affronted as Jo felt. "Have you taken a good look at her?"

Callum was still gripping Jo's hand and she yanked away, suddenly conscious of her muddy jeans, old man's shirt, and—no doubt—leaf and branch strewn hair. Shit. She was making an excellent first impression as a business professional, able to single-handedly turn the old cabin and overgrown property into a successful bed-and-breakfast, wasn't she? She could practically hear Samantha's victory chant.

She tried to fight the heat rising to her cheeks but failed, imagining how the room looked from his eyes. Breakfast and lunch dishes piled messily by the sink. A mishmash of junk littering the floor by the dish-washer. . . . She'd meant to box it up for Goodwill, but the beautiful fall afternoon had called to her. And what kind of ignoramus shows up unannounced and basically breaks into someone's house anyway?

"I'm not sure what my sister told you, or why either of you thought an impromptu, unscheduled appointment would be at all appropriate or benefi-cial"—she glared at Samantha for a moment—"but it's neither of those things. It's a Friday night, and I have plans. We can set up a time next week to meet at your office to discuss the estate and terms of my uncle's will, or, if you're from out of town, we can conference call."

Oh-so-confident Callum looked startled, and Jo made a couple more observations, all equally irritating. Time had been more than kind to him. While she'd found him gorgeous, like a rock god or something, back in the day—his tall, lanky frame had filled out with age. He looked more like a professional athlete than what her mind conjured for a lawyer. His icy blue eyes were still penetrating—and stood out spectacularly against his shock of silky raven hair— but he had just the start of crinkling laugh lines that softened his intensity. And he smelled good. Like fresh baked cookies, vanilla, cinnamon—

Callum's voice, sharp and irritated, cut through the buttery attraction melting through Jo. "You didn't arrange this? We just surprised her?" he said to Samantha.

Samantha waved her hand dismissively, and Jo wished she could lop one of those constantly gesturing hands right off. "She would've stalled indefinitely. And she doesn't really have plans. She's having dinner *by herself.*"

Like it's a capital crime or something, Jo thought.

Callum cleared his throat. "Sounds nice, actually. I'm sorry for the misunderstanding—sorry we disturbed you."

Jo didn't lie and say it was fine. She herded them to the door.

"I don't know why you're being like this. We need to talk, get this figured out, decide what works best for everyone."

"We have talked, Samantha. We disagree on what 'works best' means. Your lawyer may call me next week, anytime Monday through Friday between nine and five. I'll consult my schedule and we can set an appointment."

"Your *schedule*?" Samantha mocked.

Callum placed a hand low on Samantha's back and guided her toward the door. "She's right, Samantha. This wasn't the right way to proceed."

"And just so you're aware. If you break into my house again, I'll call the cops and press charges."

Callum turned back from the door. "I'm not sure it's so simple as 'your' house, Jo—but again, my apologies for the intrusion. It was a misunderstanding. I'll be in touch."

"Jo—"

"Let's just go, Samantha."

"Yes, *go,* Samantha. Take your slimy lawyer's advice. That's what you're paying him for right?"

Jo leaned against the mudroom's wall after they left and closed her eyes. Why had she been so rude? Yes, even after all these years, the very thought of Callum was a slicing barb—but that was no excuse. They'd been kids. She needed to let him off the hook. For her own sake, not just his.

Chapter 2

"BITCH!" SAMANTHA SLAMMED THE MERCEDES SUV's door, making the whole vehicle shake. Callum didn't agree with Samantha's pronouncement, but he was distracted. Jo. Back in Greenridge. *Jo.*

As the months turned to years after that disastrous summer—the summer he'd been stupid enough to think they'd get married and love each other for life—he'd gone away, gotten a couple degrees like his dad wanted, and eventually returned to town with plans to settle down and raise a family. Not something (understatement of the century) that had worked out well. But the point was, he'd come to terms with the fact he'd never see her again. After all, she'd been clear in all their time together that once she left Greenridge, she was never coming back.

And now here she was. In the flesh—and what flesh it was. He would've known her anywhere. And from her derisive snort at his compliment, she still had no clue how beautiful she was. Short and curvy. All that crazy, curly red-gold hair. Those warm brown eyes of hers, such a contrast to her light hair. She was like a mermaid crossed with a fairy crossed with a—

ah, he didn't know. Something sexy though. But it wasn't just her looks that captivated him. Not when they were younger, not now. She still seemed passionate and insanely optimistic about every little thing—or did according to the details Samantha had given him about "Josephine." Now that he realized the ideas about turning Ray's cabin into a bed-and-breakfast were Jo's, it sounded like she hadn't changed a bit.

Callum fastened his seatbelt as Samantha peeled out. The only thing that kept her tires from spraying a fan of gravel was how the long, bumpy driveway was mostly bare earth and potholes—showing Samantha was right about another thing, too. There was a load of work to do if the old place was ever going to be the business Jo envisioned, and it would take a long time to make enough money to pay Samantha out.

The vehicle jounced over the asphalt ridge where the winding drive joined the main highway, and Callum's shoulder banged against the window. He rubbed the painful spot. Yep, the driveway needed work all right. The house, however, wasn't as bad as Samantha made out. It had potential, though Samantha seemed to think Jo wanted to morph it into a posh hotel-like venture.

"Posh" seemed out of character for the Jo he'd loved, the girl whose yearbook write up said something like, "Most hoped for career? Pah—make love not war!" and who'd been dubbed, "Most likely to end up a hermit living off the land with no electricity." It also seemed incongruous for the woman she'd become. Who'd wear faded flannel and rubber boots and catch her own fish if striving for some uppity resort? But as he'd proven so mightily over the years: he didn't really understand people.

To reaffirm the truth of his last thought—or perhaps just to cruelly remind him of the second biggest mistake of his life, all too related to his lack of understanding—Nina's voice shrilled in his memory. "This is not about not understanding *me*, Callum. This is about *you*. You never got over her—a high school romance. You're pathetic!"

But that was ridiculous. He'd gotten over Jo Kendall. *He had.* So why was his heart pounding now? Well, it was just the surprise of seeing her again, of course, the stress of confronting his past. That was it. That was all.

"Callum?" Samantha's long nails dragged over the back of his hand. He started, but managed, barely, to not jerk away from her touch.

"I'm sorry, Samantha. What were you saying?"

"*What was I saying*?" A tittering laugh punctuated her sentences. "So many things, silly. I've been talking since we left Jo's house."

Interesting. Samantha referred to Ray's as if it did indeed belong to Jo. "I'm sorry," Callum repeated. "I guess I was distracted, thinking about your situation. Trying to figure out what we should do next."

The ear-splitting titter sounded again. "Situation, smituation. I know you'll take care of things satisfactorily. I have your daddy's word, after all."

She came to a fast, hard stop at the first set of lights into town. Callum braced himself, hand on the dashboard, and resolved that he didn't care what Samantha or his "daddy" thought of his Honda. It was a fine, reliable car, and he wasn't riding in this death trap ever again.

"Oh, don't scowl," Samantha said sweetly. "Is your father a sore point? My bad. I wasn't aware."

Not aware my ass, thought Callum. There wasn't a thing Samantha did or said that wasn't one hundred percent calculated (plus tax!)—an insight that focused him.

"So what was that back there anyway?"

Samantha turned her head, fluttered her eyelashes at him—and almost took out a pedestrian.

"What was what, back where?" She whipped into a tight spot between a red Ford and a superman-blue Toyota in front of Archer and Sons, seemingly without looking, and parked perfectly. It made him crazy that she was actually an excellent driver—for a totally insane person.

His hand was on the door, but he paused before opening it and escaping. "Showing up at your sister's, being in her house, unannounced like that?"

Samantha considered him. "I thought it would unnerve her. She didn't think I'd lawyer up. And she pissed me off. It was time to get even."

In his head, Callum gave Samantha a small kudos for honesty. At least she didn't waste her time trying to people please all the time.

A depressing drizzle had started and the sidewalk glistened under the streetlights. He was surprised when Samantha hollered for him to wait, but he did as requested—and was further surprised when she didn't continue to yammer through the window, but got out and ran—or, rather, tottered—over to him on those ridiculous high heels of hers.

She held her Gucci bag over her head and looked up at him. Staring at him beseechingly with her big green eyes, while trying futilely to avoid getting soaked, she was kind of cute. He shook his head, before he even heard her request.

"One beer," she repeated. "Mix a little business and pleasure. It'll be fun." She tapped her foot, and as she'd most likely intended, he looked down the considerable length of her long, lean leg.

She was smiling when he brought his eyes back up to hers.

"Don't let the rumors about Archer men proceed me," he muttered. "And don't misread my attention. Business is all I'm good for—if that."

Samantha's fingers danced up his forearm, then rested on his bicep. "And don't misread me. I'm not looking for a relationship. I just want a drink and a good time. We could even start by talking about work."

"I'm sorry—"

"Oh, come on. Don't be coy. You must've inherited more from your dad than just his good looks."

"God, I hope not. I'll call you Monday after I've contacted your sister."

He left Samantha pouting prettily, but looking only slightly miffed—and more like she'd received some sort of challenge—and walked around to the building's side entrance. He held up his fob, pushed the heavy door open when the light flashed green, and waited until he was safely down the dark hallway before he leaned against the wall and exhaled.

He just needed to hang in for one more job. He could do it. Get slightly odd Jo to sell, receive a fat slice of scary Samantha's share and pay off his father. Then be free. He could do it. And he would. If trying didn't make him jump off a building or something first.

His thoughts turned to his apartment's fridge and he felt himself relax. The weekend wouldn't be a total horror show. He wouldn't let it.

Chapter 3

AISHA STUDIED HERSELF IN THE white-enamel Cheval mirror by her highboy dresser, which was also white enamel with brass and ceramic ornamentation, like the desk, like the canopy bed. It was a babyish, girly set that no longer suited her, but she hadn't parted with it because redecorating the bedroom and picking out new furniture was one of the last things she and her mom had done together before her mom died.

She turned this way and that, first pressing her T-shirt against her stomach, then fanning it, trying to make it billow out. It remained snug. Soon other people would notice her "condition" no matter what she wore.

Knocked up. Preggers. Preggo. With child. Bun in the oven. *Stupid.* And why was she so big anyway? She was only three months along—okay, maybe "big" wasn't the right word. Different was more like it. Her stomach looked different. Already. And unless it was her imagination—and she was sure it wasn't—her face had changed too. It was slightly chubbier, softer.

She thought she heard a door slam downstairs and cocked her head, listening. A car engine roared to life in the driveway. Her dad, still blocked in his novel and off to the gym, she supposed. And apparently still not talking to her. Ah, well. She totally got it. If she didn't have to, she wouldn't be stuck in her head talking to herself either.

She pulled on black skinny jeans—yes, she saw the irony—that she'd recently altered, adding a stomach panel of stretchy skull print (Maternity clothes for Goth girls—it could be the new rage, yeah right!), then zipped herself into a massive black hooded-sweatshirt. She ran kohl liner around her eyes and a swath of fire engine red lipstick over her mouth. Her hair was its usual frizzy mess. She scooped it up, gave it a violent twist and shoved a chopstick up, then inverted it and pushed down—and repeated the action with another stick. "You look like a fat manga chick," she snarled at the mirror. Then felt badly. What if the kid could hear her? "Not that 'fat' or 'manga' or 'chicks' are bad things," she added.

In the kitchen, she forced down a glass of milk, a banana and two pieces of cheddar cheese. Eating breakfast, yuck, was a new thing for her . . . but necessary if she didn't want to barf. She packed wheat thins and a small jar of peanut butter into her back-pack, knowing she'd be starved like she'd never eaten in her life in about half an hour.

She paused by the computer in her mom's room—yes, both her and her dad still referred to it as "Mom's" three years later—then sank into the worn, burgundy office chair and contemplated the list she'd printed out and accidentally on purpose left for her dad to discover. She had wanted his opinion, even though she didn't want to hurt him. And he'd given it, but yes, been hurt. Didn't understand why she needed advice or information from her biological mother—or why she wanted to find out who her biological father was. And Aisha didn't understand it either. She just needed to.

She scanned the repeating surname, Kendall, Kendall, Kendall . . . twenty-two of them, all women in the right age range, all still living in B.C. There was a chance, of course, maybe even a high probability that her birth mom no longer lived in the province, but she had to start somewhere. And until she talked to her birth mom, *met* her in person, for reasons Aisha couldn't articulate, she felt powerless to decide what to do with the baby.

Ah, well. Commencing the cold calling—fun, fun—would have to wait. She needed to get to work and though the Return-It Depot wasn't her dream job or anything, she wanted to keep it as long as possible before the lifting got to be too much. She'd needed to earn and save every dollar she could right now. Getting canned for being late wouldn't do.

Chapter 4

JO CONSIDERED HER CLOTHING CHOICES, and once again cursed Samantha for launching a surprise attack when she was all grubby from a fishing trip.

She liked her outfit, but how would Callum see it? What would a *lawyer* read into it? The black silk tunic was lovely. The pendant she wore—a moon shaped chunk of labradorite on a heavy silver chain—was striking, but not over the top. She wore jeans, and not just because she didn't own more formal attire. They were practical, and made it seem like she wasn't trying *too* hard, or so she hoped.

That said, she really did need to make a better impression at this meeting, or Callum would write her off as being as eccentric as her uncle was. Normally she'd be proud to wear the title, but it wasn't a helpful label when it came to trying to inspire confidence in a business plan.

"You're a liar," she muttered at her reflection. "*Liar.*" The full and only reason she was contemplating her appearance was because Callum was still ridiculously attractive, maybe even more so with some years on him. She wanted him to think she'd held up okay, too—and she needed to appear strong, put together, and *long over him.* Which she was. She totally was.

She tromped through the house locking doors, resenting the fact that she had to, but wanting to establish the habit so that if Samantha decided on any repeats of the other day's behavior, she'd be stuck waiting on the porch.

Outside, it was raining—or, more accurately, misting. Great. Her hair would be a mess of frizz. She called Hoover, and he must've realized she was leaving the property because for once he came without being asked twice. She opened the truck's passenger door, and he jumped up eagerly, turned three circles on the wide canvas seat and settled into a crescent roll shape with a small grunt.

Jo scratched his soft ears, a total anomaly from the rest of his wire brush fur. "It's a good thing you're cute because you're a useless watch dog." Hoover grunted again and rolled to his back. "And no," she added, rubbing his belly obediently, "you're not forgiven for letting Samantha and he-who-shall-not-be-named into the house without giving me so much as a whimper of a warning."

"MR. ARCHER WILL BE RIGHT with you," the secretary, a slight, red-haired woman in a leopard print skirt and jacket, assured Jo. "Can I offer you tea while you wait?"

The woman's warm, soft voice clashed with her loud outfit. "No, but thank you," Jo replied. Too keyed up to sit, she moved about, taking in the reception area's décor with growing confusion—and a tiny bit of fascination that she tried to deny. There were enough food magazines to stock the library of the best culinary arts program. And the items decorating each shelf and hanging on the walls were what? Early century baker?

She smiled. So Callum still liked cooking, hey?

"What on earth is this?" she muttered to herself, hefting a heavy black utensil and studying it. It looked almost like a shovel, but the metal blade was dull-lipped and perfectly flat, not good for scooping anything, plus it had three decorative cut outs, two hearts, and a diamond. Stuff would fall right through it.

"It's called a bannock spade, but didn't you see the sign?"

Jo jumped at Callum's cold tone, and only then—of course, Murphy's law—noticed the glaringly obvious ivory card requesting that people enjoy looking at, but refrain from touching, the collection of antiques.

Jo carefully set the object of her faux pas down. "A bannock spade?"

"Yes. Turn of the 19th century. Scottish. Used for flipping bannock, a kind of flat bread, much like a modern spatula."

"Weird."

"Not weird," Callum said stiffly. "Collectible."

Jo raised her eyebrows, but didn't say anything. She hadn't meant to sound like she was passing judgment. "Weird" was generally a compliment coming from her mouth; too bad he didn't remember that.

After an awkward moment, she complied with his wordless invitation and followed the sweep of his arm into his office. She perched on the edge of a chair and wondered why was he being so awful. You'd think, considering their past, he'd be remotely human. But then again, maybe he felt ashamed of how he'd led her on all those years ago. Or worse—her temperature rose—maybe he thought *she* remembered and held it against him.

With that thought, an old joke Callum used to repeat constantly came back to her. She clenched her hands into fists. *If I said I liked your body would you hold it against me?* The answer, annoyingly, was yes on two counts. She had held it, her body, against him then—hyuk, hyuk, hyuk—and she did hold it, that fact, against him now. She had truly loved him. Deeply. Unabashedly. Whenever people spoke dismissively of teenage romance, calling it "puppy love," she never agreed the relationships were such lighthearted things. It had torn her heart out for years that Callum hadn't shared the depth of feelings she'd had for him. Might've even been why, after a string of flings, she ended up with Devin—an equally disastrous relationship, though for completely different reasons.

Callum sat on the corner of his desk and looked down at her.

Jo studied him a moment, then got up, crossed the room, stood close to him—and stayed standing. Let him try to use his stupid power moves, consciously or unconsciously, on someone else.

He fidgeted uncomfortably, but didn't move away. "Before Samantha gets here, tell me . . . is there any point to this mediation session?"

Jo shrugged and hoped her smile was Mona Lisa-ish.

Callum's jaw clenched and his eyes darkened to the shade of a sunless sea—and Jo wanted to slap herself for noting his eyes at all, let alone thinking about them in such ridiculously drippy way.

"Is there any chance you'll listen to sense and come to a reasonable solution, Jo? Please? Sell the property, give your sister her fair share without tying up everybody's time and resources by taking this to court?"

"Pardon me?"

Callum's face flushed. "I know you heard me."

"Oh, I *heard* all right. I just thought maybe I mis-understood. It sounded like you were insulting me, insinuating that I don't have sense if I don't give into your bullying, and threatening me with huge costs of time and financial resources if I don't capitulate to your very one-sided, incredibly self-centered 'solu-tion.'"

The cliché "if looks could kill" ran through Jo's mind and she shivered under Callum's glare, but tried to maintain a stony expression.

"I'm not a villain. I just want this taken care of quickly," he said quietly.

So he did remember leading her on and totally jilting her. He knew he was a villain—or why else would he say he wasn't one? "Why the hurry? You get paid by the hour, right? And get a cut of the property's value?"

"It's not like that."

"It's exactly like that."

"Do you know how much money that decrepit sinkhole will cost you? Samantha's filled me in on your plan and I have to tell you—it's not much of one. Greenridge has been more bust than boom for years now. Almost the whole downtown core is empty and up for rent. Two of the big hotels have gone under. What makes you think you can get a bed-and-breakfast up and running and be cash positive, especially when you have no equity, no savings, and your only real service industry experience was an owner-operated restaurant that went belly up. You have no credit, no backers, and a bankruptcy in your recent past. You're a piss poor risk."

Jo staggered like she'd been punched. She was stupid to be surprised, but she couldn't help it. Samantha—that witch. She really hadn't kept any secrets.

Callum got to his feet so quickly that Jo had to

leap sideways to avoid being bowled over. He put his hands out and caught her by both arms, surprisingly gently—steadying her, though she didn't need it. She'd already regained her footing and her composure.

"I'm sorry," he said, his voice entirely different than that of the arrogant naysayer he'd been just seconds earlier. He really was amazingly tall. And she was still taken by his great scent. What was it? Vanilla and butter? She wanted to nuzzle his neck and—

"I'm sorry. I don't know what got into me. I'm sorry," he repeated and strode to the other side of the room.

Jo was flummoxed by his abrupt change—and by the heat that coursed through her at his touch. What was wrong with her? All evidence suggested he'd only matured into an even bigger asshole than he'd been when he first ripped her heart out, yet here she was . . . what? Still finding him attractive? Good grief.

You're happily single, she reminded herself. Happily single. *Happily. Single.*

The surprising glow of happy hormones faded as quickly they'd sparked, and nerves cramped her stomach. Come to think of it, maybe that's all her unsettling response to him was: nervousness she was mistaking for something else.

A popping sound pulled her out of her self-analysis.

Callum had paused mid-stride and cracked his knuckles loudly. "I'm sorry," he said yet again. "So sorry."

Jo's cheeks flamed. It would look terrible if anyone interrupted them—both the color of beets, both in the middle of breakdowns.

She looked at the expensive grandfather clock standing sentry by a huge fern. Was this another one of Samantha's games? Was her tardiness some calculated scheme, or just her usual disregard for other peoples' time?

The other night Samantha had pretended to not know—or not to remember—that Jo and Callum had known each other, had dated, but she sure as hell knew Jo had been hurt over "some juvenile romance" (as Samantha had called it) that had run deep and held hard. And she knew Jo's weaknesses all too well. Her stupid sentimentality. If Samantha had remembered Callum's name when she came across it and chose him intentionally, knowing it would unhinge Jo—it was a low thing to do, but damn if it wasn't smart, too.

Still . . . Samantha had seemed genuinely surprised, even irritated, when Jo and Callum recognized each other.

Well, of course she did. Wouldn't be much of a strategy if she admitted knowing you knew each other right off, would it?

Meanwhile, Callum paced on, practically hyperventilating.

Do not give in, Jo lectured herself. Do not cave. Do not!

"Um . . . is there something wrong?" she finally asked, even as she kicked herself for being a sucker.

She got no reply. Callum just continued his frantic march.

"This is ridiculous," she muttered. "And it won't work."

Still no response, and she noted with alarm that beads of sweat had formed on his forehead, and his hair was damp and curling with perspiration. Was he a drug addict or something now? No, she was pretty sure he wasn't. It was weird, but she thought she knew exactly what was going on with him—but then again, what were the chances they'd both end up in the same stupid boat? No, it wasn't possible. . . .

But what if it was? She looked at Callum again, then sighed. Whatever. It was either a ploy or it wasn't, but she couldn't just let him come completely undone in front of her.

She stopped Callum about three feet from his big oak desk by placing a hand on his shoulder. "Can you sit?" she asked. "Just try—and take a deep breath?"

He shook his head wordlessly.

"It's okay if you can't—but just try. I'll sit, too."

She closed her eyes, envisioned her creek, and imagined its surrounding trees and grassy bank. Willed him to feel the calm she felt when she fished— like everyone and everything was okay, or would be.

A chair creaked. She kept her eyes closed. She didn't even open them when she heard Callum take a deep, gasping-for-oxygen breath—or, moments later, when he let out a long shuddery exhale. She didn't know how long they sat there, but she could almost feel sun on her face, smell the slightly fishy river mud, hear the Steller's jays chatter. . . .

"Thank you," he said, so quietly she almost didn't hear him. "I . . . I've been having some anxiety issues lately."

"You should take up fishing," she said, eyes still closed.

"Ah, that explains—" but whatever Callum was going to say was interrupted by a buzz that made Jo jump. Callum answered the phone and became exasperated again, almost at once. "Well, come as quickly as you can. . . . What? No. . . . *Fine*."

Jo opened her eyes when he hung up—to find him staring at her.

She shrugged a little. "So something's come up and Sam can't make it?"

"How did you know that?"

She just shook her head. "And to answer your question in a belated way, with slightly more details than you asked for . . . I think we will end up in court. I don't want my uncle's home sold. I want to honor his wishes, which were abundantly clear, if not perfectly organized detail-wise—"

Callum snorted. "That's the understatement of the year."

Jo's eyes narrowed. "And yes, I think it's a financially viable idea, even with a 'piss poor risk' like me attached to it."

"I—I shouldn't have said that—but do you understand how much money the legal mess will eat up?"

"So why don't you talk Samantha into being a human and dropping it?"

"She just wants what your uncle intended her to have."

"Our uncle wanted her to have about twenty-five thousand dollars, what he figured a quarter of the property was worth. He should've had it assessed, yes, and had an updated will that reflected the current value, yes—but he didn't."

"Right, he didn't and his wording, 'or about a quarter of the property's worth' is exactly your sister's point."

"And I'll go with her interpretation. I'll pay her. I'm just asking for time."

"You don't have time. I'm sorry. Either we come to an agreement here, or—"

"Will you at least hear me out? Samantha just sees a cash grab, and she's being stupid. She's paying you. She's the one running through money—and for what? For a quarter of a price she doesn't even know we'll get. You said it yourself. Real estate's in the toilet here, but there's still money to be made, and more importantly a life to be made here, a home, a—" Jo broke off abruptly. What was she doing? Why was she spilling her personal dreams and hopes here? Next thing she knew she'd be confessing her desire for love, true love—bah, she was an idiot!

She struggled to get back to business, forcing

herself to meet Callum's gaze, despite how flustered she suddenly was. "This is a gorgeous area, with fishing, hiking, and skiing that's second to none—all a well kept secret. With a little promotion, people will visit and bring their families. They'll come back year after year."

Callum's chin lifted and one of his eyebrows rose. Encouraged, Jo rushed on. "Maybe if someone who's not so emotionally entangled in the place hears the business plan and explains it to Sam, she'll see that I'm not just dreaming. Come back to the house. Let me show you around—when I'm expecting you."

"Fine."

"Really? You mean it?" Jo jumped up, and only just managed to keep herself from grabbing his hand. Callum was very hard to read—cold and professional one minute, a bigger wreck than she was the next, and then mere seconds later, a totally human guy—even warm seeming.

"How about tomorrow afternoon, say three thirty? I'll walk you around the place while it's still light, then feed you dinner?" She practically tripped over her words, needing them out and for him to have agreed before he changed his mind.

Callum nodded slowly, but his brow furrowed. "You do know I'm not a banker, right? It's not like I can give you any financial aid. You're not pitching to me."

Jo laughed—and hoped it wasn't a bitter sound. "If you were a banker, I wouldn't waste your time. As you so accurately pointed out, I won't qualify for any loans. What you are is my last chance—person to person. If Samantha would just give me two or three years, I know I could . . ." Jo's voice trailed off at the expression that took over Callum's face. What on earth had she said that made him so sad?

"Anyway," she finally continued. "Thank you. I'll see you tomorrow. Is there anything you don't eat?"

"Not a thing," he said.

She was halfway out the door when she swore he said something else.

"Pardon?" she asked, turning back.

He looked up from the laptop he'd bent over the moment she'd finished talking. "Nothing. I didn't say anything."

He had though. Jo was certain. And it had sounded all too much like, "Don't get your hopes up."

Well, it was too late. She did have her hopes up. She couldn't help it.

A TRIO OF FAT BOOKS lay open on his desk, surrounded by a mess of papers, and both his laptop and his desktop were in use. If anyone happened by, Callum would look industrious: a carefully constructed ruse. All he could think about—all he could see—was Jo's face when he'd laid her secrets bare. And he'd also observed the moment she passed silent judgment on him and wrote him off as a jerk—how her hurt eyes hardened and her soft lips disappeared into a tight line.

So she hated him. Not that he could blame her.

In their far past, he'd been too weak to express how he felt about her in the face of his father's disdain and his mother's worry. He'd taken the coward's way out and written that stupid letter declaring his love, but postponing their plan to run off and get married and start their life together. No wonder she hadn't bothered to respond. For years he hadn't understood her failure to acknowledge the letter, but now he thought he did.

And here, in their present, he'd invaded her space and shown up at her house unannounced. He was pressuring her into selling her inheritance, a family home that meant more to her than a quick buck. *And* he'd just finished acting like a complete psycho, ranting about the room, muttering. . . . Yet, she'd been kind to him. *Kind.*

He considered how he would've acted if someone he'd set up a meeting with completely lost it. And he thought of how Samantha acted with far less provocation and was only further humiliated. He'd never fallen into one of his "episodes," as he chose to refer to them, in front of anyone before except Nina—and since he figured she was partly responsible for them, she didn't count.

Jo calmed him down—something she'd always been good at, he recalled. It was almost like she recognized what was happening to him, but then didn't coddle him. As soon as he was fine again, she

resumed arguing with him. Didn't change the purpose
of their meeting or suddenly forsake the points she
wanted to make, using some lame excuse about
needing to be somewhere else or something. And
then, just like she still actually valued his opinion and
thought he might have weight with Samantha, she'd
invited him to visit.

Callum straightened in his seat, then stretched,
twisting side to side. He was lying to himself if he
tried to pretend any of that was why he kept dwelling
on their meeting.

It had been beyond bizarre when he'd touched her.
It was like he received an electric jolt, his physical
reaction every bit as powerful and uncontrollable as
when they were seventeen-year-olds. But that wasn't
the shocker—the shocker was that he'd felt anything
all. He hadn't been powerfully attracted to anyone
since Nina.

He was "off women," as his brother Brian always
(oh-so-helpfully) told people. A truth always met with
a variety of unwelcome comments.

"Well, keep him away from me then," their friend
Dave said whenever the topic came up, then laughed
uproariously.

At first Brian joked back, "Well, you are pretty
hot." As the months turned into a year, turned into
three years, the humor failed.

One night there'd been a beer-soaked "heart-to-
heart." Callum still cringed when he thought of it.

"You know if you really are gay, I'm all right with

it," Brian had said through the noisy din of the pub.

"Me too, buddy."

"What?" Callum looked back and forth between his best friend and his brother, and realized they weren't kidding.

"If our jokes made you insecure, we're dicks and we're sorry."

"Good to know, thanks . . . but I'm not."

"Are you sure?"

"Yeah, I'm *sure*. And if I was, I'd be fine with it but thanks for your permission."

"Dad thinks you are."

"What?"

"Well, his exact wording was, 'When's that brother of yours going to tell me he's a fag?'"

"Nice, really nice."

Both Brian and Dave were still studying him.

"I'm *not* gay. I'm just not in the mood—and there are other things in the world beside sex, you know."

"There are?" Brian asked, sounding almost serious.

"Are you still on antidepressants? They can do that."

"Wow, thanks, Dave. I didn't know you were so up on my meds. Is this what you guys do when I'm not around? Obsess about why I'm not getting any and what kind I would be getting if I was?"

Dave laughed.

Brian feigned horror. "You were on antidepressants? That *is* gay!"

Callum smiled. Idiots. Good enough guys, but *idiots*.

Brian was single and played the field in a way that put their old man to shame—but seemed happy enough. Dave was still looking in general, but currently seemed obsessed with some old flame who'd moved back to town. And himself? Well, he was—or had been until half an hour ago—totally disinterested in relationships and the headaches that came with. He recalled Jo's smiling eyes and the pendant that rested heavily between her firm breasts— breasts he'd seen more than once, lucky him. He wondered if they still felt the same, looked the same. He'd loved the color of her nipples—

His pants were suddenly uncomfortably tight. Damn. So much for being off women. But at least it proved he wasn't dead yet. Before he could think about what it meant—or if it meant anything—the phone rang. The caller deflated his tenuous libido as effectively as a bucket of ice water.

"So, what's the deal?"

"Samantha?"

"Who else?"

Who else. Like she was the only client in the world. "The deal? You mean what came of the meeting?"

"Of course!"

"Well, like I said when you called the first time, it would've been helpful if you'd shown up, then you'd know already."

"I knew I'd be missed, but it was unavoidable."

Callum knew she wanted to be asked what was so important that it detained her, but he resisted. After a breathy pause, she laughed throatily. "I guess you could say I was tied up."

He rolled his eyes. This was what he avoided staying shy of coupledom—constant, shallow games.

"So you met with Jo in all her eager, wide-eyed earnestness, I suppose?"

Jo. A memory of her naked and laughing popped into his mind. Once they'd taken turns tying each other to the wooden post of his bed with one of the silky patterned scarves she used to wear. He wondered how her sexual tastes had changed with the years, then tried very hard *not* to wonder—and grudgingly gave points to Samantha again. There was a certain appeal to some kinds of games. . . .

Samantha babbled on, but he was still hung up on the concept, *sister*. Samantha and Jo were so different it was hard to believe they were related. Back when he and Jo were together, he'd known she had a sister— had even met her once when she was incredibly inebriated. Jo had called him to help her get Samantha home from a party gone wrong, but she'd been curled up vomiting in the backseat—and all he remembered from that night was the huge mess, sympathy for Jo, and relief that her much older, much crazier, sibling lived somewhere else. He, as he'd proven, wouldn't have known Samantha if she walked right up and introduced herself. He wondered idly if they had the same parents or if they were only half-siblings—

"Callum, are you still there?"

"What? Oh, yeah, sorry."

"I pay you to listen."

"Actually, that's not quite—"

"So what's next?"

Good question. What *was* next? "Well, I'm not going to lie—"

"Wait, that makes me think you *are* going to."

Callum laughed. "Seriously, Samantha. Jo, I mean your sister—"

"I know who Jo is," Samantha interrupted dryly.

"Of course." Callum shook his head, tried to get a grip. "She's pretty passionate about keeping the place. And maybe she's onto something. Maybe you'd make more money if you hold off.... Write up some agreement entitling you to a quarter of the appraised market value in three years time. If the business is successful, you—"

"Forget it. A lot of people are into that whole 'delayed gratification' thing, but I'm not. Definitely not. Jo could sink eons of time and buckets of money into that place, find a way to go into debt with it, and it could be worth squat. You may think I'm a cold-hearted bitch—"

Callum made appropriate "No, no, of course not" noises and realized that in doing so he was lying, just as Samantha had predicted. He sighed.

"But I'm honestly trying to help my sister. She needs to be protected from herself."

Callum didn't bother pointing out that Samantha had just used "honestly" the same way he had and that he suspected it meant exactly what she suggested: that her words, unconsciously or not, were less than truthful.

"So I guess you'd be opposed to me visiting the old place tomorrow to hear her plans and to have dinner?"

"What?"

Callum started to repeat himself.

"No, no, I heard you. I just can't believe it. That duplicitous little *sneak!* She's going to try to convince you into talking me out of taking this to court."

"Well . . . yes. But she's not exactly being sneaky. She told me that's exactly what she aims to do."

"That's what always makes her plans so diabolical. She fesses up beforehand. Very disarming."

Callum shook his head, but realized he was smiling. There was something hilarious, if slightly twisted, about the Kendall sisters' relationship. He'd only known Jo as a teenager. What on earth had they been like when they were kids? Their poor parents—actually, that was strange. Neither of them had brought up their parents, only their uncle. Where were their folks?

JO'S CELL PHONE BUZZED THE whole drive home, but she never answered calls or texts while driving, much to the complete frustration and ridicule of Samantha.

When she finally pulled into her driveway, she checked her call history and cringed. Wow, that hadn't taken long at all. Against her better judgment, she hit 1-1 to listen to whatever Samantha had to say.

"You're not serious," her sister's message shrilled. "You're dating my lawyer? This has got to be a conflict of interest!"

Jo hit reply. The phone barely rang.

"I don't believe you!" Samantha yelled.

Jo laughed. "Well, hello to you, too. And I'm not *dating* your lawyer. I'm just trying to get him to see sense—and then hopefully to pass some on to you."

"It won't work."

"You're that sure you won't be able to have sense?"

"Very funny."

Jo climbed out the truck and patted her thigh. Hoover jumped down and plodded after her. "Come on, Sam. Can't we manage this without lawyers? You know I won't rip you off."

"Don't call me Sam—and no, I don't know any such thing. Money does funny things to people."

Jo snorted at the unintentional irony in Samantha's comment, but refrained from retorting further. Samantha's tone softened. "I'm not trying to hurt you. In a lot of ways, your vision is wonderful—and I know you loved Ray and that old dump."

"*But*?"

"But it won't work—and you already know how devastating it is to have a dream go south. Why would you put yourself through that again? Let's sell, put money in the bank. Cold, hard cash is a beautiful thing, little sister. A lovely, safe cushion."

Jo sighed. She knew all too well where Samantha was coming from: the same place she was. And they wanted similar things, just had very different views on how to attain them. "I don't want safe."

"And see! That's why I'm not going to wait around and have you lose the property and have both of us get nothing."

"Well, this was another productive conversation." Jo rummaged under the worn welcome mat for the house key and almost missed Samantha's next comment—almost. She straightened so quickly she got a head rush. "*Kiss him*? Of course I won't kiss him. It. Is. Not. A. Date."

"Uh huh—been there, said that. Are you making him dinner?"

"Yeah, but only so I can show I have the culinary skills needed to provide edible meals to future guests."

"So there you go."

"So there I go *what*?"

"The lighting in that hovel is low and golden, what some poor dopes who don't know better would call romantic—"

Jo scoffed and let herself into house, shutting the door behind her.

"You'll feed him a ton of good food."

"Kind of the point of *dinner*."

"You'll eat a whack of delicious tidbits yourself, and you know men. They love that whole woman-who-actually-eats thing."

Jo rolled her eyes.

"I'm serious. Don't get all hot to trot with my lawyer. He's cute and I want him."

"Well, you can have him, weirdo. To quote you, been there, done that. Not interested. I only want him to get you to see the light."

There was an awkward pause.

"It's not going to happen, Jo. You need to prepare yourself. We're selling."

Jo sighed again and her heart kind of twisted. "I've missed you. We're going to be okay whatever happens with this place, right?"

"I've missed to you, too—even though you're driving me totally crazy with your insane selfish-ness—but yeah, we'll be okay. I just don't want you to be sad."

"Okay . . . well, I guess we'll have to agree to disagree, yet again. I'll get your lawyer to call you when he's done being wowed here."

"Jo—"

"Look, I'm sorry to cut the conversation short, but I'm putting dinner in the oven. I have to go." Jo hung up before Samantha could say anything else.

Chapter 5

AISHA PUSHED BACK FROM THE computer table. Six for six and no luck.

"Are you eating with me?" her dad called.

"Yeah, I'll be right there." And with that they were on speaking terms again.

"I just don't want you to get hurt, to be disappointed," he said when they were halfway through a large pepperoni, mushroom and green pepper pizza—heavy on the sauce and double-cheese.

Aisha took another big bite, closed her eyes, and savored the spicy deliciousness. One praise point for pregnancy: it sure made eating an amazing experience.

"It's too late," she said when she'd finished enjoying the mouthful. "I've been hurt. I am disappointed. So have you. It's called life."

Her dad looked sad. And tired. She reached out and punched his arm lightly. "Oh, buck up, Chuck. It's not all doom and gloom—and I'm not looking for some big family reunion or a new mom or something like you seem to fear. I . . . I'm just still slightly shocked to find myself in similar shoes to those my birth mom walked in. And I want to know how things worked out from her perspective before I decide what to do."

"Don't call me Chuck," her dad said, refilling his glass of milk. "But yeah, I get where you're coming from. And for a dumb kid, you're pretty smart."

A demerit point for pregnancy: it makes you so damn weepy. She brushed at her eyes angrily. "I think we both know the last bit's a lie, or I wouldn't be captain of the baby bus, right?"

Her dad patted her shoulder. "Can I help you out, captain? Make calls too or anything?"

"No," Aisha said too sharply. She forced a softer tone because none of this was her dad's fault, for crying out loud. "Thanks though."

There was a lull in conversation as Charles drank his milk and wolfed down another piece of pizza. Aisha realized, pun intended, the silence was pregnant.

"What is it?" she asked.

Her dad shook his head.

"Tell me."

"I guess . . . well, I was wondering if there's any news on the Evan front." Charles hung his head, apologetic for even asking.

Aisha pushed her suddenly unappetizing plate away. "I get why you ask, but you need to stop. *No.* The answer will always be no. And you, me and the bean might as well get used to it, okay?"

"Okay." He frowned. "But just so you know, that

guy, that little piece of shit . . . he was never good enough for you."

Aisha pressed her hand against her lower back and got up slowly. If it already ached this bad now, what would it be like in a few more months? "That's kind, Dad. Thanks."

She turned away to hide more stupid misty tears and headed upstairs to hibernate in the princess cave, a.k.a. her froufrou bedroom. The hardest thing about this whole mess was how her dad never got mad at her—angry at the situation, yes. Frustrated by her inability to make a concrete choice about adoption or motherhood, yes . . . but never angry with *her*. She wished she could be so forgiving and understanding, but come on, birth control wasn't rocket science. What was she, a complete moron? Maybe stupidity ran in genes, like eye color or middle toe length. Maybe, if she ever found *the* Ms. Kendall, that's how she'd introduce herself. "Hello, nice to meet you. I only want one thing: answers to a couple questions. First can you tell me if the stupidity I've inherited is on the paternal or maternal side of my bloodline? Both you say. Oh, perfect. Second—"

"Are you talking to me?" her dad called.

"No, just mumbling to myself."

Chapter 6

JO PUSHED A LOW-HANGING HEMLOCK branch out of the way, bringing a cascade of rain droplets down on her and Callum. "Dead," she said.

Callum stopped walking, struck momentarily mute. "Both of them?" The words clawed at his throat. "Ah, Jo—I'm sorry."

Jo studied him for a long moment, beads of water shining in her hair and on her cheeks, like someone had wept over her. Fitting, he thought.

Her voice was soft as the moss beneath their feet when she spoke. "Yes, both. The sperm donor who aided in my creation was taken by pancreatic cancer just months after you and I . . ." She looked down. "My mom was killed in a car accident in Uruguay about five years ago."

They were trekking toward what Jo had described as "the prettiest spot in the world," but the wild jungle of northern B.C. rainforest was doing its best to halt their progress. Callum's leather shoes squished and squelched with every step, he was soaked up to his knees from the long grass, and he sorely regretted his stupidity. He'd worn his suit, thinking it would help him maintain a level of professional decorum—something his brain wasn't doing at all. But it was just one more bad decision, making him, as ever, ill equipped for the terrain he found himself in.

"I'm sorry," he repeated. It seemed that was all he ever said to her, but he couldn't help himself. He wished he could roll back the years and fix all the things that had caused Jo pain when they were younger, things that obviously hadn't healed with time—and then he realized he was being selfish again. Because he was one of the things that caused her pain, and he wanted that fixed most of all—for her, yes—but even more, if he was honest, for himself.

Jo continued forward, without looking back. It was like she floated above the rough ground rather than walked, and she seemed oblivious to the snarled roots that kept making him stumble. "Unless you killed them, it's not your fault, so don't say sorry."

There didn't seem to be a good response to that so he said nothing. A few minutes later, she glanced over her shoulder. "It was a long time ago, but apparently it still stings. I didn't mean to bite your head off."

He grinned. If that was her biting someone's head off, it was pretty funny. She smiled back, and he remembered how much he used to love her dimple—just one, on her left cheek.

"Are you wet?" she asked a moment later.

"Drenched."

That stopped her. "Should we turn back? I just thought—"

"That since I'd agreed to come for a tour of the property, I'd have dressed for the occasion?"

Her nose scrunched and her eyes twinkled. "Yeah, sort of."

"I wasn't thinking. It's been too long since I went hiking—but I'm good. I meant what I said at the house. I'm game to see whatever you want me to."

The beloved dimple appeared once more and Jo continued the nonstop flood of description that he'd interrupted with his question about her parents. He followed her gestures and found himself genuinely caught up in the bits of information she imparted about the various types of trees and plants they passed.

"A lot of people didn't know it, but my uncle was quite the horticulturist. He planted and preserved a variety of indigenous plants—and cultivated other, non-invasive, species that thrive here. I'd like to create little sitting areas where guests can sneak away and write or draw, work with their laptops, or even just picnic. And I thought I might put up small plaques, made from cedar or something, filled with information about the various things growing around here."

"Sounds cool," Callum said. And it did. But her plans, if one could even give them so concrete a word, also sounded more like fun, dreamy what-ifs than a firm, practical here's the market, here's the profit margin, here's the room for growth over time, business model.

They came to the end of the trail. Two ancient Cottonwoods formed a golden-leafed archway. Jo ducked to avoid a low branch and pushed a prickly pine bough out of the way, then beckoned to Callum.

Another curtain of water showered down on them as they walked through the arch, and Jo's curls glistened. He reached out to touch her hair—and stopped himself just in time. How quickly he forgot all the years between them. How quickly his body remembered the time he could touch her whenever he wanted to.

His melancholy sigh died on his lips, however, as they stepped out of the forest and into a dream.

The dense greenery gave way to a soft blue-gray world of rock and river. They stood on a sandbar the color and texture of raw brown sugar, sprinkled here and there with huge white rocks. Marshmallows in light cocoa. Butter in cookie dough before it was beaten in. . . .

Jo propped the two fishing rods she'd brought "just in case" against a stack of driftwood, then leapt lightly onto a big rock about three feet away. She held her arms out and leaned her head back. Callum could almost feel her pulling the clean, cool wet air into her lungs, and he inhaled too.

She pivoted to face him, feet still planted on the rock, and grinned. "So what do you think? Isn't it glorious? Your own private river and wildlife adventure. All the best salmon run here with the changing seasons, Coho, Springs, Sockeye, Pinks—

and Rainbow trout too, my favorite.

It's magical. That's what he wanted to say, or something equally lame—but he wasn't able to speak right away.

Jo's ecstatic expression faded and a blush heightened the color in her already pink-with-the-wind cheeks. She hopped off the rock.

"What's wrong?"

He shook his head. "Nothing, nothing. I'm just making inner notes. Does it have boat access from the road, a ramp or something?"

Jo chewed her lip and her toe nudged a black-ringed stone out of its hole in the sand—a nervous habit he, again, remembered from their youth. When she met his eyes, her own were serious. "Yep. Boat access from the highway and directly from the main driveway. You know where you parked?"

"Yes?"

"Well, if you'd gone to the left of the pole shed, there's a lane that meets up with the road to the ramp. And the best thing? The ramp's maintained by the Department of Highways."

"Because there's a small settlement of people on the other side of the river."

"Yeah, that's right. I keep forgetting you've been here forever, that you know all the exciting little places I've forgotten—or never learned about while I was here."

I'm an outsider. Different than you. I see things in new ways. She might as well have put up a banner—

except she wasn't saying any of those things intentionally and he knew it.

She picked up the rock she'd dislodged and put it
in her pocket.

He smiled at the romantic, sentimental gesture—
but her tone was all business now and that was his
fault. He was sorry for it.

"Two boats come with the property, just simple
aluminum things, but the motors are in good shape,
and I used to work for a guy who did small engine
repair. I can maintain them, no problem."

Callum consciously fought to keep his jaw from
dropping. What kind of life had she lived? Working in
a rewind shop, running her own restaurant? Hadn't
she gone to school like everyone else? "You did? You
can?"

Jo shrugged. "Yes, but a lot of sport fisherman
prefer fishing off the bank or wading into a prime
spot—and there are plenty of those around here." She
hefted the rods, turned back toward the trees, then
hesitated. "Actually"—she moved decisively left—
"let's take the road back. It's not as pretty, but it's
more practical."

The return walk went quickly because they kept a
good pace. Jo didn't leave any quiet spaces in the
conversation for idle looking about, or pause to point
out whimsical details. By the time they reached the
house, he had a good idea of how many tourists the
area attracted, what the peak months were, how many
visitors were just general holiday-takers, how many

were drawn specifically to fish or hunt, and how many were business people. She also discussed, for reasons he didn't understand at first, what the local arts community was like.

"There's a lot of potential here for retreats or small conferences or workshops," she explained.

"I'm impressed. How'd you find all this out already?"

"It wasn't difficult. We have a Chamber of Commerce."

Ah, of course. And it was a pretty rudimentary market assessment. Callum flushed, realizing his being "impressed" was a little condescending.

Jo stashed the rods in a case by the cab of her truck, and they climbed the stairs at the backside of the house. As they walked toward the door, a large porch swing on the west side caught Callum's eye. All the better to watch the sun set, he thought.

Jo paused and scooped up a wine bottle, a stemmed glass and a plate with the remains of what looked like assorted cheese from a small glass-topped table with a base constructed from the roots of a tree.

"I thought I'd caught all the mess—sorry."

He wanted to pull her onto the swing's wide seat, tuck the wool blanket crumpled welcomingly in the corner of the chair around them, and watch the sky. He wanted to apologize for how he'd disappointed her with his reaction to the river. He wanted—

He wanted.

"Come on," she said. "I think you'll like dinner a

lot. I cooked in camps for years, but I've also taken culinary art courses. I can feed a crowd, or cook up the sexiest—er, fine or intimate, I mean—dining experience for two you can imagine."

"'Sexiest' sounds fun," he said.

She laughed. "Sorry, sir. It's not that kind of establishment."

Inside the house, Callum was taken with the small changes and improvements she'd wrought in the week or so since he'd been there with Samantha. The living room, homey and comfortable to begin with, was clutter-free. Flames flickered and danced through the glass in a big-bellied black woodstove and the beaten up leather couch called to be sunk into—perhaps with one of the novels jam-packed into the shelves that lined the far wall. A south-facing window showed off a flank of gold and red deciduous trees, then a row of evergreen, topped by ridges of navy, snow-dusted mountains stretching into the chilling, purple sky.

The dining room table, a massive slab of ancient cedar, looked like it could support a feast to feed and seat twenty people, but also seemed equally, if surprisingly, conducive to, well, there was that word again, *intimate* parties.

Jo had set their places directly across from each other on the furthest end of the table. Beautifully tarnished brass candleholders stood off to the side of the plates, creating a small, personal eating space despite the grandness of the large table. He could imagine how the light would play on the soft, polished red wood.

Unfortunately, the ease they'd enjoyed at the start of the afternoon, temporarily reestablished with their small joke about sexy dinners, had died.

Jo glanced around the house's interior, but the lines in her brow and the tension in her mouth said she found none of the charm Callum was seeing. "So . . ." she said.

"So?"

She clapped her hands lightly, some decision apparently reached. "So, I'd thought I'd try to give you the experience of being a guest here—that it would be, if you'll excuse my attempt at manipulation, the best way to win you over and convince you to try to change Samantha's mind . . . but now I'm thinking you're more of a hard numbers guy. What would you prefer? Just an all-out nice evening and a taste of what I think guests would come back for—or an equally good dinner, but eaten at the kitchen table with my business plan?"

"You've developed a hard copy plan?"

"Complete with a market analysis and projected financials."

"Really?"

Jo nodded, but her eyes narrowed—consciously or not, he wasn't sure. Shit, he'd sounded condescending again. But that's not how he meant his comments, either time. He was just fascinated by the variety of divergent things she was proficient at. He did the same thing day in, day out—and had for years.

She moved out of the soft, sensual light of the dining room toward the bright galley kitchen. "Wine or coffee?"

The question should've been simple, but Callum found it anything but. His answer would reveal his choice. Wine? A night of fun and a lovely glimpse into Jo's home as her guest and, if he could be so lucky, her *friend*. Coffee? A cut and dried business dinner.

He wanted wine, dammit. And an appetite-teasing starter, followed by a rich, satiating main course . . . then, maybe even dessert. Something decadent. Would she offer different wines for different parts of the meal? Was the meal *in* parts? He couldn't smell anything cooking yet. . . .

But he didn't want to mislead her. He suspected that with her passion, if she just had some money to invest—and a little extra to carry her until the venture started to turn a profit, she would be successful. But, unless Samantha and Jo herself had steered him wrong, she had neither of those things.

And Samantha, though she looked like she could afford a financial risk, or at least to wait for her share, was convincingly adamant that she wouldn't be swayed. He could have the best night ever, believe in Jo's vision one hundred percent, but what difference would it make? The place had to be sold. He didn't want to pretend otherwise and get Jo's hopes up. She was too much of a dreamer. It wasn't his fault.

"Coffee sounds great," he said. "Thanks."

Jo opened her mouth—then closed it without speaking, nodded, and led him to a sunshine yellow table covered in papers.

"What would you like as an appetizer?" she asked, smiling and handing him a cup of some dark deep roast poured piping hot from a stainless steel carafe. "Spinach salad with chèvre, strawberries, and almonds, or pan fried zucchini cakes with tzatziki?"

"Is it too late to change my mind?"

Jo cocked an eyebrow.

"The coffee smells amazing, but if you're still offering, I'd love a glass of wine. And the zucchini patties—but only if you'll let me help."

Callum stretched with a satisfied grunt and surveyed the remains of their dinner spread out beneath the candlelight, wishing he had room for one more bite. "Well, I know what I'm telling Samantha."

"You do?"

"Absolutely. That you tried to kill me with food."

Jo leaned across the table and smacked him. He caught her hand and held it—an action that felt both delicious and slightly taboo but also completely natural and right.

"Seriously though. That steak was, well, beyond description. And those scallops? You're a wonderful chef."

Jo looked down at their joined hands resting on the cedar table, then waggled her eyebrows. "Yes, and I have the failed restaurant behind me to prove it."

Callum wanted to believe the flush on her skin was caused by him, not the wine, not the food, not the heat from the candles glowing beside them ... definitely not by embarrassment over something stupid like a business gone wrong. *Him.*

"What happened with all that anyway? From just the little I know of you now, it's hard for me to imagine you not doing well."

Jo gently disentangled her fingers from his and stood up. "Ah," she said, resting her hands on her stomach. "So good—but I don't think I left room for dessert."

"You made dessert too? You *are* trying to kill me."

Jo grinned. "Do you want to sit soft for a bit first?" He must've looked confused because she added, "Settle in the living room—you know, *sit soft*? And would you like that coffee now?"

"Not so much, no," he said. He grabbed the remaining bottle of wine and their glasses and trailed after her. A woman in jeans was well worth following, he thought—then the lawyer in him amended that statement to something more specific. Jo in jeans was well worth following.

She turned, smiling like she'd read his mind, then laughed when she saw he'd brought the dregs of the wine. "Is there anything left in that?"

"Oh, yeah, at least a mouthful or two." He pretended to swig straight from the bottle and wondered when he'd turned into such a goof. He was as hammered—and as transparent—as his brother Brian.

She plunked down in the middle of the couch. "I have a gorgeous port—"

"You *do* have a gorgeous—"

She held up her hand, but giggled. "Whoa—but if you want it, it's on the bookshelf between Mary Shelly and Bram Stoker, and you have to pour it."

"Well, I'm definitely in need of a cab anyway, and since the fare's going to be ridiculous I guess I should make it worth it."

"I'm sorry. I didn't even think—"

"Don't be sorry." He poured them generous drinks, and settled on the end of the couch, freakishly pleased Jo had taken the middle. The couch wasn't big. Her thigh was only inches from his. "I've loved every minute of it."

"Even though we didn't crack open my business plan once?"

"Especially because."

Jo laughed. "Nice."

They sat in comfortable silence, watching the fire, sipping the deep, full-bodied port—and Callum was a little shocked. He'd always remembered how animated they'd been together, how he could—and did—tell her anything and everything. How they laughed and talked nonstop. He'd forgotten until now how easy she was to be quiet with, too. How he could just sit with her, let his mind wander and not be pressured to entertain, inform, educate. . . .

"We're just like before. I feel like you never left,"

he said suddenly—then muttered almost angrily, "Wow, I do *not* need this drink."

Jo didn't contradict his words or seem put off. She just laughed. "Yeah, you're still a lightweight."

After a little while and a few more sips, she turned sideways on the couch and sat cross-legged. "You asked about my bankruptcy—the restaurant."

"I thought maybe you didn't hear the question."

"No, you didn't. You assumed I didn't want to answer, and you chose not to press."

He shrugged.

"I had a partner, otherwise known as a common-law husband."

"Oh. Well, I know about being burned by one of those all right. I have a treasure of an ex, too."

"He liked to have businesses—and all sorts of other things I found out too late—on the side."

"What? Like other women on the side of *you*?" Callum had had enough to drink that his self-censor button was thoroughly turned off. "Was he a fucking imbecile or what?"

Jo's laugh was hilarious to him, like she literally said, "Ahaahhahahahaaha" and it made him laugh too. And then she answered quietly, "I don't know. Maybe he was, or maybe I was. Maybe I *am*."

He shook his head. "No, not you. Your ideas are great."

"But?"

"But—"

"No," she interrupted suddenly.

"No?"

"Let's not talk about any ifs or buts tonight."

It was late when they finished dessert—a baked pumpkin cheesecake with a pecan bottom and warm caramel topping—and more round-bottomed glasses of port.

"You were right," he said.

"Of course I was—but about what?"

"You do make a sexy dinner."

He wanted to make her smile the way she was smiling right now every time he saw her. . . .

"Thanks," was all she said and disappeared into the kitchen with the dirty plates. She reappeared a few minutes later, a quilt in hand.

"If you want, if it's not too weird, you could sleep on the couch tonight."

"Really? Are you sure?"

She shrugged. "It'll save you fifty bucks at least—and it'll drive Samantha mental. Make sure you bill for every hour."

He laughed. "Well, thanks." He stretched out on the couch.

She snapped the quilt in the air and let it settle over him.

"I feel about eight."

"Ha—you look almost thirty-five and drunk as a skunk."

"Touché," he agreed happily.

Jo bent over him and for one blood-surging minute he thought she'd kiss him. "Good night, Callum. I had a surprisingly good time tonight."

"Me, too—equally surprising."

She was about to straighten up when he reached out. "May I?"

"May you what?"

He touched her hair. "It feels the same," he said and closed his eyes.

"Weirdo," she said, but he heard the smile in her voice and knew her dimple was showing again. "Sleep well."

Chapter 7

J O LIFTED A SMALL END table, tiptoed over to the couch, and set it down without a sound. With equal care and quiet, she slipped back to the kitchen and returned with a heavy mug and a small note she'd just written: *Hey, Sleeping Beauty! Sorry to duck out. I wanted to be here when you woke up, but forgot a prior engagement. Coffee's on in the kitchen. Help yourself to whatever you want to eat.*

She smiled down at Callum's dead-asleep form; he'd always been able to crash out like no one else she knew. Sometime in the night, he'd stripped to his T-shirt and boxers and pushed his blanket half off. A small shudder of heat quaked through her belly as she appreciated the peep she got of one long, heavily muscled leg. What did the man do all day? He didn't get his physique from sitting at a computer. His square jaw had a shadow of stubble that she wanted to touch.

Wow, creepy much? she asked herself and had to stifle a giggle so she didn't destroy her silent exit thing.

Out in the yard she whistled for Hoover, took one look at his matted fur and caught one whiff of his foul stench and clipped him to his lead. "The only con to this place—the abundance of rotten fish guts left at the river for you to roll in," she muttered. Hoover smiled happily, his tongue lolling out the side of his mouth.

Jo freshened his water dish with the outdoor tap, then washed her hands with the dish soap she kept tucked on a small shelf under the fish-cleaning table her uncle had conveniently rigged up years earlier.

"You're gross!" she said cheerfully to Hoover as way of good-bye. He wagged his tail, whining as she headed to the truck. "Oh, don't fret. I'll be ba—ack," she promised, doing a terrible impression of the Terminator—but she couldn't help it. She was in that good a mood. Maybe, just maybe, Callum was someone Samantha would listen to. And even if he wasn't, hadn't they had fun? Her stomach clenched remembering his hand on hers—how naturally he'd caught her fingers and held her hand. And those eyes of his—how they burned with every emotion that moved him like they were lit with a gas flame.

She hated, but also loved, how he seemed so much like the old Callum she had known and adored. Her Callum. Be careful, she warned herself, *be careful*— but the inner warning was more like a plea.

I thought you were off men, a small part of her wheedled.

"Hmm," she murmured aloud. Her crazy inner voice had a point, but then again, dreams could grow and change, right?

As she turned out of her driveway onto the highway, her phone rang. She was jumping to know if it was Callum, but refrained from answering. She arrived at the coffee shop on Main Street with time to spare though, and didn't see Dave's truck anywhere, so she pulled out her phone.

Rats—disappointing, for sure, but no big surprise. She pressed the Talk icon to call back, and waited for Samantha to pick up.

"Well, helllllloooo, dolly."

"Hey, Sam." Jo squinted against the sunshine attempting to blind her through the windshield. Was anything more painfully beautiful than morning sun in a frosty-cold autumn sky? "What's up?"

"I was wondering if you knew what our mutual lawyer friend was up to."

"Um, should I?" Yikes! Jo hadn't stopped to consider the conclusions Samantha would jump to if she knew Callum stayed the night, no matter how innocent it truly was.

But *was* it innocent? Or had some part of her known exactly what Samantha would think? She grinned, but before she could say something cheeky, Samantha beat her to the punch.

"So did you seduce him or what?"

"Uh . . . "

"Wait—what?"

"Um—"

Samantha shrieked. "No, you didn't. Tell me you *didn't*! I was being *facetious*. I meant seduce him into

70

thinking your ridiculous B & B plan was viable, not seduce-*seduce* him."

"I didn't seduce him in any sense of the word. He stayed over, but nothing happened."

"He *stayed over*."

"On the couch. He was on the couch! We didn't even kiss. We had a bit too much wine and—"

"Too much *wine*!"

"Maybe. Just a little. A *tad*."

"What the hell did you make for dinner?"

Jo gave full details, but before she got to describe the dessert, Samantha interrupted with another top-volume shriek. "That is too much, totally unfair. You played dirty."

"Oh come on. It's not like that. He was, he *is*, nice."

Samantha stopped mid-huff. "*Nice*, eh? That's interesting. So you like him. You actually *like* him. This isn't just about you trying to weasel him into convincing me to give the bed-and-bomb a go?"

The bed-and-bomb. You had to give it to Samantha. She was funny—but what she was suggesting wasn't. It was one thing for Jo, in the privacy of her own head, to wonder if she was feeling something for some guy—if Callum even qualified as something as nonthreatening as "some guy." It was a totally different thing, a horrifying, unacceptable thing, for Samantha to notice it.

Two large fists pounded lightly on the driver-side window, saving her from having to respond. She jumped and turned to see giant, rangy Dave. She gave a little wave and held up one finger. He nodded and headed toward The Zoo, a popular coffee shop decorated, surreally, with life-sized wire art animals.

"Look, I'm at the coffee place. Dave just got here."

"Oh, I see, *Dave just got there.* Aren't you just the busiest little entrepreneur ever? You have'em lining up."

"I do not have them *lining up.*"

"Current events have way more potential than your stupid bug-and-breakfast."

"Sam—"

"No, seriously. Just quit with the farfetched idea already and take up finding a man as your new obsession."

"Not interested."

"No longer believe you."

"I mean it, and if anyone thinks otherwise they're barking up the wrong tree."

Samantha snort-giggled. "That should be a T-shirt. You could have a tree labeled 'wrong tree' with a sign beside it that says 'No barking.'"

"I have to go."

"So go. I'll talk to you later—after I've scrounged *my* lawyer out of *your* bed."

The coffee shop was busy. Jo craned her head to see where Dave had managed to find a seat.

A laugh sounded behind her. "Got you again."

She turned to face him, forcing a smile and trying

not to feel irrationally annoyed by him. "For a big monster you're pretty adept at sneaking about."

"I got you a Chai latté, but if you want something else, no worries, I'll drink it along with mine."

"No, that's fantastic—just what the doctor ordered. Thanks."

Dave took her elbow and led her toward two black leather armchairs in the corner under the window. Two red mugs steamed merrily away on a low table.

"It's sweet you remembered me going on about how much I love Chai," Jo said, then realized he'd recalled no such thing when a confused look crossed his face.

She removed her half-length trench coat, hung it on a nearby coat tree, and sank into a seat. "Mmmm," she said, wrapping her hands around her mug and reveling in the steamy heat and yummy scent of cardamom, cloves, and cinnamon.

"So what's new?" Dave asked. "You all settled in?"

"Pretty much."

"And are you still gung ho on your hotel idea?"

"Bed-and-breakfast," Jo corrected and shrugged. "I don't know."

"I still can't believe you're here. I mean a lot of folks move away and come back, but I never expected you to."

Jo rested her lip cautiously against the edge of the mug, then set it down. Still too hot. She didn't want to rush, burn herself, and not be able to enjoy the rest.

Dave took a big mouthful. "Ow—shit! Hot!"

Jo winced and laughed simultaneously. "Are you okay?"

"Fine, fine," Dave said.

"Here put some sugar on it." Jo passed him a small package of white sugar.

"What? Why?"

"Trust me. Just sprinkle a few grains on the burnt part of your tongue. It won't magically heal it, but it will take away most of the sting."

A moment later, Dave beamed. "Hey, it worked. You're awesome."

"Yeah, sure, that's me all right. *Awesome*," Jo joked.

"Yeah," Dave agreed. "You are." He spoke without a touch of sarcasm or humor, and stared in a way that made Jo uncomfortable. Samantha had warned of this weeks ago, when they'd first ran into Dave at Safeway. . . . But, no, he wasn't really holding a torch for her, all these years later, was he?

Dave broke a peanut butter cookie in half and held it out.

"No, thanks. Pathetically, I'm still full from dinner last night."

They chatted more or less easily for half an hour or so, and then conversation dwindled and Jo stood up to go. "It's been fun catching up. Thanks for the invite—and for the Chai."

"Are you still throwing your party at the end of the

month?"

"Absolutely. Wear your fanciest duds."

Dave grinned and Jo saw a perfect opportunity to send the message that they were just friends. "And feel free to bring someone, okay? The more the merrier. I'd love to meet the special person in your life."

"Sure, if you say so. Do you want me to bring anything?"

"If there's something particular you like to drink, but other than that, not a thing."

"How many people are going to be there?"

"Um . . . twenty or so, including me and your date, or even more maybe."

"Date? I'm bringing a buddy. He wouldn't like being called my date."

Buddy? Rats, that had backfired. She tried again. "Well, great, but feel free to bring a romantic interest, too—"

"Romantic? Nah, there's no one . . . or no one *yet*."

Dave stared into her eyes intently, his face grave. Even Jo couldn't pretend not to notice it was meant to be a "significant" look.

"Oh, well, count yourself lucky, hey?" she said. "Single life is where it's at."

"I don't know about that."

Jo checked the time on her phone. "Shoot, I really have to run or I'll be late. I have a bank appointment.

I'll see you Saturday."

Dave reached for her hand and gave it a little squeeze. "I can't wait," he said.

"Yeah." She pulled away quickly. "Should be great." And with those lame words, she fled.

Chapter 8

JO LEFT THE BANK DISTRACTED—and ran smack-dab into an ornate wrought iron cage the city had put around a small maple tree, trying to protect it from breakage. She dropped her portfolio bag and almost tripped.

Yes, putting a spike through my face in a classic Jo move is exactly what I need right now, she thought as she caught her balance.

It's true she wasn't particularly surprised by the loan officer's pronouncement, a very nice woman who seemed genuinely sorry for the bad news—but somehow, being prepared for something, or thinking you were, didn't stave off disappointment as much as one might think.

Stupid bank policies. Stupider bankruptcy. Stupidest Devin—no, that was a lie. Stupidest *her*. She didn't go there often anymore—found it unproductive and unhelpful to dwell on the two-fold implosion of her relationship and restaurant. She'd spent three years working hand to mouth, wasting all her off time laid out on the couch crying or staring at the TV, unable to bear public places—and still, in the end, hadn't managed to pay everything off. She didn't care if other people declared bankruptcy. She hated that she had. And she hated that her name and her reputation were tied to that dirt bag. What an idiot she'd been. What a complete, total idiot!

Her heart hammered and her vision blurred. Oh no—*no*. It had been so long. Not here, not now. She leaned against the door of her pickup, then bent forward slightly, resting her forearms on her thighs for support.

Breathe, she commanded herself. *Breathe.*

She tried. She really did, but the air seemed thick, sticky. It caught midway down, hurt her chest, like it was something too big to swallow and she was choking—

No, it's okay. That's just the anxiety. You're not choking. You're fine. You went to the bank. You did really well. The loan officer, Michelle, was really nice—

It wasn't a big breath, but she managed a bit of air. Her vision steadied. She closed her eyes, but continued bracing herself against the truck.

One more breath, really slow—good. Feel the oxygen right through to the bottom of your lungs, lifting your ribcage—

You were professional. You have nothing to feel ashamed of it. And you did it—you went to the bank.

She was breathing normally again, and was queasy with gratitude at being able to do so. And she *had* gone to the bank. And survived. And in terms of an attack? Well, this was just a baby one—and the only flare up in months.

"So that's something, right?" she whispered. "A victory of sorts."

"Pardon me? Are you all right, ma'am?"

She looked up. An elderly man in a suit and tie had stopped, the lines in his face a story of concern and mild irritation that he might be held up.

No, that was her thing, putting it on him.

"I'm fine, thank you. Just dizzy for a moment there."

"You should eat something. I always get light-headed myself if I don't eat something," he said gruffly, moving away even as he spoke.

For some reason the practical advice, given without fanfare, struck Jo as spectacularly kind. And he made a good point. She'd figured she was fine to go without breakfast after indulging so heavily the night before, but now hunger was chewing a hole in her gut.

And she suddenly felt ridiculously fine. Powerful even. She'd gone to the bank! Endured the humiliation she'd feared. Heard the news she hadn't wanted to hear. And was fine! She had even managed to thwart her panic before it overwhelmed her. Lunch—on her, ha ha—was definitely in order.

She was about to climb into her truck, when the stupid cage around the poor tree caught her attention again. There was some sort of symbolism at work here. And it was a striking image as well. She hesitated for a second, then thought, What the hell?

She'd just spent ten minutes propped up, trying to breathe, what was one more embarrassing pose?

She grabbed the camera she always kept in her bag, removed the lens cap, and checked the sidewalk for dirt. It was clear, except for a few dry leaves that scuttled across the cement like crabs in the light breeze. Jo lay down on her back and took two shots. Sat for a moment and skidded her butt closer, leaned back, and shot again. Saw the angle of a specific branch—shot once more.

She remained planted on the ground and reviewed her pictures. Then smiled. The last one was good. Black metal pickets, banded together with heavy rings, tried to confine the growing tree—but it stretched and reached, far surpassing the unnatural restraints, and exploded into the brilliant blue sky with leafy branches of fervent color—orange, red, gold-kissed-greens. . . .

Jo clambered up to her feet again, said excuse me to a couple of people walking by, and dusted off the seat of her jeans.

Now what did she feel like having?

Pizza? No. A good old-fashioned deli sandwich? Nah. A street over, there was a new-to-her café that advertised Pad Thai. Just the thing. Definitely. Something she never cooked for herself.

She didn't bother to take the truck. It was only a couple blocks away.

Halfway there it struck her. She'd thought of Devin, of what had happened between them, for all of a second, for the first time in weeks and weeks and weeks. And it hadn't spiraled into an obsessive thought cycle. And she hadn't cried. Shitty bank appointment or no, things were looking up.

In the restaurant, Jo took a two-seater table hidden away from the rest of the diners by a half wall and an extraordinarily leafy ficus tree. Moments later a waitress arrived with a pot of green tea and a heaping plate of noodles and shrimp that Jo had ordered and paid for at the counter.

The server disappeared, and Jo closed her eyes to savor the gingery, fishy goodness for a moment. Then she tore open the paper package holding her chopsticks.

The ficus tree shook lightly as someone sat down on the other side of wall, blocked from her view—but not from her hearing.

"Thanks, it looks amazing," a familiar masculine voice said.

She tried to resist the urge to peek and confirm what she thought her ears were hearing? Callum? Here?

"Enjoy," chimed the same server who'd brought Jo her meal. "Will someone else be joining you?"

"Not today."

"Then do you mind if I steal this chair for another table?"

"Not at all."

Jo could refrain no longer. She took a big mouthful of noodles—oh, man, they were delicious—stood up a little and peered over the wall. It was Callum all right. His face wasn't visible, but she'd recognize his crown of blue-black hair anywhere.

She settled back into her seat. She'd like to approach him, but she already had her food. It would be kind of weird. But then again, she was kind of weird, so . . .

"And how is everything?"

Jo jumped as a second server appeared by her elbow. She hadn't realized there were two sets of stairs to the small landing.

"Really good so far," she said.

"Can I get you anything else right away?"

"No, thank you. I'm fine for now."

Callum's head popped over the wall. "Hey, it's you. I thought I recognized your voice."

Jo grinned. "I just noticed you a minute ago, too. I was trying to decide if I should disturb you or not."

"You definitely should've disturbed me—and you should've this morning, too."

"Ha, yes. Sorry to disappear on you like that."

"Are you meeting someone?"

"No—well, I was, but it's done now." Jo motioned vaguely toward the door. "I was just running around, stopped for a quick bite."

"Mind if I join you?"

"Not at all."

Moments later he was pulled up to her tiny table, so close their knees touched, his own plate of Pad Thai nearly resting against hers.

She held up her mug. "Green tea, too?"

"What else? Great minds and all that—cheers." They clanked porcelain cups.

"Do you come here a lot?" she asked through another mouthful of noodles.

"A fair bit. My office is really close by."

After a few minutes of eating and chatting about the food and the décor, Callum's foot started tapping.

"Nervous?" Jo teased, then realized from the shadow that crossed his eyes he was. "What's up? Is it something I said?"

Callum shook his head, and sank his teeth into his lower lip for just a second. Random desire and a wave of heat rippled through Jo. Oh, how the body had a memory all its own. The things they used to do. . . . *She* wanted to bite his lip. She set her chopsticks down. "Seriously, what is it?" she asked, her voice embarrassingly rough.

"I—well, do you think we should talk about, you know. . . . What happened between us, and what didn't happen, all those years ago?"

Jo's body responded again, but this time it was nerves not lust that jangled her senses. She did want to know why he'd given up on her, why he'd bailed, but she was also afraid to hear it. Didn't want to know the ways she hadn't measured up or been good enough for his dreams for the future.

She shook her head. "No, let's not. What's the benefit? We were very young. I for—" She stalled and changed tracks. "Let's leave it at that."

Callum's eyes blazed, like "leaving it at that" was the last thing he wanted to do, but then his phone buzzed. He read the text message, and slid his cell back into his pocket without responding.

"Well, I think—" His phone rang shrilly, interrupting whatever his thought was. "I'm on lunch," he said without a greeting. "What do you need?—No, that's fine. I'll be back in half an hour." He drummed his fingers on the table. "Samantha Kendall? No—her sister. That's right. *Jo.*"

Jo speared a large shrimp with concentrated effort, feeling like she was eavesdropping though it wasn't like she could avoid hearing. "Do you need some privacy?" she whispered.

Callum glanced up, and she was a little shocked by the ferocity in his glare. "No, not at all," he told her, then directed his attention back to the phone. "It is not. Not in any way—no. And I told you. I'll talk to you soon. Fine. Fifteen then."

He ended the call, shut his phone off, and laid his napkin over his plate.

"You're not going to finish?"

"Lost my appetite, sorry."

"Is it something to do with me—or Samantha?"

"No . . . yes—not really," he said. "Just my dad. He feels your and my 'acquaintance' is a conflict of interest."

"That sounds like a thought Samantha planted."

"Oh, don't worry. He doesn't need help thinking I've screwed up—wow, though, sorry—I'm not trying to be super negative here."

Jo held up her hand. "No apology needed. Family stuff. I get it."

They were quiet a moment and Jo kept eating—no way she wasn't going to keep enjoying her food—but after a few more bites, she put her chopsticks down. "So you ended up working with your dad after all, hey?"

"Yep." Callum pushed his chair back and stretched. Jo tried to focus on his words, not the long, taut lines of his body. "Archer and Sons, a.k.a. him, me and Brian—only Cade was smart enough to escape. He threw 'sons' into the name practically the day we were born. You probably remember me complaining about him—and his expectations—ad nauseam."

Jo didn't bother to deny it. "And you don't like it anymore than you thought you would?"

"It?"

"Law."

"No"—he shook his head—"I don't. And it's funny, but very few people ever ask me that."

"Most people probably think you're set for life, living the dream."

Callum huffed and stood up. "Well, the set for life part's right anyway. What I was supposed to be was mapped out from day one."

Jo ate one last shrimp—so garlicky, so good— then got to her feet as well. She was done, too. "Do you want me to walk with you?"

He looked uncomfortable.

"Another time then."

"Actually, yeah . . . that would be better. Is that all right?"

"Of course." Up close, without their fragrant lunches between them, he smelled like lemon peel and sugar. How did he always smell literally good enough to eat?

They parted ways on the sidewalk, and Jo walked to the corner. Waiting for the light so she could cross the street, she glanced back just in time to see Callum pause in front of his office doors.

She framed her mouth with her hands to amplify her voice. "Hey!"

He turned, spotted her, and lifted his own hands in a silent question.

"If not a lawyer," she hollered. "*What*?"

Callum shot a look at his office building's door, shook his head lightly, and jogged over to her.

The walk signal lit up, but she didn't step forward.

Callum leaned in, almost like he was going to kiss her. "A baker, practically forever, just like when we were together, if you can believe it."

Of course. Another way he hadn't changed. Sugar and spice and everything nice.

"Oh, I believe it," she said.

His mouth was inches from hers and the heat in his eyes made her giddy. "And I've wanted to do this again forever, too," he said.

His lips pressed against hers and she made a little

"oh" sound—surprise then thrill zipping through her as his arms went around her and his tongue opened her mouth.

They broke apart a minute or two later and for once she was speechless. Then he said, "Thank you," which made her giggle.

"My pleasure," she said as he ran a finger along her jaw.

A stocky man appeared on the sidewalk in front of Archer and Sons, arms crossed, glaring.

"Um, is your dad, uh, still huge and scowling, and prone to wearing charcoal suits?"

"And balding now?"

"I think so . . . "

"Yep, that's him," Callum said.

"From the look on his face, I'd say he definitely feels this is a conflict of interest."

Callum put his finger to her lips. "Well, he's only half right. I'm definitely interested, but I don't have any conflict."

He loped away in an easy stride, and Jo crossed the street, then smiled all the way back to her truck.

Chapter 9

JO SPENT THE NEXT WEEK laboring through her to-do list. For every one thing she did, another crucial need became more obvious. The bathroom was spic-and-span, but so old and worn it didn't look clean. She priced out a renovation, planning on real stone tiles and natural wood that would call the river to mind, and felt a bit discouraged—especially since, realistically, the house needed a minimum of another two additional bathrooms besides.

She sorted through a bunch more of the never-ending boxes of junk that filled the five spare bedrooms from floor to ceiling, loading discard items into her pickup, repacking and labeling things to be sold or given away. It was hard not to be discouraged when day after day, it looked like she'd hardly made a dint.

On Friday, she enjoyed a late lunch of pumpkin soup and dark rye toast with lots of butter, took stock of what she'd accomplished and contemplated the remainder of the day. Two o'clock. She had a few hours before the light faded. She could take the truckload of stuff into town and drop it off at the

Salvation Army, then stop by the Unemployment Office and see what jobs were posted. She had checked her funds online using the public library's Wi-Fi the day before, and though she'd be okay for another couple months, thanks to Uncle Ray's cash gift and her own paltry savings, she didn't want to exhaust that money entirely.

Man, she wished Samantha would soften up sooner rather than later. If she was going to open in the spring, she needed the ball rolling now. Every week of waiting pushed her opening date—and the opportunity to generate income—back that much further. And besides, it was excruciatingly difficult to refrain from just jumping in and starting the work, but she really shouldn't push her luck. She probably shouldn't even be living in the house, though so far Samantha hadn't made too much of a stink.

She wondered what Callum's opinion on all this was—his real one, not his careful I'm-your-sister's-hired-counsel shtick.

And then, as always the past few days—heck, every other minute—when her thoughts ran to Callum, her body went to remembering. His chin grazing her cheek. The smell of him. The velvet softness of the initial pressure of his mouth, then its demand—

She stopped the thought there. She was never going to get anything done this way. But even reminding herself of that, she couldn't help but wonder one more thing . . . also *again*. Why hadn't he called? Or, perhaps the more pertinent question: why hadn't she called him? But she knew the answer to both those, didn't she?

He'd obviously kissed her on impulse, an impulse he now regretted—and she didn't want to hear it and have her fantasy crushed. She didn't regret their kiss. Quite the opposite, in fact. Just like in days of old, when it came to Callum Archer, she only wanted more.

She traced her index finger back and forth across her mouth then sighed heavily, startling Hoover. He grunted and rolled over into a deeper nap. All this ruminating wasn't helping her get on with her afternoon—but it did change her mind about going into town. She knew what she wanted to do instead. She'd worked hard all week. It was time to play.

The river was a slate-colored ribbon, almost black beneath the trees shading the pool Jo was about to sink her line into. She was glad she'd worn gloves. Yes, the tips of her fingers were pink with cold since her woollies were nipped off below the knuckles for dexterity's sake, but the rest of her hands were warm.

She smiled at the red and white bobber floating serenely for the most part, but spinning out and away and back every so often as it caught a small current. A lot of people used weighted foam bobbers now, but she liked the old school look of the little ball—and the memories it kindled. How many trout had she and Ray grilled over an open fire on this very spot of riverbank?

Overhead a crow cackled and hooted. Laughing at her or with her? Either way, the sound made Jo grin.

She gripped her rod between her knees for a moment, freeing her hands to pour hot chocolate from a dented stainless steel thermos. Life was so good here. Why had she ever left? Well, she knew why—but what would it have been like if she hadn't?

What if Callum hadn't chickened out? What if she'd had the guts and the maturity to stick around and see what happened instead of fleeing? Would they have gotten married, after all? Had a whack of kids? Ended up with lives they loved instead of merely tolerated or survived? Maybe she wouldn't have ended up getting conned—

No, no, she would have. . . . Well, maybe not by Devin, specifically—but she would've made some other equally disastrous decision. It was just where her head was at, and anyway, there was no going back and remedying the past. There was only how you lived in the present—and what you hoped for and worked toward for the future.

Her line jerked tight, and the bobber disappeared beneath the surface of the water. Shoot! She dropped her stainless steel cup, sending hot chocolate splattering, and yanked the rod up, hard. Then waited. The bobber reappeared. Double-shoot! The little fighter had escaped. She smiled. It never got old. A shame about her cocoa though.

The crow above her chuckled again—no, wait. That wasn't a crow. It was a human. Jo turned her head, studied the tree line, then swung her gaze to the space she knew opened up into road, though it was pretty much impossible to make out unless you knew where to look.

"I thought I might find you here." Callum's voice came through the trees and though Jo couldn't see him yet, her heart skipped.

She wished she'd worn nicer clothes, but then again, if Callum really was remotely interested, he might as well get used to her in man pants and rubber boots. The look was, as Samantha would say, Jo's signature style.

"Hey," she said, raising a hand as he stepped out of the bushes.

"Any luck?"

"No, but I can feel it turning around now that you're here."

"Heh," he said. "That's a nice thing to say." He smiled at her. She smiled at him. Yikes, they were the lamest people ever. Thank goodness Samantha wasn't there to bear witness. And double yikes, she hoped Samantha wouldn't read her feelings when they met up next.

"I dropped by because you weren't answering your phone, and I wanted to see if I could take you to dinner or something."

"I'd love to—" Callum's eyes lit up, then dimmed as she continued, "but I already have plans with Samantha."

Callum made a face she didn't quite understand,

but didn't have time to ask about because her bobber disappeared again. She yarded on the rod to set the hook. The tip strained down. "Oh, that feels like something all right."

"Can I do anything?"

"No, no, not yet—thanks." She reeled. The fish fought like crazy. She reeled in some more. There was a flash of silver under the water. A tail broke the surface with a splash. Her line spun. She reeled in again. The fish—a glittering beauty with a black-speckled back—came bucking and twisting out of the water.

The small net Jo had brought with her appeared under her catch.

"Thanks," she said. A minute later the fish was laid out on a flat rock. Jo stuffed her gloves into her pockets, then pulled a knife out of its holder on her waistband. She drove the blade through the top of the fish's spine in one quick, hard motion, then held it up for Callum to admire—but he looked a little green around the gills.

"Not a fisherman?" she asked.

"Not so much. A fish eater though."

She lowered her prize to the rock again, made an incision just beneath the gill plate, and cut until she felt the spinal column. She flipped the fish over and made a similar cut, but this time she cut right through, removing the head. Next, she held the fish belly up, inserted the tip of her knife into the little hole above its anal fin and cut along the body, opening a nice straight line between the fins.

She pulled out the guts and air bladder, leaving them in a pile along with the head for her laughing crow friend—then scored the blood line running along the spine several times. Finally she grabbed a toothbrush from her tackle box and squatted by the river, sloshed the fish through the water, and briskly brushed the blood out of the small cavity until all that was left was lovely peach-pink flesh.

She gave thanks in her head, slid the little five-pounder into her basket, and rinsed her hands at the water's edge. When she straightened, Callum was staring at her.

"What?"

He shrugged.

"No, seriously. What?"

"I see why you and Samantha don't get along."

Jo packed up her lures and clicked the tackle box shut. "And how's that?"

"I can't imagine Samantha baiting a hook, let alone braining a fish she'd just caught and gutting it and cleaning it in five minutes flat."

"Under three, actually."

"Pardon?"

"I can clean a trout in *under* three minutes."

"Impressive." Callum laughed.

"Darn tooting it is."

"'Darn tooting'?"

"Sorry. I slide into gumboots and a mac jacket and turn into a hick. And hey, just thank your lucky stars I used a knife."

"Meaning?"

"Usually for a small trout like that I slide my thumbs into its mouth, lace my fingers in a locked position around its back, and break its neck."

"Remind me never to piss you off."

"You wouldn't fit in the pan. You're safe." Jo handed the net and tackle box to Callum, and gathered the rest of her stuff. In the fifteen minutes or so since he'd arrived, the light had already changed. Evening fell earlier and earlier these days. Too early.

They took the road back, figuring it would be lighter than the forest. After a bit, she broke the silence. "I'm sorry."

"Sorry? For what?"

"My fish killing, cleaning, and subsequent neck-breaking conversation. Maybe it's kind of gross if you're not into it."

"Are you kidding me? Hunter-gatherer woman—totally sexy."

"Uh huh," she said, but was flattered. Maybe he hadn't meant his "You and Samantha are nothing alike" comment badly.

They stopped and he helped her lift a large branch, broken and thrown by the wind, off the gravel road.

"We're far more similar than we are different. In fact, in a lot of ways, we're exactly alike," she said when they resumed walking.

"I think so too—oh, wait, you mean, you and Samantha?"

Jo nodded.

"Yeah, right."

"I'm serious."

They were nearing the fork in the road that led back to her place or away depending on the route chosen. He stopped moving.

She raised her eyebrows.

"You couldn't be more different. She's all about name brands and flash. You're all about home cooking and living off the land."

"Nope. We're completely focused on the same thing—creating a home and building something to securely call our own. Just what that looks like to each of us is a bit different."

"*A bit.* You're pretty generous toward someone you can't stand."

"What are you talking about?" Jo was so flummoxed she dropped her rod. She scrambled to grab it, but the heavy vines and undergrowth immediately hid it from view.

"You and Samantha hate each other. You're nothing alike."

"Ah, sorry, no. Not at all." Jo found the rod, straightened up, and searched his eyes. He was serious. She shook her head. "That's the furthest thing from the truth. Yes, there's this freaky issue about the estate and a question that needs resolved. Will Samantha be brave and take a risk—"

"And there's no judgment in the way you worded that."

"Um . . . I don't mean there to be. Yes, okay, we're different in some ways, sure. But we love each other. Even when our parents were alive, in practical terms, we were each others' only family save Uncle Ray—and we hardly saw him because he wasn't that into kids."

"You mean because he was a drunk and the courts wouldn't let him raise you?"

"Wow." Jo shook her head again and resumed walking—at a faster pace. "I'm confused. Did you come here to start a fight? I don't get it."

"No, I came to invite you to dinner, only to find out you're hanging out with the sister I thought you hated."

"So what's setting you off? That I'm busy when you deign to drop in at the last minute, or that I don't loathe my blood kin?"

"Neither." Callum practically scowled. "I just don't understand why I have to be part of this mess then. If you guys are so lovey-dovey, why can't you resolve this yourself? Why do I have to be dragged into it?"

They'd reached the house, but hovered by Callum's car instead of heading inside. Jo fiddled with a piece of twine hanging off her fish basket's handle. Yes, her and Samantha's conflict was bound to be awkward and a bit confusing for Callum. "I kind of hate to say this, but I think the very reason Samantha hired you is because this way if anything goes south, I'll focus my sorrow and anger on the legal system, the *lawyer*, rather than on her."

"And will you do that, Jo? If you don't get your way—and I don't see how you will—are you going to be angry with me?"

Jo crossed her arms over her chest. She guessed she knew which way the wind was blowing now, didn't she? He didn't think she stood a chance. "I hadn't thought about it until now, but I guess as long as there really was no other way and every possible avenue had been fairly considered, I wouldn't hold it against you."

"Not exactly reassuring." Callum smiled but it was a sad look, and Jo didn't see a trace of I-want-to-kiss-you-again in it. "And really, *exactly* the same as your sister? It's hard to believe."

"I guess." Whatever that means, thought Jo.

"Okay, well . . . I'll see you. Have fun with Samantha tonight."

Jo watched Callum's departing taillights until they disappeared around the corner. Not even a rain check? Wow. Something had changed between them within minutes.

She bit her lip, a worm of shame and embarrassment squirming through her. Really *nothing* had changed between them. This was just her, yet again, imagining a connection or attraction between her and Callum where none—or at least none strong enough to merit the weight she gave it—existed. She sighed heavily on her way into the house to wash up. *Would she ever learn?*

Chapter 10

DAVE REEKED AND SWEAT DARKENED the armpits and the back of his blue T-shirt. He dropped his racket on the bench. The clatter made Callum flinch. "You a glutton for punishment or what? I'm always going to beat your ass, Archer."

"Yeah, yeah." Callum gulped from his water bottle, then picked up his towel and looped it around his own sweaty neck. He'd really thought he might win when he agreed to a second match. "You suck."

Dave laughed. "It's not my fault you don't understand how best of three works. You don't play again when the other guy's already shown you he's the better man."

"Yeah, yeah," Callum said again.

"Look, I'm sorry I'm an asshole when I always win."

"Oh, trust me, buddy, it's not just when you win."

"Ha." Dave shoved Callum, and Callum was more than happy to shove him back.

After they'd showered and changed back into street clothes, they met up in the café next door to Dave's gym.

"So what's up with you these days anyway?" Dave asked over one of the green energy juices he'd ordered for both of them, while they waited for salad rolls and Udon soup.

Callum took a big mouthful and set his glass down. "Ugh, that tastes like something a lawn mower spit out. Not much, why?"

"Eat to live, man. Don't live to eat."

"Save your motivational health-speak for your health groupies, okay?"

Dave splayed his hands in front of him and leaned back. "Bit more green juice and a lot more gym time, and you might win a game once in a while—and you'll live longer—just saying."

"Who says I want to live longer?" Callum said, but he did take another slurp of the green swamp-mess. "And anytime you want a real challenge, to do some actual physical labor instead of just playing with your balls, let me know."

"Funny," Dave said, but both he and Callum grinned at the continuation of their ongoing argument about what was better for overall strength and fitness—concentrated gym workouts or manual work like pounding nails, building fences, etc.

"I'm serious about the labor. I want to make a shed before the snow flies."

Dave waved the invitation away. "Brian says you're obsessed with some woman."

"That's what I love about this town, gossip at the speed of light."

"So there is someone?"

"I don't really know . . . maybe." Jo's face flashed into Callum's mind and he grinned a little. But then he remembered the confused, hurt expression he'd put in her eyes during their last conversation. He sighed.

Dave didn't seem to notice. "You kissed her yet—or more?"

"What are we, sixteen?"

"So you have!" Dave finished the rest of his green swill in one big gulp, obviously finding it less unpalatable than Callum did. Nothing new there. For good friends, they'd always had divergent tastes.

"It's complicated."

Dave grinned. "You're not updating your Facebook status here. Give me details."

Callum finished off a salad roll in two bites. "It kind of blew me away actually. I know her—knew her before. We just reconnected recently, but I've never been with anyone like her."

"Been with as in—"

"No, dipshit. As I've said a hundred times, not everything is about sex."

"Not everything," Dave agreed, seeming sad about the fact.

"She's . . . totally different from most people in this town."

"She's not from around here?"

"Used to be. She was the one who got away—"

"Really? Mine too." Dave launched into a big tale about a girl he'd crushed on in high school—and that explained his question about Callum's love life; he had one of his own he wanted to talk about.

"Did I know her?" Callum asked.

"No idea—but have no fear. I want you to meet her this weekend."

Wow, it was serious then.

"She's throwing a dinner party Saturday night with her sister. It's perfect, hey? If things don't work out with your lady, my girl's sister can be your back up."

"Oh, great. *Thanks.*"

"No problem," Dave replied, completely oblivious to Callum's obvious sarcasm.

Callum shook his head. Poor guy had it bad.

"So you're in?" Dave asked.

"In?"

"To going. I said I'd bring a friend."

"Sure."

"I'll drive."

"Even better." Callum grinned. "Unless you wanna get kazooed—then I'll take over."

They set a time, and Dave headed back to work—to teach a relaxation yoga class or something. The idea of Dave leading anyone, let alone a group of people, through relaxing *anything* was always hilarious to Callum. Dave was one of the most hyper, most competitive guys he knew.

It wasn't until Callum was back at his desk, staring at a stack of files he needed to refresh himself about, that it hit him. Sisters. Used to live in town, newly moved back. A dinner party. Hadn't Jo mentioned something about a dinner party, too? *Dave had a thing for Samantha?* Now that was a couple he never would've predicted in a million years. But opposites attract and all that—and it wasn't like he had any track record picking a relationship that worked, so why not? And if Dave was smitten, maybe Callum was wrong about her. Maybe Samantha wasn't the spitting emotional replica of his ex-wife Nina. He wanted to call Jo and ask her what she knew about Dave and Samantha, but it wasn't the right time. He'd ask her at the party—the party he was suddenly really looking forward to.

Chapter 11

JO OPENED THE DOOR BEFORE Samantha finished knocking, but Samantha didn't enter right away. Instead she placed an arm casually against the doorframe and posed, as if considering the crush of noise and bodies and stringed lights twinkling in the house.

In a fitted black dress with a plunging neckline and sky high heels with ribbons that crisscrossed her ankles like the ties in a bustier, Samantha was gorgeous and perfectly put together as always—but maybe a tad overdressed for a small town, back road get together. Jo welcomed her warmly and motioned her inside.

"Good grief," Samantha said, still not moving. "You really went all out. How much is this little shindig going to set you back? What's on the menu?"

Leave it to Samantha to kill the casual, fun party mood right off.

"I told you it was a dinner party, get-to-know-the-townsfolk kind of thing. What were you expecting? Canned soup for six?"

"There are close to twenty cars out there!"

"The event grew. What can I say?"

"You? You can say nothing. I can say plenty." Samantha's voice softened. "Come on, Jo. . . . Didn't Callum talk to you? There's no way you can hold onto this thing. It's not going to happen. You shouldn't have moved in. It's gone to your head."

Jo nodded. The last sentence was true anyway. "Get in here, so I can shut the door. You're letting the cold air in." You *are* the cold air, is what she wanted to say.

"I don't want to see you hurt."

"Why can't you let yourself dream a little? We could run it together—"

"No. I like a nice fat bank account—something no one can foreclose on. You're making the same mistake you made all those years ago, just in a different way."

"Sam—"

"No," Samantha said again. "You're happy to be just Jo. I'm *Samantha*. And you know I'm right. Hasn't Callum talked to you at all?"

Jo didn't like how it was the second time Samantha had asked that. Had she and Callum reached some set-in-stone conclusion?

"Talked about what?"

"The will and selling, of course. I know you guys chat about God knows what else, but I don't care about that. What I do care about is—"

Whatever else Samantha was going to say was cut off by another knock on the door.

"You've invited more people?"

Jo shrugged and smiled even more broadly.

"I'm getting a drink," Samantha said in a tone that made it sound like a threat.

"Knock yourself out," Jo said and opened the door.

Dave beamed, big, blond and bearish. "Hello!"

Callum slouched behind him, glowering—almost as tall, but leaner and dark and brooding, like a sexy vampire—albeit a huggable looking vampire in his oatmeal-soft sweater.

"You're the sister having the dinner party," Callum growled in response to her cheerful greeting.

Dave turned to stare at Callum. "I told you that in the car, man. *Jo Archer*."

"I thought you had them mixed up," Callum said, bafflingly.

Jo laughed lightly, trying to lighten the tension that she in no way understood.

"Well, now that we've established I'm me and I'm having a party, won't you come in?"

"Wait a minute—" Dave's eyebrows shot up as he studied Callum's surly expression, then he shot a glance at Jo and changed his mind about whatever he was going to say. "Later, man," he added cryptically.

They all stood awkwardly for another moment or two. What on earth had happened that she wasn't privy to? Well, whatever it was, it was going to stop. She had guests to attend to.

"Just toss your coats on the bed in the room to

your left, and follow the noise to the living room. I'll be right on your heels. I just need to check on something."

The guys removed their coats and disappeared as ordered.

Jo slipped into the nearby bathroom, leaned against the door, and exhaled slowly. "You can do this, Jo. You can totally do this," she muttered.

She wasn't sure if she'd convinced herself, but her words gave her the boost she needed to at least step away from the door. She didn't need to use the toilet, but she washed her hands to give herself the extra bit of time, then dampened a washcloth with cold water and pressed it to her burning cheeks and brow.

"Regardless of what comes of it," she whispered at her too-pink self, "business connections, future reservations, or just a nice one-time evening, eating great food and making friends, this was a good idea." That line finally broke through her insecurity.

People would have fun. That was good enough for her. And should she manage to bring Samantha over from the dark side—a possibility that seemed more and more unlikely—well, nothing could be better for potential business than memories of a great party, right?"

The dining room was humming with laughter and chat.

"Omigoodness, Jo. These are to die for. Did you make them yourself?" Selina, one the few other people Jo remembered from school, now a reporter with the local paper, waved a smoked salmon and cream cheese stuffed pastry.

Jo nodded. Another woman, one whom Jo had just met—Beth from the bookstore—also gave raving praises of the appetizers, then added, "Thanks so much for inviting me."

"No, thank you for coming," Jo said. "I'm so happy you're here. I hardly know anyone yet, so I invited tons of people because I was scared no one would come."

The three of them surveyed the crowded room, and Selina giggled. "Guess you miscalled that one."

"Yeah, you didn't need to worry," Beth added. "There's no nightlife here, so your invitations will always draw a crowd."

"Sheesh, make her feel special or what?" Selina laughed again.

Beth blushed. "I'm sorry. That's not how I meant it. I just meant people are pretty friendly here, and who wouldn't be flattered to get invited out?"

"That's sweet, Beth. Thanks," Jo said.

"Jo?" a male voice asked at her ear.

She turned. "Glen—hello! I'm glad you could make it."

"Me, too. I've always been intrigued by this old homestead. Your uncle was forever buying tools."

"You're telling me." Jo laughed. "The shed's packed with them—and the bedrooms, and the crawlspace!"

"Yep, that was Ray all right." Glen tugged the arm

of a plump, pretty woman with short red curls. "And this is my wife, Melanie."

"Nice to meet you, Melanie. Glen talks about you all the time."

"Yeah, stuff like, 'Where'd that woman put the blue slip,' and 'Hey, if you want to charge stuff you can't afford, talk to the wife,'" Melanie joked.

And so the night went, full of small talk, and enough food and drink that no one got bored. Jo congratulated herself on forgoing a formal sit-down meal. The buffet-style courses encouraged mingling, and if someone wasn't seated near someone they enjoyed talking to—or who didn't talk—they weren't stuck in one spot, miserable, all evening.

Dave shadowed her most of the night which was helpful because he had the kind of easygoing, life-of-the-party personality that joined small cliques of chatters into larger ones and left quiet groups noisily joking. He also appointed himself her "kitchen slave" and helped her bring out new dishes and carry empty ones away—something Jo found both kind and practical, so she wasn't sure why he was rubbing her the wrong way.

Callum remained cool and distant, though he did laugh once or twice at things she said. . . . Maybe he was just shy in a group? Or maybe her gut—that she foolishly kept fighting—was right and he was an ass. Maybe he was still the kind of guy who declared interest where none really existed, and she was still the same dope who fell for it. She needed to stop giving him the benefit of a doubt!

Later, as couples started to trickle away, calling cheery good-byes with promises to visit again or to have her over, and the house slowly emptied, Jo was ready to call the night a full-blown success.

And then Samantha struck.

Jo had noticed her social butterfly sister was in her heyday all night. Yes, she hit the drink table a bit heavily, but that was just Samantha. The woman could hold her liquor like no one's business—so shock practically knocked Jo down when Samantha staggered over. Literally *staggered*. Then raised a glass.

"I'd like to raisa toassst," she slurred. "To my sister."

The few people still there complied merrily, lifting their glasses in salute.

"Only my sister—" The last word came out *sis-ssstah*. Samantha burped, then giggled, holding one hand over her mouth.

Jo was by the door to the kitchen, too far away to grab Samantha by the arm (or hair!) and drag her out of the room before she completely embarrassed herself. Jo's armpits prickled with sweat.

From where he was leaned against one of the wide cedar pillars that marked the dining room's change into living room space, Callum met Jo's eyes. He nodded once, then moved toward Samantha.

Too late.

"Only *Josephine* could think of opening this place.

Sure her food's good, the best maybe, but she doesn't have any money." Samantha laughed like she'd told a hilarious joke. Callum took her arm gently, but she shook him off and snarled, "I'm not done my toast!" She raised her glass again. Its amber contents sloshed, but didn't spill. "And have you seen the rooms? There are holes in the floor in some'em. You can see dirt! And the room she slept in when she was a kid? Gaps around the window big enough to stick stuff through."

Callum started, and his eyes narrowed at Samantha.

The cheerful hush that had greeted Samantha's first line, "I have a toast," changed to a watchful, uncomfortable silence. Then someone whispered, "Well, I guess we know who got poor old Ray's genes." There was a very slight, very uncomfortable titter.

If Jo's face burned any hotter, she'd burst into flames—but honestly that would be preferable to the gush of tears filling her sinuses. *Don't cry. Don't cry. Don't cry!*

Jo put the heavy crockpot of mulled apple cider she'd been about to carry into the kitchen down on a side table, and readied herself to take on Samantha.

Dave stepped forward then, his voice cheerful and booming. "Oh, don't be such a drama queen, Sammy. Any monkey can do a bit of fix up. It just needs elbow grease—and look at what Jo's done already. Give her the winter and none of us will be able to afford to stay in the place."

"Don't call me Sammy!" Samantha shrieked.

Jo appreciated what Dave was trying to do, but he was missing the point. Jo could care less what Samantha said in regards to her plans; she only cared that her sister would be mortified the next day. She didn't need Samantha to stop bashing her. She needed her to stop slurring, to not have a melt down—to say something funny or gracious that pushed away the wary, growing-judgmental expressions appearing on the surrounding faces.

Callum's intense blue eyes met hers again, and she remembered something long forgotten. He'd helped her out during a similar crazy Samantha moment when they were teens. That was actually how they'd met for real, in a way deeper than being aware they attended the same school. Was that the first time they'd gone for coffee? Such a grown up thing that had seemed, going for *coffee*.

Despite the current situation and stress, Jo's stomach tightened with remembered excitement. How flattered and exhilarated she'd been—

Her inner reminiscences were cut short by two guests who raced for the door, citing the time and a babysitter they needed to get home as their reason for leaving. Another couple jumped on that inspiration for their equally quick exit.

The room was down to about nine people—including her, Samantha, Callum, and Dave.

Samantha chuckled suddenly as the drunken pendulum of her emotions swung yet again. "But here's to big dreams, little sister. Here's to you!"

There was a weak chorus of "Hear, hear" and "Cheers" from the few remaining guests.

Jo forced a smile and made some joke that she couldn't remember later, but that smoothed the mood a little—though everyone except Callum, Samantha, and Dave still left immediately. No quiet conversations into the late hours then. That was okay. She was suddenly wiped out anyway, the happy adrenalin she'd run on all night, drained.

Dave grabbed the crock of apple cider she'd put down. "You okay?"

She nodded. "Oh, yeah. Totally. That's just . . . Samantha."

"I'll help clean up."

"No, no, it'll take hours—"

"I insist, m'lady." Dave ducked his chin as he spoke, smiled in a way Jo figured other women would've found charming, and disappeared into kitchen.

Separated from her by the table—and by something else, something growing bigger by the minute, though Jo still couldn't comprehend what it was—Callum stood staring at her. Her eyes locked with his. She wanted to say something, but felt rebuffed by his blazing expression of what? Hurt? Anger?

He placed his hand on Samantha's shoulder. "Let me give you a ride home. I came with Dave. I can drive your car back for you."

"Really, you'd do that?" Samantha simpered. Jo

was going to have fun harassing her about this—or maybe she wouldn't joke about it. Maybe she'd try, again, to get her sister to see it was time to do something about her imbibing. Still, the night could've been much worse, given Samantha's history—and then it was.

Samantha moved forward, swaying unsteadily on those damned heels of hers. She reached out and clutched Callum's arm, tittering. A flame of jealousy sparked through Jo with an intensity that shocked her. She's just trying to keep her balance, she thought, but could only see Samantha's pretty hand buried in Callum's soft sweater.

"You don't need to go out of your way. Samantha can crash here."

"In one of the rooms with holes in the floor?" Callum asked, a glint of something sharp in his voice.

Jo winced. What the hell was his problem?

"You're sooo sweet, Callum," Samantha cooed. "Let me just skip to the lady's room and freshen up."

Skip? Jo would pay to see her manage that. If Samantha didn't fall on her face before the night was through, just trying to walk normally, Jo would eat her words.

Samantha, completely belying the amount of alcohol she'd ingested and her recent bumbling, deftly— and sexily, Jo observed grumpily—slid her heels off one by one, picked them up by their ribbons, and yes, fairly *skipped* out of the room.

Callum and Jo were alone.

Something metal clanked against something else metal in the kitchen.

The ticking of the clock on the wall, a noise that should disappear unless focused on, was deafening. Or was that the sound of her heartbeat? Was it that audible?

This is stupid, Jo thought. She took a few tentative steps toward Callum, and he met her at the end of the table—the place he'd spontaneously taken her hand— what, a mere week ago, really?

She was close enough to touch him, and she wanted to, how she wanted to! But their past, distant and recent, and his rigid posture, made her refrain. He tilted his head, studying her.

He smelled of expensive aftershave, and though it smelled good, it was no vanilla and butter. Something in Jo's stomach tightened—apprehension, not lust. There was something wrong. His nearness felt different than it ever had before.

He ran his fingers lightly down the side of her face, tracing a line from her temple, over the slope of her cheekbone, across the hollow of her cheek— stopping by her mouth. His touch lingered for a moment and he leaned in. Jo was sure he was going to kiss her again. The tightness in her stomach relaxed into a warmth that tingled through her lower parts. Good grief, how she responded to him.

For one stupid, stupid moment she dared to hope that she'd been wrong, was paranoid, that maybe everything was fine between them. She lifted her face.

Then he whispered, "I should never have kissed you. And I wouldn't have if I'd known you were seeing my best friend."

Wha—the word half formed in her mouth, but only a surprised sound escaped.

"It's a small town. Even if I didn't know Dave personally, did you really think I wouldn't find out?"

"But—"

With impeccable timing as usual, Samantha called, "Callum, I'm ready," and her footsteps, soft and confident, padded down the hallway.

Callum, who'd pulled back at the sound of Samantha's voice, bent near again. But Jo—whose heart, dammit, was beating more furiously than ever—wasn't fooled this time. She stepped away.

Increasing the distance between them didn't protect her from his furious words, however.

"You led me on," he growled. "You shouldn't have kissed me back."

Jo barely slept. The bed felt wrong. Her blankets were first too cold, then too hot. It was too dark. If she put on a light in the hall, it was too light. She made herself chamomile tea with milk—and then had to pee. Despite her tired muscles and absolutely-past-spent emotions, she couldn't turn off her brain.

Should she have confronted Callum then and there? His attack—okay, "attack" was a bit strong—but his misguided notion was so far off base that at first she'd struggled to understand what he was getting at. When she did realize what he was saying, Samantha was there, clamoring for help finding her jacket, and then Dave appeared on the scene, asking where she kept the dish soap—weird in and of itself because it was in plain view by the sink.

Dave.

He'd seemed hurt when she pushed him out the door the same time Callum and Samantha left.

"I'm wiped, Dave. Thank you so much for all your help. I'm just going to do the rest tomorrow," she lied—though not intentionally. At the time she hadn't known she wouldn't be able to sleep and would proceed to clean in a wild frenzy of irritation and nerves.

She frowned and rolled over again as she recalled Dave's parting words and his touch on her arm. "I had a great time tonight. I don't want it to end. Do you want to finish it off with a night cap or something?"

Callum scowled even more darkly at the suggestion. But his response wasn't why she'd practically pushed Dave out the door, or was it? Would she have invited Dave to stay a bit and unwind with her? Probably, actually. It would've been fun to talk about the good parts of the night with someone, and might've lessoned the impact of the bad parts that threatened to overwhelm the fun memories. So all in all, maybe it was good that Callum had clued her in about Dave's going public with his misinterpretation of their relationship—even if Callum was an idiot and asshole for the way he did it. She kicked herself for not heeding her suspicion in the coffee shop and dealing with Dave overtly, instead of trying to hint.

And what emotion creased Callum's forehead when Dave finally gave in and left—pleasure or confusion? And why did she care what it was? Stupid! She punched her pillow and folded it, then rested her cheek on the cooler side. Callum should've asked her directly if she was seeing Dave, not just assumed. He should've asked if she'd kissed him back—oh, crime of crimes!—when she was dating someone else. She had less than no desire to be with someone who jumped to conclusions. She didn't have time to waste with someone who wasn't upfront with himself or others.

So about her and Callum and the tiny torch she'd been carrying for him again against her better judgment?

"Consider it burned out, baby," she mumbled. *"Burned out."*

She finally fell into a fitful sleep around four in the morning.

Chapter 12

ON THE ELEVENTH CALL, AISHA got lucky. She said
her piece, aiming for a casual, optimistic tone, striving
to keep the futility she was starting to feel about the
process from leaking into her words.

The woman's voice on the other end of the connection was hesitant and wary, as if anticipating some
sort of scam. "I don't know . . . you might be looking
for my second cousin. I heard she had a baby that she
gave up for adoption. . . ."

Aisha tried not to hyperventilate with anxiety or
excitement she wasn't sure which—and really they
were pretty much the same thing, weren't they? She
paced, phone pressed so hard against her ear it kind of
hurt, and gave the woman her birthday.

The brief pause before the woman answered made
Aisha feel somehow sure her details fit. "It's possible,
I guess," came the reluctant affirmation.

Don't sound like a psycho; don't sound like a
psycho! Aisha commanded herself twice, then took a
long steadying breath and put a smile into her voice.
"Thank you so much for your help. I know it's a long
shot, but do you by any chance have a contact number

for your cousin?"

"*Second* cousin," the woman corrected, making Aisha decide the two women weren't close. She did provide a phone number though—and a possible address. "But I wouldn't get your hopes up. It's been a long time since our paths crossed—and she moves a lot."

Aisha scribbled the information onto a pink sticky note, then ended the call and sank shakily into the couch. She had a lead. Her first real lead.

Chapter 13

SAMANTHA AND JO EACH GOT a large breakfast blend coffee at the Starbucks kiosk—and Samantha popped a couple of ibuprofen. Jo balanced her to-go cup carefully on the grocery cart, while she dug for a quarter to unchain the thing from the rest of the long line. Finally set, caffeine in hand, shopping cart ready for action, they made their way into the busy store. It was packed. Had everyone in town left their weekly shopping until Sunday afternoon? Jo sighed. Seemed like it. She slammed items into the metal buggy as loudly as she could. The canned tomatoes and tins of chickpeas clanked satisfactorily.

"Do you mind, Jo, seriously?" Samantha moaned. "You're killing me. My head feels like it was ran over by a small truck last night—then stuffed with gauze and glass splinters."

"Very descriptive, Samantha. And *good*. You deserve it." Jo put the largest box of spinach spaghetti noodles she could find into the cart, gently this time. No point breaking perfectly good pasta because of her sister.

"Okay, so I had a little too much to drink last

night. Sue me."

Jo shook her head. "How about we call a truce? I'll give you half the value of the property, not just a quarter—but lend it to me. I'll buy you out in three years—for a way higher amount than you'll receive if we sell now."

Samantha pressed her French-tipped fingers against her temples. "You're persistent. I give you that."

Jo consulted her list and grabbed a jar of marinated artichoke hearts. "Anyway, I didn't ask you to join me just to nag you some more about Uncle Ray's."

"You didn't? Well, too late."

Jo ignored the jibe. "Last night, before you became a slobbering idiot—"

"Ouch, was I that bad?"

Jo scrunched her face almost sympathetically. "No," she finally said. "You were pretty bad, but I've definitely seen you worse."

"Thanks a lot." Samantha laughed and didn't wince; the painkiller and caffeine must've kicked in.

"You should send Dave and Callum thank you cards. They headed you off before you really got going."

Samantha studied the label on a box of heat-and-serve mattar paneer, then tossed the package on top of Jo's growing pile of groceries. "Did I mention the gap between the window and the wall?"

"Yes." Jo gritted her teeth.

"And the holes in the floors?"

"Yep."

"The issues with the roof?"

"Uh, no—"

"And what about the crazy ass bats in your belfry?"

"What?—*oh*. Ha, ha, very funny."

"So consider yourself lucky."

Yeah, *lucky*, Jo thought as they turned into another aisle and Samantha picked up a jug of unsweetened cranberry juice.

Jo stopped rolling the cart and fidgeted with her coffee cup. "Do you remember that guy I was madly in love with the two years I went to school here?"

"Yeah, vaguely."

Jo reached for a box of oatmeal.

"Oh, wait, don't tell me, it was Dave? I didn't realize you guys had a fling—but it's more than obvious he still has a thing for you."

"No, *not Dave*. We were acquaintances, that's it. And if he has a 'thing' for me now, it's completely one-sided." Jo regretted bringing the topic up at all. "Do you need anything else here? I'm ready to hit the produce section."

"No, I'm good, and don't change the subject." Samantha commandeered the cart and steered toward the fruits and vegetables.

Jo trailed behind and didn't say a word.

"I told you the minute we laid eyes on Dave that he—" Samantha stopped moving so abruptly that Jo careened into her. The coffee she was holding sloshed, but thankfully didn't splash Samantha. Jo would never have heard the end of it.

"Wait a minute, wait a minute! If not Dave, then who—*Callum*?" Samantha was so loud, several shoppers turned to stare.

"Shhhh," Jo hissed.

"So it is Callum! Are you kidding me?" Samantha's stage whisper was barely better than a yell. "*Callum Archer* was the big catch who slipped away and broke your heart?"

"Don't cheapen a fishing metaphor by sticking him into it."

"I can't believe this. What stupid small town bullshit and dumbass luck. The lawyer I happen to pick is some guy you used to roll around in the hay with—and now you're resuming your relationship?"

"Would you forget about yourself and your plans for five minutes?" Jo paused by a bin of tomatoes. "And no, we're not together, not even close."

She continued to browse, while filling Samantha in on the details of her and Callum's reacquaintance. She didn't entirely trust Samantha to be unbiased—but what could she do? She needed to talk to somebody.

"So that's it," Jo finished with a shrug and a lame recap. "We had a great time, we ran into each other by accident a day later—he kissed me—then nothing. He surprised me at the river, was super sweet—then acted off. Then he attended the party with Dave and acted *super off*, like I'd betrayed him or like I'm with Dave or something. I don't get it. What do you think?"

Samantha plucked a red grape from the bunch Jo had selected, wiped it on her denim-clad leg, and popped it into her mouth. She didn't comment until they were almost at the check out. "When you ask, 'What do you think' . . . do you mean in general about the two of you so far, or about whether I think his kiss meant anything—"

"So you don't think it meant anything? Shit, I knew it."

Samantha shrugged. "I'm sorry . . . and maybe it did, but maybe it was just a heat of the moment, spontaneous I-had-a-good-time-let's-try-on-a-kiss-for-fun thing."

Jo twisted a strand of hair around her finger as they got into line. That was a possibility. She sighed. Was she the only old-fashioned fool left in the world, who still took a kiss to mean something, to mean *a lot*? It hadn't felt like a casual kiss, but she'd be first to admit she was the furthest thing from knowledgeable on the subject these days.

The line rolled forward and Samantha followed suit. She and Jo were shoulder-to-shoulder now, and she glanced at Jo sympathetically. "Or maybe it was for old time's sake. You said it yourself, you guys were pretty hot and heavy back in the day."

Jo wanted to say, *It wasn't just about lust* (Though there'd been plenty of that too, she admitted in her head)—*we were going to get married*, but the words and her belief in the truth of them, apparently even now from the way it stung to think about—were too embarrassing.

"And maybe it just felt like more to you than it meant to him because of your past. All your old emotions stirred—but his were untouched because they've been, as he proved back then, different than yours all along."

Jo nodded. Samantha with her typical razor-sharp astuteness cut through all the bullshit and emotional blah-blah-blah that always snagged Jo.

They finally reached the counter and started putting their groceries onto the conveyor belt.

"I'm sorry if that hurts, and I could be totally wrong. Maybe he felt everything you did—excitement about starting anew, trying again, this time as adults—but he just got scared."

"That's kind, but I suspect you nailed the truth with one of your other guesses. Totally explains why he was being so weird. I was probably embarrassingly transparent and my instant doe-eyed interest freaked him out."

The cashier greeted them, and Jo ended the conversation with that thought. She was tired of talking about it anyway, and hated that a big part of her had hoped Samantha was going to say, "Are you kidding? He's crazy about you," and then use her considerable talent for cutting to the quick to show why that was true.

"Still want to do lunch?" Samantha asked on their way out of the store. "I'll buy."

"Sure, why not?" Jo shrugged. "Do you want to stash the bags in my truck, then walk somewhere?"

They were almost at the small Indian restaurant they'd mutually agreed on, when Samantha broke into Jo's glum thoughts. "You could always ask Dave."

"What do you mean? Ask Dave what?"

"Well, you and Dave are friendly, right?'

"Yeah . . ."

"And he and Callum are good friends?"

Jo walked up the concrete wheelchair ramp instead of taking the stairs and held the door open for Samantha. "Apparently."

"So ask Dave out right. Did he or did he not give Callum the idea that you and he—Dave, I mean—are a couple?"

"Oh." Jo stopped in the doorway. "Maybe that *is* what happened."

"Yes, maybe," Samantha agreed, but then her voice took on a warning tone. "But regardless, my other suggestions are still plausible. I know you loved Callum once—but you were kids. You have no idea what kind of man he grew up to be."

"You're right," Jo said, but her mind was already skipping ahead. She'd call Dave as soon as she got home. Obviously he'd inadvertently given Callum the wrong idea about their friendship; she'd get him to clear things up and see where things led with her and Callum.

Chapter 14

THE AIR WAS CRISP AND the sky was robin egg blue. Gold and brown leaves crackled under Jo's snub-toed walking boots on the Millennium trail—a path built along the edge of town by the City to celebrate the year 2000. She took a deep breath of the clean, delicious air, and tried to ignore how happy Dave looked—something that, of course, wouldn't bother her except that a minute ago, he'd tried to take her hand. She evaded him by stooping to tighten her laces, but you didn't need a Psych degree to read his body language and emotional cues.

"Smells like snow," Dave said.

"Yeah, it does," Jo agreed, smiling despite herself. "I forgot about that—that you can actually smell snow coming."

"Ah, you city kid."

"I was hardly a city kid."

He shrugged agreeably, a gesture that was quintessential Dave. It irked her. Why did he have to agree with every single thing she said? And then she was irritated at herself for being rankled by something so innocuous. Why couldn't she like nice, kind, easygoing Dave? Why was she still drawn to Callum? Oh, well. It was a pointless question. Might as well ask why fish swim. They just do. And she just was. She was about to clear things up with Dave, when he spoke.

"I'm glad you asked me to go for a walk," he said.

She nodded and shoved her hands into the pockets of her fleece-lined nylon jacket. "Yeah, about that," she said.

"I feel really close to you," Dave continued like she hadn't spoken. "Like I did when we went to school together."

He'd felt close to her in school? News to her. "Oh yeah?" she said.

"Yeah, but I always wanted more."

Jo walked backwards, so she could face Dave but keep moving. "Listen Dave, you're a great guy—"

"Oh oh," Dave said. "Not the 'great guy' line. Things haven't changed for you at all since you came back? Since we started spending time together again?"

Jo shook her head and was about to say, "No, sorry," when Dave held up a hand. "Wait, don't say it out loud. Don't write it in stone yet. Just give me a chance. Let's keep hanging out and see what develops."

Jo kicked at a large rock that didn't belong on the path and sent it off into the ditch. "Yeah, about that. Have you been telling people we're dating?"

Dave stopped in his tracks. "What? No, of course not."

Jo studied his face. He met her eyes without flinching. "Why?" he asked.

Why indeed? she thought.

"I don't know," she said. "It's just Callum. He . . . " Her voice trailed off. He what? Had kissed her and blown her off? Had seemed pissed off about her and some imagined relationship with Dave?

Dave sighed heavily. "Let me guess? Callum's acting all territorial about you and odd about me?"

Jo turned away and resumed walking frontwards. "He seemed to have a misguided idea about you and me, yes—"

"But why not you and me?" Dave interrupted. "You're not seeing anyone else, right?"

Was she seeing anyone? No, not really. Only in her imagination. The one where people took physical affection as a sign of something deeper. One where staying up all night talking and laughing was special—and unique to two people. One where—ah, what was the point? No, she wasn't seeing anyone. But also, no, she wasn't interested in Dave, and she wasn't going to lead him on and pretend that could change.

"Not specifically, but—"

Dave made a fist and pumped the air in celebration of some perceived victory. "Yes!" he said. "I knew you weren't. I told him you weren't." His eyes narrowed. "Just because he's a player doesn't mean everyone is."

Jo was confused by Dave's words and by his change of expression—hard and almost angry. Most un-Dave-like. "What do you mean *he*?"

"Callum."

Jo picked up her pace. "So you guys did talk about my dating life?" She tried—and thought she failed miserably—to keep her voice conversational and detached.

Dave's big shoulders lifted in an exaggerated shrug. "I'm not sure how it came up—" His cheeks reddened. "Okay, that's a lie. I told him how much I liked you."

"Oh." *Oh.* She tried not to frown too offensively. No wonder Callum had been confused and assumed she might like Dave back.

"He said I should be careful, that 'a woman like you' always has a bunch of fish on the line."

Jo almost tripped on her own feet. "He said *what*? Why would he say that?"

"I don't know." Dave's eyes were round with concern. "It was out of line and I said so."

"Then what did he say?"

"Not much. I just figured he was being his usual self. Wanting to eliminate the competition and all that."

"The competition?"

"Sure." Dave's breath showed white in the chilly air, but Jo was burning hot all of a sudden.

"I'm sorry. I still don't get it. What do you mean?"

"You know." Dave paused to zip up his jacket, avoiding eye contact. "He's a typical guy and it's a small town. When new flesh moves in, he wants first chance with it."

"*New flesh*? He said that?" Jo was on the verge of shouting.

"Not in so many words, but it's kind of common knowledge. He's an Archer, after all."

Jo remembered all the rumors about Callum's dad. How she'd been so humiliated for Mrs. Archer and she'd only met the woman once or twice. But Callum had been the opposite of all that when they were teenagers. He vowed he wanted one woman, *her*, for life. But then again, look how that had turned out.

"Yeah, and he told me you and him had a thing back in school."

"He did?" Surprises like barbs on a hook kept tearing at her.

"Yeah. Said it was weird to have you back—and to meet your sister. Said he can't decide which one of you is hotter." Dave cleared his throat. "Said he might have to try you both."

Oily hot shame spread over Jo's flesh. She wriggled her shoulders trying to shake it off. Why should she feel bad because some guy was an objectifying creep?

"He . . . he wasn't like that when . . . *before*," she said. It was work to push the words out. Painful work.

"No," Dave agreed. "He's one of my oldest friends, but he's changed a lot, and we don't see eye-to-eye on everything. Not even close."

They'd come to the end of the trail. It was either turn around and backtrack to the vehicles, or trek down the highway and take an extended return route. Jo wished she could teleport away instead of choosing either, but since that option wasn't available she started retracing their steps.

They walked in silence, Jo lost in black thoughts about how silly and naïve she was in her approach to life. How many disappointments—and how many heartrending failures to correctly read what kind of person someone was—did she have to suffer to realize she was bad at relationships? Beyond bad, actually. Terrible.

"People will always meet or exceed your lowest opinion of them," Samantha was known to say. And Jo had tried to talk her out of that point of view a zillion times, but maybe Samantha was right. Dead right. New flesh, indeed. Hotter or not? What a—

"I'm sorry," Dave interrupted suddenly, about halfway back.

"For what?" she muttered distractedly.

"You know, for telling you all this, especially if you like him again."

"Are you kidding?" Jo wrinkled her nose like there was a bad smell. "We were stupid kids, playing at being grown up. I was surprised he was still in town, and it's always disappointing to find out someone's turned into a creep, but it's nothing to me personally."

Dave searched her eyes, then smiled and patted her shoulder. "Yeah, well, I'm still sorry."

"Thanks."

"Hey, Jo?" Dave asked a few minutes later.

"Uh huh?"

"I feel kind of bad about what I said about Callum. He's not a terrible guy. He just had a number done on him by his ex. It changed him."

"Don't worry, Dave. I'm not going to hate your best friend. I just know better than to think we could rekindle anything. I'll be fine. I promise."

"Okay, well . . . good."

Back at their vehicles, both parked near a picturesque candy shop housed in a remodeled train station, Dave touched her shoulder again. "So how about it?"

Jo felt her brow furrow grouchily, and she forced her face to relax. None of her stupidity was Dave's fault. "How about what?" she asked.

"My proposition?"

"I'm sorry?"

"You know, to give me a chance?"

"Ah, Dave, come on. Please don't make this awkward."

"Not awkward, I promise." He shifted his feet and crossed his arms over his chest, tucking his hands into his armpits.

"I don't like how you're purposely not hearing me. I'm not into you."

"No, I get it. And I accept it—but let me try to change your mind."

Was he kidding? *I accept it—but let me change your mind?* Argh! Jo sighed. She was done with this day. So done. "I can't tell you how to feel, Dave—or how not to. But you're barking up the wrong tree. I'm not interested in dating you. And I won't be. I don't know how to be more plain than that."

"But you'll still hang out with me?"

"I don't know. Maybe." Or maybe not. She needed to think about it.

"Good enough."

It was like she'd actually said she'd go out with him. Shaking her head, she climbed into her truck, started the engine and roared away, without saying a polite good-bye. She needed to work on being much less Jo-dumb and accommodating and much more Samantha-smart.

Chapter 15

C ALLUM TURNED ON THE EIGHTY-INCH flat screen, set
out a bowl of kettle chips, and grabbed a couple cans
of Coke from the small black fridge in the entertain-
ment console.

"Shit, I love this TV." Dave settled into one of the
deep Italian leather chairs, stretched his legs and
rested them on the low, highly polished burl table in
front of him.

Callum looked around his opulent living room, but
could hardly appreciate it. All he could see was how
the house and its furnishings tied him down. He never
should've let Nina convince him to take a huge
mortgage and loan with his father. He'd have been
just as happy living in a condo until his student debt
was paid off. His father held that loan too, dammit,
and it was still a grossly sizeable amount because he
and Nina went on extravagant holidays every year,
drove fancy cars—well, he didn't anymore—and
bought crazy furniture, choosing to pay back a
pittance every month and continue to wear the golden
handcuffs his dad happily held the key to instead of
paying down debt. He tried to go to the bank and

refinance through them—but even with his salary, they all but laughed. Now Nina was long gone, but he continued on in the monster of a home that kept him tethered to his father and bound to a job he hated— unless he sold it, paid everything off with the remaining equity, including Nina, and started over. But that would mean . . . *starting over*. Admitting he'd taken on more than he could chew. Facing that every decision he'd made as an adult, right from spurning Jo, had been a mistake. . . .

"Earth to Callum. *Callum*!"

Callum jumped. "Uh—what?"

"I called your name like five times. Pass me the chips, dude."

"Right, yeah, sorry." Callum handed the bowl of chips to Dave who took a big handful, then shook the dish at Callum.

"No thanks. I'm good." Callum settled into his own seat and reclined.

"So what's up with you anyway?" Dave asked, but kept his eyes focused on the blaring truck commercial.

"Nothing. Everything." Callum cracked his knuck-les. "I want to know what she said."

"You're going to give yourself arthritis doing that shit." Dave finally glanced Callum's way. "And I told you. She didn't say much."

Callum felt like a big tool. Why was he getting Dave to be his go between anyway? Why didn't he just call Jo and apologize himself? Because he was a coward and a jerk, that's why. When Dave offered to clear the air and smooth things over with Jo on his behalf, he'd jumped at the chance.

"So what did you say? Did you tell her I was really sorry, that I know I don't deserve it, but I'd really appreciate a second chance?" *Don't you mean a third chance?* a harsh voice muttered in his head.

"I tried." Dave averted his eyes again and took another big handful of chips.

Callum studied him. "Something's rotten in the state of Denmark, old friend."

Dave rolled his eyes, but still looked shifty. Callum's spine stiffened. "I'm serious, what's up with you? What happened?"

Dave clenched and unclenched his hands a couple of times. "Don't take this too hard."

"Take *what* too hard?" Callum's heart hammered. "Of course I won't. Tell me already."

"I brought up the topic of you and her, and, well, she basically said the past was the past, that you guys aren't 'stupid kids, playing at being grown up' anymore—"

Callum fought to mask his hurt and must've been half successful because although Dave shot Callum a look, he continued. "And she said she was surprised you still lived around here, but that it's nothing to her personally."

"Really? She said *that*—that's what she said?" Callum felt like he'd been kicked in the balls. He rocked back in his chair, a little dizzy. Thank heavens for small mercies. At least he hadn't completely humiliated himself by apologizing about his misinterpretation of her and Dave's relationship. So what if she hadn't kissed him behind someone else's back? It was just as bad to return his kiss out of . . . what? Some sort of ego trip? Or pity? *See, Callum still has it bad for me. Poor sucker.* Her response hadn't felt feigned—but then what did he know? He had enough pent up affection and never-diminished attraction for her to fool twenty people. Maybe in his pathetic hopefulness, he'd projected the feeling it was mutual onto her.

Projected. Shit, he was an ass. He really needed to stop with the self-help books.

"Are you all right, buddy?"

"Yeah, sure. Great."

"Okay. . . ." Dave didn't sound convinced.

"I'm just surprised is all. I thought—ah, never mind." Callum crumpled his freshly drained cola can in his fist, then set it on the table. "So that's that, hey? I guess it's better to find out she's not into me now instead of later, right?"

"Yeah, you don't need another Nina, man."

So there it was. The elephant in the room. Even Dave was drawing a comparison between Jo and Nina. How could he be such a shitty judge of character, time and time again?

"What time's Brian coming over?"

"Eight," Callum said, glancing at the clock. It was ten to. He couldn't wait. Then Brian could entertain Dave, and hopefully the two of them wouldn't notice if he tuned out for a while. He got to his feet. "I made a pizza earlier. I'll go throw it in the oven."

"Sounds great. You're the best."

"Yeah, yeah." Callum imagined his future stretching out ahead of him, an unchanging pattern of daylight hours filled with a job he hated and evenings dictated by whatever was on TV. This was his life. Confirmed bachelor. Sex only in his lame imaginings. The highlight of his week being game nights with his equally lonely, but posing-as-if-they-weren't-lonely-at-all friend and brother.

No laughing wife who enjoyed working in the kitchen as much as he did. No little blue-eyed mini hims or curly-headed mini hers running wild in the yard—

Good grief! So now he wasn't just gloomy because he wasn't dating Jo, he was back to being miserable about not marrying her? He made himself sick.

Callum slid a huge eight topping pizza onto the middle rack in the oven. Why did he feel almost as bad as when he'd first lost her? They'd only seen each other a couple of times the last few weeks, and most of those had been chance encounters. They hardly knew each other.

Callum's hands shook and his breathing sped up. He leaned back against the counter to steady himself. His heart felt like it was skipping beats, and his stomach clenched and gurgled. He didn't know if he should stay put or run to the bathroom just in case. He grabbed a tea towel and wiped his sweating forehead. At this rate he wouldn't be able to watch the hockey game with Brian and Dave. The glare from the TV, combined with Dave's and Brian's shouting and cheering, would send him over the edge.

He leaned harder on the counter and lowered his chin to his chest. "Come on, Archer. Get a grip." The stern words just made it more difficult to breath.

Jo popped into his brain. What had she said to him at the office that day?

"Take a deep breath"—that was it. Everyone said that though: *Just take a deep breath, calm down*—as if it was that simple. Light-headed, he tried to suck in some sort of oxygen, got nothing. It was stupid advice. Why had it worked coming from her?

"It's okay if you can't . . ."—maybe that was it. How she said it. Despite the stomach-turning anxiety threatening to undo him, he smiled at the memory of her voice. "Just try," she'd said, like it was no big deal whether he succeeded or not—and then she'd joined him, like it would help her as well. "I'll sit, too."

Callum didn't know exactly how long he stood there in the kitchen by himself, or when his breathing and heart rate returned to normal, but they did.

Well, look at that. A therapist he used to see had encouraged him to find some sort of mental touch-stone, a person or place he could think about when an attack started that would hopefully soothe the symptoms before they got out of hand. Callum thought it was nonsense, but now? Now maybe he'd found one—and she wanted nothing to do with him. He sighed heavily. Maybe it was just as well because if she was like Nina then he needed her back in his life like he needed another hole in his head.

The oven's timer beeped and he opened the glass door. Garlicky tomato sauce and the aroma of melted cheese, onion, and spicy meats and shrimp made his mouth water. Weird. He was even going to be able to eat now. And he arrived at another conclusion, too.

Jo wasn't like Nina. She just wasn't. No way. Callum pulled the pizza out, and let it rest before slicing it into fat wedges. Dave was out to lunch. If Jo was like Nina, thinking of her would *not* calm him down. Even if he was an idiot, he refused to believe his subconscious would be tricked.

"What are you doing in here, bro?" Brian hollered from the doorway.

Callum jumped. "Making you knuckleheads food."

Brian held up his hands. "Whoa, okay. Don't shoot." He disappeared again, and Callum grabbed napkins.

Who knew what Dave had actually said when he talked to Jo—and whatever it was, it probably came out wrong. Besides, like he'd just been contemplating, they didn't know each other very well anymore. Jo could've meant her comments, cold as they sounded, merely as practical truth. They *had* been dumb, or he'd been anyway.

He arrived at another decision, and it made him

smile. So what if he was starting at a lower rank in her heart than she already had in his? He'd known that was the case forever, ever since she'd ignored his letter asking her to wait for him all those years ago. But she was back. And she *hadn't* seemed completely closed off to him when they reconnected. Maybe she exaggerated her disinterest to Dave, feeling odd about him bringing it up like they were kids in school. It was okay that she wasn't smitten. He was up for the challenge.

Feeling a lot better about the night, he grabbed the platter of pizza and hollered at Dave to come carry the plates.

"What are you, my wife?" Dave grumbled.

"You wish you had a wife, loser," Callum said.

"Like you don't."

"I don't just a want 'a' wife, no."

Brian, who'd piled into the room along with Dave, stopped mid-step to the counter. "You have someone specific in mind?"

Callum grinned. "Maybe."

"Who, you old dog?"

"A gentleman never tells. Grab the chili pepper flakes, will you?"

"Dude, really? You're not going to tell?"

"The game's started, man. Hurry up," Dave called over his shoulder as he left the kitchen, plates in hand, and Callum realized that yes, it really had. Indeed. And round one would involve two things. First, him manning up and doing his own talking. Second, determining, once and for all, what kind of person Josephine Kendall had grown up to be. And he wasn't going to lie. He couldn't wait to put time into finding out.

Chapter 16

Jo STUDIED THE FINAL BEDROOM with a critical eye and sighed. This was the room she'd used the random summers and two marvelous school years she'd lived with her uncle. It was unbelievable how much it had declined in the time since. But maybe her standards were lower then—or maybe, so desperate to have a home life of any kind, holes were a small price to pay. Samantha hadn't been lying. Gaps around the ancient single-paned window showed daylight, and today— Happy Winter!—a windrow of powdered snow lined the baseboard. She had hoped the snow would hold off until December, but no such luck.

She shook her head. Yep, this room was absolutely the worst of the lot, but the others weren't much better. Samantha was right again. No one could stay in the place as it was. Hard work, applying order to the chaos, and the kind, forgiving glow of soft lighting had gotten the living room and kitchen to a lovely state, as the guests at the dinner party would attest. And the room Jo slept in was fine, not spectacular, but closed to the elements, at least—as was the one Uncle Ray had always used. But the rest of the place? The more she got a handle on Ray's copious piles of stuff, sorting and selling and hauling it away to the dump or Goodwill, the less easy it was to ignore problem areas. The ramshackle state of the house became more and more obvious.

Her and Samantha's attempt to be civil and get along, despite their opposing goals, continued to be contrived and fumbling, but it was no wonder Samantha gave her whole-hearted blessing and permission to remove the junk. It only furthered her cause. It didn't necessarily get Jo closer to her goal of a bed-and-breakfast, but it did get Samantha closer to hers: a saleable property.

Jo grabbed the notebook she used to jot down things that needed done and approximate costs. What she needed was a partner, though she couldn't believe she was even considering that route again. But it would be different this time—a formal business arrangement, with a written up contract and crystal clear black and white terms. And maybe "partner" was the wrong word. *Backer* was better. She needed someone with cash. She knew she could give them a good return on their investment. She knew it.

The best way to fix the snow-pouring-into-the-house issue would be to install a larger window, in a frame that wasn't falling apart with dry rot, that fit the hole properly—but she didn't think she should spend her money on new glass just yet. . . . She'd cover it with plastic for now. She was reaching for her measuring tape, when the phone rang.

"Hello, Jo?"

Callum's low voice on the other end of the line did more than sidetrack her from her immediate goal. It tightened her stomach with anticipation, then made her furious for having that reaction.

"Jo?" he purred again.

She closed her eyes and leaned against the wall. "Yeah?" she said.

"Are you okay?"

Like a hunter could actually care for the meat he chased—but dang, if he didn't sound sincere. She needed to be very careful around him. She didn't have his leathery heart. "I'm fine, Callum. What's up?"

"Uh . . . " Mr. Smooth hesitated for a moment, perhaps slowed by the coolness of her tone. "I, well . . . I used your suggestion last night. It was really helpful. Thanks."

"And what suggestion was that?"

"Um, you know, to breathe."

"Sorry?"

"I was having one of my stupid anxiety attacks and usually nothing helps," Callum spoke very quickly and Jo empathized, though it was the last thing she wanted to do. "But then I remembered in my office, how you managed to help stave it off—"

"Being told to breathe is nothing genius. Everyone says that. It's useless. It was just luck that time."

Callum laughed and Jo's breath caught in her throat at the sound of it. "That's exactly what I thought, 'Take a deep breath'—totally unhelpful. But it was the way you said it, followed by "Just try," like it wasn't a win or lose, succeed or fail thing. You were so casual about it."

Jo slid down the wall until she was seated on the floor. She pulled her knees to her chest and wrapped one arm around her shins. "And that helped?"

"It was brilliant!"

She chuckled, just a little.

"I'm serious. I recalled what you said, started pondering how the heck it had worked, and then, practically before I realized it, I'd stopped freaking out."

"I'm glad." And she was. She wouldn't wish anxiety attacks on her worst enemy and Callum wasn't her enemy. He was something infinitely more dangerous—someone she liked too much. Still. She closed her eyes. "I'm glad," she repeated. "Very happy for you. Sincerely. But I have to go. I'm in the middle of something."

"Sounds fascinating. What?"

Jo sighed. "Measuring windows."

"I have the day off. I could help."

She wondered at the lines he used. Surely offering to help with reno prep wasn't a lady-killer's usual repertoire, but maybe that was what made him so good at it? That he seemed above suspicion.

"No thanks. I'm good." Good at being alone for the rest of my life, thank you very much! She thought of his face, though, and his ridiculously good smell, and only half of her was fooled by her adamant inner declaration.

"Okay . . . you're right. I shouldn't pretend nothing happened. I'm sorry, Jo."

"Pardon?"

"I was a jerk, and I'm sorry I hurt you—and put a damper on your party. I just . . . I thought you had a thing going with Dave, and, as I'm sure he told you, I was jealous. I acted like a testosterone filled idiot. It won't happen again. I was, I *am*, ecstatic you kissed me back, for whatever your reasons were. I think that's what made me crazy. I thought we were, you know. . . ."

"No, I don't know. Thought we were what?"

"Hitting it off, maybe like old times."

Jo picked at a thread of denim that had worn through a thin part on the knee of her jeans. *Like old times.* Like when she waited and waited and waited to hear from him, ready to go anywhere with him, have a life with him, only to be worse than crushed?

She had to give it to Callum though. Despite all Dave had told her, she couldn't hear a false note in his sweet words. It was now or never, but she needed to be clear—and could only hope he got the message quicker than Dave who had already called five times and left three messages today. Thankfully she recognized his number and let them go to voicemail. She realized she was stalling. Why was she worried about potentially hurting Callum? He was the one with all the power to inflict pain because she was one who, stupid and shocking and slightly pathetic as it was, still cared for him. Her high school "sweetheart." What a loser she was!

"Look, Callum, I know it's exciting, two new women—'fresh meat' so to speak—in a small town and all that, but, well, I can't speak for Samantha. . . . She might give you a whirl, but not me. I'm not in."

There was a second's silence. "Um, I don't know what you think I was asking, but I'm not interested in Samantha. At all."

Well, like he would admit he was pursuing both of them. Of course he wouldn't. She gave a small derisive snort before she could help herself.

"Sorry?" he said.

"Callum, you, me . . . We want incompatible things, and that's all right. Different strokes and all that."

He laughed, but it wasn't a happy sound. "Different strokes? Wow, the eighties are still alive and well."

She shook her head, couldn't hold back a small smile. "I like those lame old reruns, okay?"

"Okay," he said, but she wasn't sure what he was agreeing with: that it was all right for her to like retro sitcoms, or that they wanted different things. She was only further confused when he spoke again. "Can we at least be friends? Don't tell me you're so well connected already you couldn't use someone to gab with occasionally, or to bang nails and take orders. . . ."

Jo's heart hurt. She did want a friend, other than

Samantha who had a definite fun side but who thought pretty much every activity Jo really enjoyed was disgusting and/or too much work. And she was making other acquaintances that would hopefully grow into friends, true . . . but so far Callum was the easiest and most natural to be herself around.

You're setting yourself up for another big fall, part of her brain warned—but a softer, more soothing inner voice contradicted the advice, Ah, you can handle it.

"Are you still there?" Callum asked.

"Do you promise not to try and change my mind about being just friends?"

"I can't promise, no, but I'll do my best. That said, should you feel moved to seduce *me*, let me just say—"

"No," Jo replied more firmly to his teasing than she felt. "No flirting either."

"Yes, like I was saying . . . I would have to say a very stern, 'No,' to any seduction attempts because we're just friends, so gosh woman, stop jumping all over me like that. I mean it. I said, no. Quit it!"

Jo giggled.

"Hmmm," Callum murmured. "I think I changed my mind. I vote for a little bit of flirting."

Oh, yeah, this "just friends" thing she was pretending was possible was already working really well. "*Fine*," Jo said.

They hung up after making plans for the next day. Apparently Callum had worked in construction during the summers of his university years and kept up his skills with random do-it-yourself projects—which explained his shoulders and made him a very handy new . . .

Friend, she reiterated in her head, remaining on the floor a moment. She repeated the reminder aloud. "He is just your *friend.*"

FRIENDS. WELL, IT WAS BETTER than *not* friends and for a moment that was exactly what Callum had been sure she was going to say—in stronger words.

Her comment about her and Samantha being new "meat" nagged him. Had he somehow implied he felt like they, or women in general, were interchangeable? Nothing could be further from what he thought. He considered calling her back to ask about it, but decided not to. Maybe Samantha had mentioned flirting with him, and Jo had thought it was two-sided and wanted to confirm there was no interest on his part before they pursued a friendship.

For the first time in a long time he couldn't wait for Sunday, even though it meant the workweek would arrive more quickly.

You have a bad attitude, Archer, he said to himself, then surprised himself with the thought, *Dad's right about that at least.*

He decided to make calzones with the leftover pizza dough and toppings he had in the fridge. They'd be an easy, quick lunch to reheat at Jo's the next day.

As he washed his hands in the bathroom sink, he met his own eyes in the mirror and his observation about his attitude came back to him. It was time to change. Past time, actually. It wasn't fair to ask Jo to be friends—or anything else—with someone as lazy, cowardly, and stuck in a rut as he was.

Oh, lighten up. You're not *so* terrible, something whispered into his consciousness. It was almost a shock to have his thoughts say something positive.

He was at the counter, rolling out dough, when he realized the encouraging voice in his head had been Jo's. As if cued, the phone rang and he saw Jo's name on the call display.

He wiped his hands on his twill apron and grabbed the phone.

"Hello again!" he said, knowing and not caring that his excited tone revealed how thrilled he was to hear from her.

"Hey, Callum," she said softly.

His old standby negativity crashed back, full force. She'd reconsidered. Of course she had.

"I'm so sorry," she continued, fulfilling his doom and gloom prediction. "But I can't be your friend. I just can't."

He was about to let it go. He didn't need to be rejected over and over. It was like asking to be repeatedly hit by a car, or to have your head slammed into a brick wall again and again. She wasn't into him—and he didn't want to add pressuring someone to conjure up feelings that weren't there to his list of personality flaws.

Yes, he was about to let it go all right. Except that he couldn't—not until he knew he'd done all he could, been as honest as possible, about how he really felt. The few times he'd spent with her had been more fun, less stress than anything he'd done in . . . well, almost since they'd first broken up.

"Thanks for understanding. I'll see you—"

"Wait!"

For a second, Callum wondered if he was too late because she was so quiet, but his phone showed the line as active.

"What?" she finally said.

"Come on. I won't make it difficult. I promise."

She laughed wryly. "Just being friends is never difficult for one person."

What was she saying? Could she possibly mean it would be harder for her than him to stay mere friends? His heartbeat spiked in happy, hopeful excitement— then he calmed himself. No, she probably meant it would be easy for him to feel friendly toward her, but she'd have to work at it. Did she hate him so much?

"Take a chance," he said. "You never know. I might surprise you. Besides, I never thought you'd avoid something just because it's difficult."

Jo snorted. "I don't know if that's a good quality or not, but for better or worse—" She broke off, stammering, "I didn't mean that marriage wise."

"Of course not, of course not." Was she thinking he wouldn't be able to forgive her for ignoring his proposal? He wanted to end the confusion right there, to announce, "Hey, by the way, I forgive you for breaking my heart all those years ago," but it seemed too weighty a comment for a conversation establishing if they could even manage to be friends.

"So?" he asked.

Silence.

"What if we stow the issue for bit?"

"I'm listening."

"What if we don't decide anything yet? We don't need to make some firm declaration of friendship—or of anything else. What if I show up tomorrow to help you and happen to bring lunch? I mean you'll need to eat sometime, right?"

Jo was silent yet again. How he wished they were having this conversation face-to-face, so he could at least read her body language.

"And down the road," he continued, nerves making him speed-talk, "if hanging out is uncomfortable or not good in some other way, say the word and I'll move on. Despite how I might seem right now, I can—and will—take no for an answer. This is just me wanting to make sure you know how I feel, full disclosure and all that. I really like you, Jo, and it's confusing because I don't know if my feelings are just transference from before, or if they're real."

He thought he heard a quick, almost pained inhale of breath from Jo's end and rushed on so he'd have everything out before she hung up. "I don't want to pressure you, but it felt like, I mean the few times we've visited, I thought . . . you seemed to have feelings too. It's terrifying and may be years too late, but let's just see."

There were a few more beats of quiet, then Jo spoke and Callum's blood surged. "Well, you know how I hate to eat . . . but I should keep my strength up. I do have a lot of chores." The smile in her voice made him lightly punch his leg. Yes!

"So tomorrow, nine-ish?"

"All right . . . I guess."

She still sounded smiley, so he took a chance on one small joke. "And no last minute after midnight calls to cancel, right?"

"Fine," she said with mock annoyance, then added more softly, "Good night, Callum. See you tomorrow."

"I can't wait!" he said before he could contain himself.

Jo was laughing at him as she hung up the phone.

Chapter 17

THE WOODSTOVE PUSHED OUT LAZY waves of heat, and the flames behind the glass were a shimmering haze. Head propped on a cushion from the couch, Jo stretched out on the living room rug, a beautiful hand-tufted gold, navy and burgundy oriental carpet she'd found rolled up in the shed, protected by plastic wrapping.

She couldn't believe how quickly time disappeared. November was flying by. It hardly seemed possible. Snow for the winter would fall in earnest soon—no more of these hit or miss flurries or brief stints of wet flakes. The weatherman was calling for eighteen inches over night. Crazy! How long had it been since she'd seen that much snow?

But the changes in the weather weren't really what shocked her. It was how the hours she and Callum spent together were accumulating—and how she could never get enough.

The past few weeks he'd been at her side pretty much whenever he wasn't at work, and despite Dave's dire repeated warnings and Samantha's chronic skepticism, Jo felt pretty good about things.

Like her thoughts called him to her, he strolled back into the living room with a decanter of port and two glasses. He handed her one and filled it when she nodded happily.

"This is getting to be a tradition."

"Traditions are good."

"Are they?"

"Totally." He smiled, filled his own glass too, and sank down beside her on the rug, so close that his hip rested lightly against hers.

"It's an amazing place, Jo. You're right."

"Of course I am—but a lot of it's thanks to you. We got a lot done, especially the last few days."

Callum nodded and closed his eyes, basking in the heat from the stove. "I thought I'd never be warm again," he said.

"Aw, poor baby," she said lightly, sleepily. "Want me to kiss it better—" Jo broke off, suddenly wide-awake.

"Do I want you to *what*?" he teased.

"It's a figure of speech," she retorted.

"Fine, fine—but remember, you made the rule: no flirting."

"Ha, funny."

"It sure is cold though," she said a few minutes later. "The plastic is going to help a lot."

"That's me. A winterizing genius."

"Yep." Her eyelids were heavy again. "The fire feels so good, doesn't it?"

"The best." Callum moved to lie on his side, facing her, head supported by his propped elbow.

"Your hair looks like spun copper and gold in the firelight," he said.

"So like wire, hey? Gee, thanks."

His eyes crinkled.

The deep, rich port mellowed her well-worked muscles, and the combination of the pretty setting, glowing fire, and Callum's ever-yummier-to-her scent cast a cozy spell.

"Are you flirting with me, sir?"

"Nah," he said. "If I was flirting, Ms. Kendall, you wouldn't have to ask."

"Good to know." She rolled from her back to her side, mirroring his position.

They looked at each other for a long while, then Callum's eyes dropped from her face, traveled the length of her body, and rested on her dove gray corduroy pants.

"What?" Her mouth twitched as she waited for some smart comment.

He didn't say anything, but his brow creased.

"*What?*"

"I was just wondering—all day, actually," he finally said. "Ah, never mind."

"No 'never mind.' Tell me."

He shrugged and placed his hand on her knee, then ran it lightly up the top of her thigh.

"Oh," she said, surprised—and instantly warmer.

Callum kept his hand on her leg. "So that's what they feel like. I haven't worn cords in forever."

She smacked his hand away, laughing. "Seriously? Has that line worked for you? Ever?"

Callum's eyes widened in feigned innocence. "Line?"

She shook her head, then sipped from her glass. "Joker."

He shrugged. "Seriously, you can rock a pair of cords. Who knew?"

"Well, everybody, of course. Duh! Corduroy is awesome." She turned her face to hide her smile. She had warned herself in vain about not falling for his flattery. She loved every bit of his corniness.

There was a crackle and whoosh as one of the logs in the stove burnt through and the burning stack of wood and coals shifted.

"Ahhh," Callum said at the same time, stretching his arms above his head. "That's it for this guy. I've gotta hit the hay, or you'll be peeling me off the floor."

Such a nice back, Jo thought as she watched his muscles move beneath his soft cotton shirt. "Already?"

"Yeah."

"You could . . . well, you can stay if you want. The couch, as you know, is mostly comfy."

Callum got to his feet, shaking his head—ruefully, Jo hoped. "I'd like to, but I'm under a serious no flirting restriction, so sleepovers are probably out too."

Jo blushed. "I wasn't inviting—"

Callum touched her cheek. "I know you weren't. I'm just saying I wouldn't sleep a wink lying here on your cold couch."

Jo snorted. "Trust me. My bed is way colder than the couch."

Callum grinned. "Now see—I could make a comment about that too, but nope, I'm not even going there. See my mighty willpower?"

"I see your mighty something all right."

Callum eyes glinted. Jo clamped her hand over mouth. "Don't even go there, weirdo!"

He laughed, then nodded with a exaggerated sigh, his eyes still dancing.

"And you're good to drive?"

"Absolutely. I only had the one—and it was small, not like your two mugs full."

Jo grinned. "Hey, you poured them. I just drank them."

She leaned in the entrance until Callum had his jacket and boots on, and threw him a glove that fell out of his pocket.

"Thanks," he said, holding it up like he was toasting her with it.

"Thank *you*," she said. "I've had a lot of fun this week . . . friend."

"Me too, *pal*."

They both laughed and Jo slammed the door after him. She wrapped her arms around herself, shivering from the cold that gusted in as Callum slid out—or that's what she told herself caused the shiver anyway.

Really, her body felt the furthest thing from chilled, and it was like she could still feel Callum's hand on her leg.

Friends, indeed. She had to say though, smiling as she headed off to bed . . . Callum really didn't show any signs of being the playboy Dave said he was. He was funny, yes, and helpful, yes . . . and occasionally both of them broke the no flirting rules a little, yes . . . but none of it felt like a big farce to get into her pants. He seemed real. Genuine. Like his words that night on the phone about really liking her were sincere.

She bit her lip and a touch of her happy glow faded. *Real and genuine.* That's how she'd felt about him when they were together before, too. What were the odds she was actually right this time? Her happiness brightened again—pretty good, actually. Wasn't that how odds worked? They increased in your favor the more chances you took?

Nope, not even close, airhead, muttered her inner grouch. An old math exercise involving dice came back to her. Sure, the probability of producing rolls that totaled a specific number could be higher or lower, depending how many single digit combinations added up to the sought after sum. But when rolling a solitary die, no matter how many times you rolled, your chance of getting a specific number was the same each time you rolled.

She plumped her pillow, then hugged it to her chest. So what if affection wasn't logic-based? That didn't invalidate her analogy at all.

Chapter 18

MORNING LIGHT THE COLOR OF tea with milk poured through the gap in the curtains. Callum stirred and stretched, then settled again, letting his Egyptian cotton sheets and feather duvet seduce him back to the sweet, slightly bizarre dreams that live between nearly asleep and nearly awake—dreams that centered, always, on Jo. If every day could begin with thoughts of Jo, or better yet, *with Jo herself,* life would be so good—

The phone rang. Callum checked the display. Dave. Again. He ignored it and rolled over.

A few minutes later, the phone rang again. He still ignored it. Then once more. Finally he picked it up. "Dave, buddy, you're killing me. I was trying to sleep."

"So Dave calls you first thing in the morning now, too? Noon and night aren't enough for him?"

Callum bolted to full consciousness. Nina. She was like a cattle prod to the groin, armpits and any other tender parts.

"Ugh," he said out loud.

"Pardon me?"

"What do you want, Nina?

"I've heard you're seeing the Kendall sisters."

"You need to rephrase. What are you getting at?" Callum squinted at the clock again. Not early enough that he could fairly expect her not to call. Rats.

Nina exhaled in an exasperated wheeze, like he'd been stalling for hours and hours, holding her up. "Are you *dating* one of the Kendall sisters?"

"No."

The speed and lack of hesitation in his answer must have convinced her.

"Are you working for them?"

He paused. Damn.

"Are you or aren't you? It's a simple question."

"I'm just wondering how it's any of your business."

"So you *are* handling their freaky uncle's estate." Nina sounded like she'd won the Pulitzer or some equally lofty award. "Someone told me you might be."

"There are like, what, ten lawyers in this town, and only three that specialize in estate law. Your power of deduction is uncanny."

"Was it a valid, well planned will?"

"Are you on drugs? Taking something by prescription perhaps?"

"Why? What do you mean?"

"You have to be on crack or something equally mind-altering if you think I'd ever tell you about a client's will, estate, or pretty-much-anything-ever-you-name-it."

"Aw, Callum," Nina said softly. Callum could almost imagine her hand running along his arm as she crooned. His stomach turned a little and he jumped out of bed. The last association in the world he wanted was Nina and his new bed. "Come on . . . I'm just trying to be of service to our newest residents. If that dump is legitimately theirs and they want to unload it, I'm their realtor. I've already got a buyer."

Of course she did.

Well, at least it explained why she was calling. For business. What a relief.

And something else she'd said was interesting—but what? He pressed speakerphone, set the handset on the dresser, and pulled a T-shirt over his head as he tried to recall the comment that caught him. Nina kept up a steady bullet-fire of one-sided conversation: why she was the best representative for the property, why she was number one in the region, why he should give a shit—no, wait, that was what he wanted her to explain, but knew she never would. Oh—now he remembered what it was that struck him.

"You said someone told you I was the Kendalls' lawyer. Did they say the firm was handling the estate or did they specifically mention me? And who was it?"

He could practically see her pout. "I don't see how that's important."

"You're right. It's not. I'm just curious," Callum said, knowing indifference was the best way to get her to talk. He hadn't been attached to her hip for eight years and not learned any tricks. "Anyway, I have to get off the phone. I have a—"

"Dave," she said quickly. "It was Dave. Happy now?"

Happy? No, not at all. Why would Dave talk to Nina about him in any regard, let alone tell her something that put her back on his case and gave her reason to nag and harass him? He'd make sure he returned the favor—maybe with a big old slap to the head.

"Well, if that artsy one still has the deluded idea she can operate some kind of a hotel or something. . . ." Nina drifted off, like she was making an unspoken threat, and Callum noted she said "artsy" in a tone most people would reserve for "murderer" or "drug addict"—and he would've disapproved of the smug, judgmental attitude then too.

"If she still has the idea, then *what*?" he asked wearily.

"Just that I hope you have the good sense to say no when she comes around with her hand out."

"What are you talking about?"

"Don't play coy. I know exactly who she is—that fast little piece you went out with in high school."

Callum would've laughed at Nina calling anyone else "fast" and made a crack about the pot calling the kettle black, except that he was so outraged on Jo's behalf. "You don't know anything, Nina."

"Oh, I know plenty. I know you still have a thing

for her. You never stopped—and she'll figure that out pretty quick, if she hasn't already. So who's she going to come to for capital to help make her dreams come true? Well, soft touch Callum of course."

"Where are you getting this stuff?"

Callum's stomach twisted again at the smugness in Nina's cackle. "Wouldn't you like to know?"

"Yes, I would. That's why I asked."

"Maybe I overheard it from the talkative little bird herself."

The conversation was quickly falling into their classic communication meltdown. Any second now, they'd do away with any pretense of civility and start a shouting match. But even seeing the pattern didn't stop Callum from biting. He couldn't let Nina smear Jo like that.

"Jo's not going to come to me for money."

"Oh, *Jo*, is it? And really, she's not? You're so sure about that?"

"I'm sure."

"So she has you out there playing house for what—kicks? She's not trying to woo you into some dead-end financial catastrophe?"

Playing house? Who was feeding Nina this crap? Had she snuck around spying, after Dave inadvertently linked Callum to the Kendalls? Whatever. It didn't matter.

"She's not the first woman—and she won't be the last—to look at you and think your family's money is worth an investment of her own."

Not the first because you beat her to it, you mean, Callum thought. "Unless you had some other reason for calling, we're done."

"No. I'm coming to the office to see you."

"Make an appointment."

"I will."

He hung up, not believing for a second that Nina would show up. She was only fishing. It was the problem with commission-work—for greedy, climbing, bottom feeders like Nina, at least. It made everything in your life something to be bought or sold. Nothing had value without a price tag attached.

He tried not to scowl as he shaved, but it was hard not to.

"Don't let her get to you," he muttered, rinsing the blade under the tap and going in for another quick swipe near his sideburns. But it was too late. She already had. And he wasn't surprised. Getting to him was what Nina did best.

All that aside, however, he couldn't stop wondering how she knew so much about Jo's plans. Had she overheard Jo chatting to someone in town? Or worse, *had* Jo hinted a financial partnership with him was in the future?

No, she wouldn't use him like that. They were friends. They talked about almost everything. She was an open book.

Of course you think that. What's she going to do? Tip her hand right away and show you she's a conniving opportunist? The poisonous thoughts oozed into his head in Nina's voice, and although he didn't want any of his old bitterness or current worries to taint the sweetness of their new friendship, details of a recent conversation between him and Jo came back to him, choking him: what would they each do if they could do anything at all, no money or time or physical constraints.

"I'd create my dream retreat right here," she'd said, lifting her arms and spinning to encompass the cabin, outbuildings and wild jungle that made up Ray's place. Even frozen, the place was a jewel-green wonderland. Listening to her, watching her, feeling her excitement and energy like it was his own, while frosty, pine-clean air coursed through him, a big feeling of possibility had welled up in Callum. In that moment, he was purely happy just to be alive. "Uncle Ray wasn't perfect, but his house was my haven—and the closest thing to a permanent home I ever experienced. I was loved when I was here." Her eyes glowed, and Callum had wondered, *had hoped*, that her smile bloomed with memories of Callum's old love for her, not just those of good times with Ray. Now, however—though he hated it about himself—Callum wondered if her answer hadn't been a bit calculated.

"I'd run it as a bed-and-breakfast, yes, but I wouldn't have to worry about stupid practical things like staying in the black and being cash positive. It would miraculously run itself, and I could let people come and stay who needed to—no money, no problem." Then she'd laughed and said what now seemed the most damning thing of all. "I guess what I need is a kind benefactor, hey?"

At the time, idiot that he was, he'd thought it was a lovely, altruistic dream and said so, before launching into his long-held fantasy about a bakery and treat shop.

"That's perfect for you!" she'd said. "And I could buy your amazing goodies for my guests." He'd thought her extreme delight was sincere—and, super lame, it had made him mist up. She was the first person to ever express any enthusiasm for his idea. Everyone else thought he was nuts.

"What? You're going to work sixteen-hour days so you can feed cookies to snot-nosed brats and still barely scrape together a mortgage? Better plan on selling your big house on the hill, boy. That's not a career, that's called being a wife," had been his father's oh-so-enlightened comment.

Nina's had been worse. She'd simply said, "No."

Even Brian and Dave, who understood so many other things about him, didn't get it. "Dude, you're a lawyer," Dave always said. "Why would you give that up?"

Over the years, he finally stopped mentioning the bakery plan, ever—until Jo came back.

But talking to Jo, *why* he'd want to cook and bake for a living wasn't even a question. She totally got it. Totally got him—

Ouch! Stinging pain cut off that joy-triggering

realization. Callum set his razor down and leaned into the mirror, tilting his jaw to see the damage. Blood beaded on the firm ridge just below his ear. Damn it— considering how distracted he was, he was lucky he'd got through this ritual without looking like a mummy. He pressed a small piece of tissue over the nick, slapped on aftershave, and padded out into the kitchen to make coffee.

Was it remotely possible that Jo *was* playing him? Getting him excited with her enthusiasm, bringing him to a spot where it would only seem natural that she'd ask him to back her as a business partner because they were such close . . . friends.

No. Callum shook his head and ground the dark roast beans longer than needed. Jo wasn't playing him. She wasn't the type. She might try to avoid uncomfortable moments—just one more way they were alike—but she wouldn't purposely manipulate him.

Nina just knew him too well, and her not wanting to be with him didn't mean she wanted him to be with anyone else. This was one more of her control games, or even, possibly, something she sincerely believed. Nina would think Jo was up to something because that was how Nina lived—befriending those who could help her get something she wanted, cutting ties with those who stopped being useful. But not everyone was like that. They really weren't.

The coffee had finished brewing and smelled wonderful. Callum poured a big mug, added a generous amount of heated cream, and headed out to the large deck that overlooked the yard and gave a wonderful view of the small town in the valley below.

The sky was orange and pink in the distance, and gold-tipped clouds tiptoed across it. He felt warm despite the cold, and finally let himself just enjoy reliving the evening before. How fun and sweet Jo was—authentically, he was sure of it. She didn't have the ability to keep secrets or foster hidden agendas. She was the opposite of Nina in every way that mattered—and *that* was something he'd put money on.

Chapter 19

JO SAT AT THE KITCHEN table, picking at a fruit plate she'd made for breakfast, staring out at the pouring rain—or what rain she could see, through the fog of condensation on the poorly insulated window. Part of her wished the snow would return. It was December, after all, and she was ready for it now.

And she wished it wasn't a Tuesday. And she knew why she wished it wasn't. Callum worked a longer day than usual every Tuesday because he traveled to a nearby community to represent Ministry of Children and Family cases that Archer and Sons held the contract for. She wondered idly why she hadn't asked about what he did in court, what type of work the cases involved, etc.—but then again, she already knew why she didn't. Callum's eyes flattened when anyone brought up law, and his shoulders tensed.

She wondered if he was aware that even physically he didn't want to be a lawyer anymore, and smiled as she imagined what his response would be if she asked. How he'd open his mouth to deny it, then close it again without saying anything. Then he'd laugh—

and finally speak, only to disagree, to deny it . . . and eventually he'd admit she was right.

Callum Archer. Callum Archer. Callum Archer! The only person she'd ever stayed up all night talking with—countless times as a teenager, and then again, how many times this month? Her first kiss, and maybe, if she was lucky, the last man she'd kiss, too—

Oh, no, wait a minute—

She dropped the apple she'd been crunching and had a horrible epiphany—but one that put a grin on her face that wouldn't leave. Samantha, as usual, darn it anyway, was right.

Just last night she'd accused Jo: "You've fallen for him. Don't waste your breath or my time pretending otherwise."

Jo, of course, had "wasted" her breath and used up some of Samantha's oh-so-precious time explaining that she absolutely was not, could not, and would not be "falling" for Callum . . . and failed to convince Samantha one iota.

"Uh huh," Samantha had replied. "Tell someone born yesterday."

Jo picked up her apple again, and took a huge bite. And her feelings weren't even terrifying. They were . . . lovely. She would tell him soon—and pray it was still mutual. It was hard, so hard, to let herself trust that this really might be it: a relationship that could last. After all, no rule in the universe dictated that the one you loved would love you back—and while she'd forgiven the boy for breaking her heart, she didn't know if she'd survive the man doing it again.

She took another bite.

In love. Really? Fancy that. And it also explained why she was meandering about the house like a fool instead of getting down to work. The last of Ray's . . . *treasures*, to be polite, that she'd postponed dealing with while she and Callum cleaned, repaired and winterized weren't going to take care of themselves.

In love! Could it be true? She'd be lucky if she got one box sorted. She tossed her apple core in the compost bucket and headed to the back room—now the sole bastion of Ray's remaining hoard. Progress!

Jo made it through two boxes—deciding everything in them, except one small hand-carved box she recognized as Ray's handiwork, was going to the Salvation Army—before she got distracted from her task by the phone ringing.

She stood up and stretched, her hands pressed against the base of her spine, then grabbed the phone from where it sat atop the stack of boxes.

"Jo, hi!"

"Hello, Dave."

"You recognize my voice now," he said, mightily pleased.

"Or call display tipped me off, I'll never tell. What's up?"

"Well, we haven't visited for a while and the power's down at work, so I have a free day . . . wondered if you wanted to get lunch or take a wander some-where."

It was true that they hadn't hung out a lot, only twice, in fact, since his declaration of interest. And that infrequency was fully intentional on Jo's part, though Dave had been good to his word and not brought up romance again. She'd registered his occasional moon-eyed stare, however, when he thought she wasn't looking. "I don't know. I'm pretty busy today."

"Working on the place? I could help. I'd like to have an in with Greenridge's up and coming hotelier."

"It's not a—" Jo had been about to say *not a hotel*, but what was the point? She'd told Dave her dream was to own a bed-and-breakfast not a hotel, and had explained the difference, multiple times. It was interesting how he proclaimed to have this eternal burning desire for her, when he had no real interest in anything she talked about. And that was good— proved his infatuation would fade as they spent more time together and he realized they weren't a good fit.

"No, I've pretty much got the house as good as I can without any money, and the winterizing's done too."

"Wow, you got a lot done in a short time all by your lonesome."

Jo held the phone between her chin and shoulder to free her hands, pushed one of the emptied boxes out of the way, and opened a new one. "Well, I can't take full credit."

"Samantha helped? Weird. I'd never pick her as someone to get her hands dirty."

"No, you're right about that—literally anyway. It was Callum. He had some banked days to use up, and he knows about this stuff, so he popped by a bit."

"Ah, *Callum*," Dave said in a knowing tone that rankled Jo immediately.

"Yes, *Callum*. And you know, since we're on the subject, your description of him doesn't seem to fit him at all."

"My description?"

"You implied he's a womanizer. From our talks, it doesn't seem like he's so much as dated since he and Nina broke up."

"Well, I guess you only call it dating if you're interested in seeing the person again."

That stopped Jo for a second because it was true. Real playboys never admitted to having relationships. How many "clients" had Devin slept with—and stone-faced lied about—even when confronted with proof?

"I never had a relationship with any of those people. I never cared about them at all," he'd said, like it was a valid defense. Still, Callum was not Devin. He just wasn't. Not in a million years. In fact, no matter how bitter or jaded she sometimes wanted to be, not many people were Devins, period. Thank goodness.

Jo still hadn't managed a response, when Dave spoke again. "And the other thing is . . . actually, never mind. You're a grown up and you know what you're doing, but we're friends, right? Don't friends look out for each other?"

The "grown up" comment was ridiculous and obvious, and yes, friends looked out for each other, but Dave's version of "friendship" felt more like an obsession to control her. She didn't say anything confrontational, however, because she wanted to know what, if anything, Callum had said to Dave about her.

"Yes, there are definitely things we need to discuss, so how about it? Meet for lunch?" Dave asked.

Jo glanced at her watch. Eleven thirty-five, and she could use something more substantial than fruit to tide her over till dinner, plus she could pick up some more boxes—ones for the small amount of to-keep items.

"Yeah, all right. Sounds good, but give me time to clean up. How about a quarter to one at Don's?"

"Excellent. See you soon."

The cheery warm restaurant was already decorated for Christmas, which seemed too early for Jo's tastes, and was packed full of chatty late lunchers just arriving and early diners trying to finish up and leave. Jo inhaled the savory garlic and onion goodness in the air and sighed happily. She was starving. Good decision to meet Dave here!

And speaking of Dave, in keeping with his overly eager self, he'd arrived early and claimed a small booth in the back. She slid onto the espresso brown bench across from him, then turned to scan the wall-sized blackboard behind her that featured the regularly changing menu.

"So what's good here besides everything?" she asked. She'd discovered Don's a week ago with Callum and was already hooked.

"I'll have whatever you have." Dave smiled.

"Well, sheesh, that's no fun. How can I be jealous of what I didn't order if you get what I get?"

Dave laughed.

"No, seriously. And what if I order a salad, no dressing, and that's it because I'm not very hungry?"

"I like salad."

"Oh, you're hopeless," Jo grumbled, only half joking.

Their food came, loaded plates of pulled pork enchiladas, refried beans and mixed greens salad with the most amazing dressing Jo had ever tasted. She got down to serious eating, while Dave took his time— and scraped away the sour cream drizzle and the beans.

She shook her head. He grinned again.

"So what are these 'things' we 'definitely' need to talk about?" she asked when the edge of her hunger was dulled.

Dave pushed his yam fries around his plate.

"Are you not feeling well?" Jo asked. "You're not eating—"

"No, no, nothing like that. I just don't want to get in the middle of anything."

Jo leaned in to hear him better and matched his

low tone. "Get in the middle of *what*? You're starting to worry me."

Dave looked away as if uncomfortable and trying to come to some sort of inner decision. Eventually he sighed and met her eyes.

"If I tell you something, do you promise not to tell the person it involves that I even whispered a hint about it? And do you swear not to hold it against me if . . . if I made the wrong decision in telling you? I want to believe in the guy, but like I've said—"

"You're talking about Callum."

"I am." Dave nodded and finally took a big bite of food—at exactly the last minute Jo would've chosen him to.

"I promise, of course. *What is it*?"

"First I have a confession."

"I'm listening."

"I already knew you were spending a lot of time with Callum."

"You did?"

Dave nodded again. "And I'm disappointed, of course, but I get it. He's Callum Archer. Lawyer. Big shot. Great looking. Funny. Plus, you guys have a history. . . ."

"Uh, Dave?"

"Yeah?"

"Cut to the chase."

"Anyway, he told me you guys were officially seeing each other."

"He did? That's weird."

Dave's brow furrowed. "Why?"

Jo took a big sip of her lemony brewed-in-house iced tea. "No reason."

"He also told me how much he's enjoyed helping you fix up Ray's, and how it really suits him. He used to want to run a bakery. Did you know that?"

"Yeah." Jo smiled, remembering her and Callum's recent conversation and knowing it wasn't a case of "used to" at all.

"So, well, here's the thing. He's hoping you'll ask him to invest in your project—to buy into the business, or, at the very least, let him front you the money to get it off the ground."

"No way," Jo said. "Not going to happen. He can forget it—and so can you."

Dave's eyebrows rose. "You won't even consider it? Why not? You're desperate for cash, and Callum said if you don't come up with a real solution soon, the place will be sold. You know that."

Jo nodded just as a curvy, sweet-faced server popped by. "Would you like that wrapped to take home?"

Jo nodded again. "Yes, please."

Dave had hardly eaten anything, but said he was done, too.

"You don't trust him, is that it?" Dave asked the minute the server left with their dishes.

"No . . ." said Jo. "That's not it at all. I . . . well, I hadn't even thought of Callum as a potential partner that way."

"Not 'that way'—as in not in a business way, but in some other way?" Dave interrupted.

You had to hand it to Dave. Some things he caught pretty quickly. She hadn't even realized what it sounded like she might be saying. She blushed.

"Let's talk about something else, please. I don't want Callum's money. Never have. Never will."

"Even if it means having your dream fail?

"Dreams can change."

"But you'd take your sister's money."

"That's different. If she wanted in . . . well, I thought it could be a healing thing for us."

Dave nodded and asked if she was going to finish her water. She shook her head.

"Mind if I finish it then?"

"Knock yourself out," Jo said motioning for him to go ahead.

"I think you're right," he said, crunching on a piece of ice.

"About?"

"About not offering Callum a piece of the action."

"It's not like that either. I'm not trying to hog anything."

"Oh, I know—and besides, it's okay. He'll be disappointed, but he'll find another pet project. He always does."

"He does?"

"Yeah, he's always investing in some screwball cause or another. It's one of his good qualities, actually. Really generous—though sometimes I worry he's too comfortable with people asking for handouts. If he sought out specific investment opportunities, that'd be one thing—but he seems to feel just the opposite. 'You can't get if you don't ask' is his motto."

"Dave, why are you telling me all this?"

Dave met her stare steadily. "I don't know exactly. I mean I like you and all, as you're well aware, but if I ever convince you to give me a chance, I don't want it to be because I prevented you and Callum from finding out if you were right for each other."

"And knowing my past and what happened with Devin, you think me and Callum running a business together would be a good thing, a safe thing—for either of us?"

Dave fiddled with the straw in the now empty water glass. "I'm not sure. It could totally blow up in your face. That's why I was hesitant to even bring it up, but then again, maybe you're the woman he was waiting for to make a life change." Jo snorted. Dave ignored her. "Go with your gut. If you feel that strongly about not having him involved, don't get him involved."

"Okay . . . well, thanks."

Dave shrugged. "No problem."

Chapter 20

JO THOUGHT ABOUT HER CONVERSATION with Dave all the rest of the afternoon. He was one of Callum's oldest friends, and if he said Callum was interested, he'd know.

But was *she* interested? Could she risk everything again? It wasn't just a matter of another business. She'd learned the hard way what to avoid and what to make sure you got in writing. But for her it wouldn't just be a business. She wanted it to be her home. If she invited Callum to invest, to partner in the B & B, that's really what she'd be asking: to make a home with her. And *that*? *Now*? It would be crazy. It was way too soon. It was, like she'd told Dave, not going to happen. Or so she'd decided, until Callum stopped by that evening unannounced.

"I'd say I'm sorry for the surprise visit, but I'm not sorry one bit," he said, grinning. "I had to see you. Is it a bad time?"

"Never. You get a special show-up-whenever-you-want card because of all the help you gave me."

He stepped inside and pulled off his snowy boots and jacket. He was wearing her favorite sweater—the soft oatmeal thing—and she wanted to hug him. "Is it laminated?" he asked.

"What?"

"My card. I want it to be official. You know, *laminated*. Durable."

Jo laughed. "Yeah, I'll get right on that—and you're in luck. I was just making a fire."

"Perfect timing," Callum agreed, rubbing his hands together. "It's awful out there."

"So that's the reason you came over—because it's awful out there?" Jo teased.

"Of course. What else would drive my motives?"

"No idea. None at all." Jo wanted to kiss the cute smirk off his face.

Callum carried an armful of logs from the wood box by the entranceway into living room, and set them down by the stove with a satisfied grunt. "There. We should be good for the night."

He glanced at the DVDs scattered across the coffee table. "You were going to watch a movie."

"I was thinking of it."

"Could we make popcorn?"

"We could."

"I thought you'd never invite me!"

"Uh, yeah, I didn't."

"Details, details."

Jo felt something so warm, happy and silly heat up her belly that she started laughing.

"Woman, what's gotten into you now?" Callum asked, but she couldn't answer. Smiling like he knew exactly *what*, he headed off to the kitchen.

Reappearing shortly with a big bowl of buttery popcorn, he settled beside her on the couch.

Jo leaned across Callum, grabbed the remote, and pressed play. Haunting intro music started. "It's a scary one," she warned.

"Good, then I can make you hold me and it won't be flirting."

Enough was enough. How long could she deny her feelings? "Oh, no, it will be flirting. I promise." She looked down a moment, then brought her gaze up to meet his.

"In that case, I should tell you something," he said in a somber tone.

Jo's stomach flipped. "What's wrong?"

"It's just, well, I'm already feeling kind of terrified."

"Oh, you are, hey?" She was about to say something else, but the expression that suddenly crossed Callum's face—all soft-eyed and half-smiling—made her inhale instead.

"Jo, before we watch the movie, seriously now, I do have to say something."

"Okay . . ."

"I love being here with you. Everything about our times together and this place is . . . well, wonderful. Thank you."

For a second, Jo was almost dizzy. And then she was perfectly calm. Perfectly sure. She'd been silly to hesitate. If he loved this place as much as she did, it was only right to share it.

"Callum . . . "

"Yes?" he whispered.

"I, well, I was thinking today . . . and I agree."

"You do? Well, that's good." He laughed softly. "Can I ask *what* you agree with?"

"Yes, of course—sorry. I'm just excited." She shook her head to clear it. "I feel exactly the same way. I love having you here, too. This place—well, it's just right somehow—like it's already ours."

Callum had been nodding and smiling, but his expression suddenly closed just a bit—though Jo didn't notice right away, only realized it later, in hindsight, when she replayed the moment back and back and back.

"And well, I know you have money to invest in things—and that you like to."

Callum's face reddened. Excitement, she thought, misreading him so badly that she'd weep about it afterwards.

"There are various ways we could arrange it. We could do just a straightforward loan with a decent interest rate to make it worth your while, or you could buy shares—or," she said, her heart beating so rapidly she could feel it in her throat, "you could . . . well, I thought . . . we could—"

On the TV, the movie's storyline kicked in with a groan of thunder, a mighty crack of lightning, and the sound of a massive tree splintering. Jo jumped. Her hands flew to her mouth. Something was dreadfully wrong.

Callum bolted to his feet. His face was scarlet, his voice so quiet it was difficult to hear.

"That's what *this*—" he gestured wildly around the room, "was all for? You and me, all this time . . ." His voice broke and when he spoke again, he was almost yelling. "It was about money? Hitting me up for cash for your make-work pipe dream?"

Jo just shook her head. She couldn't find words. This couldn't be happening. What had just happened? What *was* happening?

"She told me you were grubbing for money, but I said absolutely not—that you were never about the money. That was one thing I was always sure about."

In the shadows of the TV world, someone started screaming and didn't stop.

Jo found her voice. It was raspy and sore like she'd been the one wailing. "Get out. Now."

Callum crossed the room in three angry strides, then stopped. Turned back. "*You're* the one who's pissed off in this scenario? Are you fucking kidding me?"

Jo leaped up too, her muscles tight to the point of being painful. She opened her mouth, but nothing came out. She swallowed hard. Clenched her fists. *Do not cry. Do not cry. Do not cry.* When she finally managed speech, her throat was hot and aching. "You don't know me at all, do you?"

Callum stared at her, then suddenly went pale. "Wait—"

"Oh, that's your favorite word, isn't it? *Wait.* I waited for you before—and I've waited for you these past months, always giving you the benefit of the doubt when you were hot then cold, hot then cold. I'm not waiting anymore. I'm not waiting ever again. I was an idiot to think you'd change."

He started as if jolted by an electric shock. "What are we talking about—then or now?"

"Now, then, if, when—everything's connected." Jo shook her head. "I keep wanting us to be different, to be ready for each other, but we're not. And we never will be. You're always going to be looking for an excuse to bail, and I'll always be waiting for you to leave me again."

"But—"

"No buts. Do you know how much I loved you, how I mourned you?" She rushed on before he could interject. "And the past few months, no matter how I fought it, I still loved you. And I wanted to tell you more than once—but a little part of me kept saying your favorite word—*wait.* Thank God I listened— well, until tonight anyway. Don't worry. It's not a mistake I'll make again."

He deflated. His shoulders slumped, and his limbs, rigid just seconds before, almost seemed to disjoint. She didn't care and she didn't feel pity.

"I, I—" he stuttered. "I thought, I mean . . . I'm sorry. I misunderstood."

She pointed at the door. "I don't care, and I don't want to have this conversation anymore."

His eyes narrowed. "Of course you don't. You never want to talk about anything uncomfortable."

"*I* don't? Thanks for the genius insight, Kettle."

"Listen to me. Please."

Jo settled her weight on one hip. "*Fine.*"

She let him bumble through another mumbled apology and jumbled explanation of what he'd thought she'd meant. She heard him out. No one could say she didn't.

"Well, you're right," she finally interrupted. "I didn't want your money."

"Well, you did—just not in the gross, greedy way I, like an idiot, first thought."

She snorted.

"And as for back then, that night . . . you can't put that all on me. I got scared, yes, and maybe I should've talked to you in person, yes again, but—"

Maybe he should have done it in person instead of just not show up?

"You think?"

"Come on, Jo. It wasn't all my fault."

"It wasn't?"

He shook his head, and his mouth opened again, but Jo waved him silent. Her stomach was nauseous with roiling anger and hurt.

"Enough, Callum." She wrapped her arms around herself. "We had our chance. Maybe it's natural to always wonder if things could've been different—but they weren't and they aren't. The only way to live is to continue moving forward, finding new challenges, making new plans when old ones don't work. It was a mistake for either of us to think we could have what we used to have back."

"Don't say that. That's what you said about us screwing everything up and not getting married when we were kids, that it was for the best, but—"

"Yes, that is what I said, isn't it? Interesting."

"No, please—"

"Good-bye, Callum. Keep well."

He made no move to leave, so she did.

In her bedroom, door firmly closed, she waited and waited—and finally heard a rustle of movement in the hall, then the exterior door click open and latch shut.

She listened to the night's deep silence grow and grow, and her heart felt as stripped and bare as the boards beneath her feet. Callum was gone.

Chapter 21

AISHA WALKED TO THE SUNNY spot in the living room and spun slowly, like a model on a catwalk, then flicked her flat-ironed hair over her shoulder. "So, whaddya think?"

Her dad tilted his head, appraising her. "What did your friends think?"

Aisha rolled her eyes. "You can imagine, I'm sure."

Kathleen had strolled right past her, not recognizing the preppy look Aisha sported. Jade had snorted in complete disagreement at Aisha's defense that she was still herself, just "new and improved."

"I just don't see why you feel you need to change who you are to meet your birth mom. You were fine the way you were. I like your curls. I like your emo Teddy Bear shirts. They're way less creepy than this Stepford wife look you've got on."

Aisha snorted. "Most parents would be thrilled if their kid, especially their pregnant kid, started dressing more like a grown up and less like a 'ghoul.'" (She'd actually had a teacher refer to her that way once—until he saw the essays she came up with and was forced to acknowledge she had a brain.)

Charles looked down at his own T-shirt and faded jeans and sighed. "Growing up shouldn't mean turning into somebody else."

"Even when you don't like your old self? I'd love to grow into someone else."

He sighed again, heavier. "Why don't you at least let me take you? Why do you have to bus alone? You're six months pregnant—and it's winter for crying out loud."

"Consider it my early-graduation present to my-self."

"So you've finished then?"

"Yep. Everything's in, I'm just waiting on marks. It's the only thing I did right considering. If I'd gotten knocked up even a month or two later, it would've been really hard to arrange the correspondence classes to work properly."

"It's not the only thing you've done right, sweet-heart."

The thin winter sun that had been lighting the floor where Aisha stood disappeared behind a cloud. The room went gray and the temperature cooled instantly. She shrugged.

Charles sank into his recliner. "Fine, take the bus trip, if you insist. But please, for the love of every-thing that's still good in the world, stop wearing the god-awful pastels and matchy-match pants and shoes. You're killing me and your mother would be beside herself."

Aisha smiled at his "matchy-matchy" criticism because it was a line stolen directly from her lips. "Mom would love it. It would be a relief."

"She absolutely would not, and *it would not*. She'd want you to keep being yourself, whatever that looked like, not wear a costume and try to be someone else."

"Is that even true? I've always felt bad I went to the wild side when she got sick."

Her dad shook his head. "No, she loved how zany and full of life you always were—skull jewelry, piercings and all. She wouldn't want you to lose your nerve or edge because of one unexpected setback."

Aisha studied her reflection the blank TV screen that took up one wall. The girl looking back at her was pretty in a tame pink lip-gloss sort of way, and she looked nice, not haughty or stuck up. Best of all, even with her no-doubt-about-it-baby-bump sticking out yay-far, she didn't look like a screw up. But straightening her hair wasn't going to straighten out her life, was it? And being pregnant wasn't criminal. Just a blow to her pride, that's all.

Aisha's voice was a bit froggy. "Okay, okay. I admit—these shoes totally suck, and pink pants? Who invents these things? And you're right about the trip, too."

A small smile lifted her dad's mouth, but it fell from his face at her next words. "I'll wait till February. Right now, I'm still good to work. It's dumb to leave when I can still take extra shifts."

Her dad opened his mouth to say something, then closed it and only nodded.

Chapter 22

PALE RAYS OF SUNLIGHT, IF one could call it sun not just the absence of complete dark, crept through the slats of the blind above his desk. Callum turned on his desk lamp, but the small bulb wasn't bright enough to dispel the gloom and shadows. He should have turned on the overhead light, but was too lazy.

He picked up his phone and listened to his messages—three. The first pertained to something he'd already dealt with, so he deleted it halfway through. The second required more energy than he had at the moment, so he saved it. The third? He hung up midlisten.

"Ah, Nina, the gift that just keeps giving . . . or rather, trying to take," he muttered, then raked his hand through his hair. It was time. Time to deal with Nina once and for all.

He got up, cracked his knuckles, and left his office. He was scared, but he was also, amazingly, calm. He couldn't believe he was sticking to his decision to change aspects of his life, and of himself, that he didn't like. That in and of itself was already a change. Before, he always chickened out.

Callum approached his father's office at the end of the hallway and rapped sharply on one of the big oak doors.

"Come in," his father commanded.

Callum complied, unsurprised that his father was there so early in the day. He'd inherited his insomnia from someone.

"What, you don't call before coming?" From anyone else in the building, the comment would've been a joke. Not so with Duncan Archer. Callum didn't know if his father could joke, actually. If he could, Callum had never heard him.

"We work in the same office, Da, come on."

"You know I prefer being called Mr. Archer in the workplace, Callum."

Like there were so many people around to hear them at 5:30 a.m. Callum almost said as much, but knew it would be pointless. Usually he just avoided calling his father anything in public—or in private.

"You're in early," Duncan said approvingly.

Like this was even slightly unusual.

"Yes." Again, easier than saying what he was actually thinking. He wondered, with no small amount of self-disgust, if he was ever going to stop taking the easiest route, the path of least resistance.

Yes, yes, he was, dammit. Right now, in fact!

"I'm done. Da. Finished."

"This again? Are you kidding me? Every couple of months you pull this Mary-boy routine. It's time for you to grow up."

"And by that you mean, be like you, right?"

Duncan's square jaw relaxed into a smile, and laugh lines creased by his eyes. He almost looked good-natured if you didn't know better. "Oh, that would be a terrible thing, eh? Successful. Powerful. A known name."

"Known all right."

Duncan shrugged off the insult and insinuation. "You could do a lot worse than ending up like your old man, boy."

"Pulling the father/son card, really? And when we're in the *office*."

Duncan's grin became a grimace.

But Callum wasn't done punching. "It's pretty easy to be the biggest fish when you're in a small pond."

"I'm assuming you came for an actual reason? If yes, get on with it. If it's more prattle you're after, call your mother."

It was amazing how a person never got used to some things. How they continued to hurt even after a spot was rubbed so raw you'd think there wasn't a nerve left.

"Leave Mom out of this. I don't know why she stays with you."

"And that's why you're a shitty lawyer, Callum. You don't understand what makes people tick. She hangs around for the same reason you're standing here even though you'd rather be anywhere else."

Callum lowered himself into a chair when his

father said "standing here." Duncan ignored him.

"Your mom talks a pretty line of lovely sounding gobbledygook but I write the checks. Big ones. How long do you think she'd last without my roof over her head? How do you think those paintings of hers would taste in lieu of groceries, or wrap around her shoulders instead of clothes?"

His roof. The guy acted like she was some impostor, not the woman who'd loved him, or at least put up with him, and raised his three sons.

"I didn't come here to fight with you."

Duncan let the lie stand.

"Like I said, I'm finished here. For real. I'll give you the house back to erase my debt, and since it's worth more than I owe—"

Duncan made an irritated throat clearing sound.

"I'm asking you to pay the cash settlement Nina feels she's entitled to and the courts agreed with."

Duncan shook his head. "No, you brought that one to your bed. You finish kicking her out of it."

Callum stood again, and Duncan lumbered to his feet as well, planted his hands on his desk and leaned forward, glaring. Callum felt about eleven. His dad could've been a pro-wrestler, probably still could be, actually. He still stood almost as tall as Callum, added years not affecting his spine or his deportment one whit, plus he had a good fifty pounds on Callum, all muscle, not fat.

"I'm sick of playing this little game every couple months. Are you serious about quitting this time? If yes, an interesting CV landed on my desk last week . . . someone I'd consider replacing you with."

Callum tried his best not to show it, but he was surprised. A bit anyway.

"Write a letter of resignation. Give me four weeks of your time, if you can, and make sure you clear as many of your cases as possible, especially get rid of the two lunatic sisters. Waste of time—no money there. The old guy was smart enough to put it in both the girls' names before he kicked, so court time isn't necessary unless you're stupid and can't get that younger one to see sense and agree to sell and have a probate judge sign it off without a hearing."

Ah, so he had looked over the Kendall file, after all.

"And about that house of yours. Don't mix business with personal. You work at the firm, so quit at the firm. You want to wriggle out of your debt or your mortgage with your mother and me? Put up a For Sale sign and hope you can unload it. Then you can pay me back, pay Nina out, or keep paying monthly alimony. Not my business. Miss a payment to me in the meantime though, and I'll start the paperwork to foreclose."

"You would."

"Yep, son, I would." Duncan sat back down, rolled his white shirtsleeves up over his hairy forearms, then perched a pair of reading glasses on his nose. He peered up at Callum over the rim of those spectacles. "Was there anything else?"

Callum knew a dismissal when he heard one, gave a curt nod, and headed for the door. He turned back when he reached it, however, conscious of eyes on his back. Sure enough, Duncan had been watching him go.

"What now?" his father asked.

"I'm taking a personal day."

Duncan didn't speak for a good long time. Finally he raised his hand and waved it once. "Of course you are."

Callum opened his mouth to say one more thing, but Duncan had dropped his gaze and returned to work, his pen moving calmly and quickly across the page like his concentration on his task hadn't been interrupted in the least.

Chapter 23

JO LOOKED OUT AT THE heavy snowflakes swirling in slow motion and was beyond grateful that Samantha had agreed that using the small amount of cash left to each of them to fix the floors made sense. She was also pleased to have found a decent part-time job. It only paid a few bucks more than minimum wage, but she lived simply and for the time being had no rent and no mortgage. It would be fine—and the best part, of course, was the type of job it was. Imagine getting paid to point people to the best places to fish—and imagine what she'd learn from Eddie, the old timer who ran the Hook and Lure. And, if, if, if—so many big ifs!—*if* she actually did get the bed-and-breakfast off the ground, she could advertise her own business there. She'd already asked.

"I wish you'd stop grinning like the cat who ate the canary," Samantha snapped. "You look like you've turned into a total nutter instead of just a partial one."

"Nice," Jo said. "Real nice." But Samantha's bark couldn't ruin her day. She was probably just feeling threatened.

"The dump does look half decent," Samantha muttered a moment later with narrowed eyes and a frown, confirming Jo's suspicions. She took a seat at the bright yellow kitchen table, and as she did Jo noticed something that gave her pause. Sam's eyes were wet.

Samantha wasn't a crier. It was a point of pride for her actually. "What's the point?" Samantha always said. "All those years boohooing didn't help us when we were kids, don't see how it'd help now."

Jo didn't know if she herself was naturally a crier or not, but years of following her big sister's lead made her feel weak when she succumbed to tears—and horribly uncomfortable when others did. What was she supposed to do? What should she say?

"Are you crying?" she asked unhelpfully.

Samantha glowered and her jaw tightened. "No, I'm not *crying*."

Jo tried a ginger pat pat on Samantha's shoulder.

Sam yanked away, which Jo would've taken as a positive sign, except that Samantha made a furtive wiping motion at her right eye like she was trying to obliterate an errant tear.

"Okay, who are you and what have you done with my sister?"

Samantha whipped around to face Jo again. "Seriously? That's all you've got? I'm distraught here and you're like, hyuk, hyuk, hyuk?"

Jo settled into one of the chairs across from Samantha. "That's better. Now that you're back to your usual soft and gentle self, tell me. What the hell was that about?"

Samantha let out a heavy sigh. "I just feel badly."

"About what?"

"I know you want this, Jo—and I know why."

"So enlighten me."

A touch of a smirk lifted Samantha's mouth. "You know I will."

Jo nodded glumly.

"You want to create a cozy, close-knit place where everybody knows your name thing—"

"You make me sound like someone off that old TV show 'Cheers.'"

"Dibs on being Carla," Samantha said and returned to her main point without missing a beat. "I get it. I want that, too. Who wouldn't?"

"You would want to be Carla. I'm Woody."

"You *are*. You're so right!" Samantha actually looked proud.

Jo raised her eyebrows and shook her head. "I was joking—but seriously, why can't we create a home here, a niche? Together. It will be great. You're wrong that a person can't just decide to build themselves a home and a life and have it work out."

Samantha pursed her lips. "Really?"

"I'm not forgetting about Devin, but good grief, if everyone quit trying to make their dreams come true because of some heartbreak or disappointments, no one would ever achieve or do anything. You've got to get back on the horse."

"Bah," said Samantha. "I hate horses."

"You're hopeless. And if you'd be honest—dead, cold, completely hardcore truthful—you'd admit this place could totally be all that I envision."

"Maybe, but also maybe not. And you don't have the money to pull it off. You just don't. We don't. Even if this place belonged solely to you, free and clear, and it was just a matter of start up costs, I wouldn't lend them to you."

Jo studied her fingernails. "Harsh," she said, finally glancing up.

Samantha's green eyes were sad. "It's not because of your disaster with Devin, if that's what you're thinking."

"It's not. I know it's not personal. We just view the world differently."

"So you'll be okay when Callum calls?"

"What do you mean?"

"Callum will contact you to set up a meeting. He's going to tell you we're listing the property. There's no other choice—unless you really want to take it to court, and you'll lose, Jo. We both will. It will just cost bags more money, take years of our lives—to get the same verdict."

The phone rang practically the instant the words were out of Samantha's mouth.

Jo picked it up—and yes, it was Callum. And yes, he was calling to set up a meeting. Jo agreed on a time, then asked if he needed or wanted to talk to Samantha. She thought she heard him start to say it wasn't necessary, but she was already passing the phone to Samantha. She didn't want to talk to him for another minute, and she couldn't bear to sit still in the house another second either—the house that felt more like home than any other place she'd ever lived that was really, truly going to pass out of her hands and into someone else's. And Samantha? Well, she needed a break from her, too. Yes, she understood where she was coming from, but it didn't make it hurt any less. Not at all.

"Jo?" Samantha's voice trailed after her.

Jo hesitated in the entranceway, but only because it was near freezing and she needed to throw on a jacket. "The meeting's at ten tomorrow morning. I know. Let yourself out, okay? I'll see you then."

If Samantha answered, Jo didn't hear her. She grabbed her rod, whistled for Hoover, and slammed the door behind her.

CLOUDS, LOW AND DARK, HAD rolled in during the night. A steady, driving rain, icy-cold and penetrating, wouldn't let up. It was the only thing she disliked about Greenridge—how it would snow, rain away the snow, then snow again. Visibility was nil, and even though it was supposed to be daylight, someone had forgotten to notify the sky. It could easily have been approaching night. Ahead of Jo on the road, some idiot cut off some jackass who was going way too fast for the conditions. There was a brief flare up of horns and road-rage gestures.

So far the whole day fit her mood. Fit her luck. Fit everything, Jo thought, noticing with irritation that even though she was plenty early, Samantha had still beat her there. And so had a little lime green Mazda sporting Realtor decals.

Jo's finger caught in her seatbelt as she was un-buckling. She pretended it was the smarting pain that triggered tears.

She opened her door, but didn't climb out right away. Instead she tilted her head back, and willed the stupid sea of saline to stay put. She wasn't going to walk into Callum's office wearing her disappointment and sadness like a big, red I-just-cried clown nose.

When she had a tight line on her composure again, she climbed out of her truck—and sunk past the rim of her shoe in a puddle of slushy goop. Awesome. The day just kept getting better and better.

Callum's secretary was nowhere in sight, but his door was ajar. Jo made her way toward it, then froze as she heard her name, coming not from Callum or Samantha, but from someone else's mouth altogether. Jo assumed it was the realtor who owned the green car. And she didn't like the woman's tone, or her dismissive laugh, one bit.

"You guys just don't get her." Now it was Callum speaking. Oh, that was rich. She inched closer, dying to know what it was that mystery woman and Sam supposedly didn't get about her—that Callum supposedly *did*. "So she's a bit of a dreamer. It's not

like she has any control over that side of her personality. She can't help herself."

The realtor—Jo's mind created a gym-fit body and
highly made-up face to go with the high-pitched,
bossy voice—snorted with derisive laughter. "Isn't it
her job, if she actually wants to run a business, to curb
her imagination and look at facts?"

Jo added to her inner picture. The realtor had an
upturned, bulbous nose—quite unlike anything seen
on a human's face before, decidedly pig-like, in fact.

Callum spoke again and Jo could almost see him
shaking his head. "Part of the charm of the place
would be what her creativity added to it. She's in the
planning stages. It's not her fault if she got a bit
carried away. She feels before she thinks."

"It is problematic if she tells every Tom, Dick, and
Harry what her so-called plans are before she even
owns the place—no, worse, when she knows full well
she'll never own the place!"

Samantha was horribly silent throughout the ex-
change—probably because she agreed with the awful
busybody. Jo pressed her teeth into the knuckles of
her clenched fist, and leaned against the wall to steady
herself.

"So what? So she acts on her heart before her
brain kicks in—"

Jo didn't want to hear another word, but she was
paralyzed. This was Callum's idea of defending her?
Holy crap, what would he say if he wanted to make
her look like the most incapable, inept, absolute loser

of a deluded never-stand-a-chance business wannabe?

"To not calculate every frigging line, starting with hello—it's refreshing, that's what, and you should try it sometime. You're only sniffing around the property because there's a buck to be made, a buck you won't see if Jo and Samantha don't sell."

"Look, I came by because I thought you could be an adult and give me some information. That's what adults do, they take their careers seriously. Sue me."

Callum muttered something like, "Wish I could."

There was an explosive exhale, the bitchy realtor or Callum? And why on earth was Samantha still being so quiet? Had they knocked her unconscious or something? Jo had never witnessed a conversation where Samantha let more than three lines pass before jumping in with her own contribution.

"You're an ass. Thank God we're over."

"Ah, Nina, finally—something we agree on."

Nina. As in Callum's infamous ex? Jo's curiosity was less intense than she would have expected.

"I don't have any actual power—as you so love to point out—but for what it's worth, I'm going to suggest the Kendall sisters go with absolutely any realtor in town besides you."

"Typical," Nina said. "Even now it's about your petty personal issues. I'd make them the most money of anyone off that godforsaken lump of land, but you'd rather make it all about you."

"Don't let the door hit you in the ass on your way out."

Nina didn't bother to say good-bye. The partially cracked door flew open all the way, and she stormed through—a flap of expensive overcoat, a clack of heels, and a wave of some delicious, pricey perfume. Jo felt like she'd been hit by a truck.

Mercifully, Nina didn't notice her cowering in the corner by the shelf of cooking magazines, just continued her furious departure through the waiting room and out into the main hall.

Jo remained huddled against the wall, but made a decision. No way was she keeping the ten o'clock. She didn't need to see Callum. He and Samantha could mail her any documents that needed signed—oh shit, think of the devil. Samantha's voice floated up from the hallway Nina had just exited into, making Jo jump. She said good-bye to someone, and then she was in the room, looking at Jo oddly.

"Uh, Jo? What's up?"

Jo tried to unstick herself from the wall casually. Samantha's silence in the office finally made sense. She hadn't been present.

"I, um, I'm feeling really sick all of a sudden."

"You look it. You're totally green." Samantha rushed over and offered an arm.

Jo waved her away. "I'm . . . I'll be all right. Just need some air."

"Is it something you ate?"

"I don't know, maybe—or a flu."

"What can I do?"

"Nothing. I should've just called, shouldn't have

come in. You keep the meeting with Callum, let him know it's all decided, and—"

Typical of the whole blooming day, Callum picked that moment to hear their voices and step out of his office.

"Hey, you two. I'm ready for you. Come on in."

Eyes focused on the floor, Jo shook her head and gently pushed Samantha forward.

Samantha held her ground, didn't budge. "No, I think we should do this together. If you're too sick, we'll reschedule." She glanced at Callum as if to confirm this as a possibility.

"Of course we can reschedule, absolutely. No problem."

Jo shook her head again. It was worse than pointless to put it off. If they wouldn't go through it without her, she might as well suffer but be done with it. "No, it's fine. It's *fine*. Just show me where to sign."

Chapter 24

CALLUM PACED HIS OFFICE, REPLAYING every minute of his meeting with Jo and Samantha again and again. But no matter how he tried, he couldn't bear how Jo treated him so coldly—no, worse than coldly. She acted like he wasn't there—no, that wasn't quite it either. She answered his questions politely, spoke when answered to, wished him well and thanked him courteously for his time when she left—

Yes, that was it. That's what felt so off. She treated him like someone she'd just met, barely knew—like a lawyer hired to take care of a fairly straight forward estate, so long as it wasn't contested, which, yes, technically, is exactly what he was, but still . . .

Her eyes haunted him. He'd always known they changed color with her mood—but he'd never seen her in such a bad one. They'd been a flat muddy brown, devoid of even a trace of their usual amber sparkle.

Maybe his mistake had been in trying to encourage her to think about the possibilities about what she could do with the money once her uncle's property sold.

"You could buy a nice little house, maybe one with a guest room or an in-law suite. You could start out with a miniature of your bed-and-breakfast idea and grow from there."

He'd actually felt a stab of physical pain, her glare was so piercing. He definitely should've expressed his regrets and left it at that, not attempted to problem solve.

"I'm sorry, Jo," he'd said. "I know this feels like a big loss right now. I know how it feels to have a dream die."

"It doesn't *feel* like a big loss, Callum. It *is* a big loss. And maybe some people find comfort in discussing things in poetical terms like losing dreams and finding them, but right now I'm not one of them. I'm devastated that my uncle's home will go to strangers. Coming into money too late to save it is no consolation—and it's also none of your business."

His face burned remembering her expression. He'd looked to Samantha for help, but she'd just shrugged and looked away, feeling, maybe, as guilty as he did.

Because that was the thing. If he had nudged Samantha harder to reconsider, maybe she would have.

He stopped pacing and hung his head. The problem was that would've been poor counsel. Nina, as ever, was wrong about him. He did take his career, albeit his soon-to-be-caput career, seriously. He would never advise clients to do something that wasn't in their best interest. Jo, no matter how wonderful her dreams were or how good the potential for profit was on paper, didn't have the capital to get her plan off the ground. If she held that against him, wouldn't forgive him for not jumping in with her on it, well, what could he do about it?

Chapter 25

THE FRONT LAWN WAS IMMACULATE and well tended, despite it being the time of year most people ignored their yards. The decorative shrubs were wrapped in burlap that remained, regardless of how battered it was by the heavy rains, resilient and protective. The flowerbeds were mulched, and the grass was short and brilliantly green, no doubt mowed the very last day of the season. It was amazing how even in winter, unless snow covered it, Greenridge was, well, *green.*

Callum stood on the equally clean walkway—no cracks, no weeds, no debris soiling the first impression of the mighty Archer house—and knew that inside, the house would be equally pristine. Appearances were very important to his father and no one could argue: Duncan Archer's home was beautifully appointed inside and out, and to some, may have even seemed welcoming. As if to further perpetrate this falsehood, a large hurricane lamp, complete with a glowing electric candle, sat amidst an arrangement of various evergreen boughs, holly with red berries, and cheerful ribbon by the front entranceway.

Some people he knew entered their parents' home

as if it was still their own; Brian and Callum always rang—which is exactly what Callum did now.

A moment later, four paws tap-danced to the door, and there was an excited snuffling sound. Callum could practically see the black button nose beneath the door—Trixie, his mom's Sheltie. She was the only thing Callum had ever seen his mom be resolute about: *I will always have my dog, Duncan.* And she did. Trixie was her third that Callum had known. The first, "Sable," who'd been elderly when Callum was born, had passed away when Callum was in grade one. Then there was Millicent, a.k.a. Millie. She'd enjoyed life to a ripe middle age in dog years before a nasty cancer claimed her. Trixie was five and totally living up to her name—still as full of tricks as when she was a pup. A dog's love is a pure, devoted, uncomplicated affection and Callum understood his mother's adamant stance. He hoped Trixie lived to be thirty.

"Is someone here, Trixie?" Callum's mom, Caren, asked as if she addressed an equal. Trixie yipped, "Yes, yes."

Callum grinned, but shook his head. Now even *he* was imagining the dog could talk. Caren cracked the door open a slit, saw Callum and opened it further, a smile warming her cornflower blue eyes and pale-as-milk skin.

"Callum—this is a nice surprise." She held her arms out to him and he hugged her obediently, noticing as he always did, how small she was, how fragile feeling. It seemed impossible that this little woman bore three sons that all grew to be over six feet. She stepped back and looked him up and down. "You look well."

A pang of guilt hit him—again, nothing new. It was a shame he saw her infrequently enough that she always commented on his appearance, seeing him with new eyes each visit instead of ones that were long familiar. And he would notice changes in her too—fluctuations in weight, in countenance, in how she was styling her hair.

Caren Archer was fifty-seven, had three adult sons born two years apart, now ranging thirty-three to thirty-seven, and a difficult husband—yet, physically at least, she always managed to look untouched by life and could pass for a woman, a pretty woman, twenty years younger.

"You look good too, Ma." She was barefoot in jeans and an oversized man's white business shirt, not his father's though, not *that* oversized—her work uniform. "Are you busy painting? Should I come back?"

"Yes, and no. Your timing's great. I was just taking a break."

She led him to the kitchen, bypassing the great room, formal living room and dining room. "Would you like to chat here, or in the studio?" she asked, pouring two fat mugs of Earl Grey tea and doctoring them both with honey and lemon.

He shrugged. "Either works." The cozy kitchen

alcove, a jumble of house plants, mismatched garage sale furniture, unwashed mugs and cookie crumbs, and "the" studio, which was really *her* studio—off limits without an invitation—were the only spaces in the house that truly belonged to her. She claimed them, used them, and resisted the intrusion of others into them with the territorial passion of a teenager.

She nodded and padded off through the house once more. "The studio then."

They entered the room and quick as a wink, she handed Callum her mug and turned a large canvas standing on an easel toward the wall before he could glimpse its surface. He frowned in question.

"Just something new, something silly. I'm not ready to show anyone yet. Sorry."

Callum stepped back. *That* was something new. Caren was rarely shy about her paintings—dismissive, yes, or almost embarrassed it seemed, but not . . . covert.

"Is it an extra cutting-edge mountain range?" he asked—and immediately regretted the asshole question. What was he, his father?

Points of color flared on Caren's cheekbones, and that was also a surprise. He was used to his mother being unflappable—almost to the point of being spacey.

"I'm sorry, Ma. I love your work. I didn't mean anything. I'm just not used to you being private."

Caren took her mug back, sipped her tea, but didn't absolve Callum or acknowledge his apology.

"My *work*," she said with a bitter inflection he didn't understand. "Good one."

She settled into an ancient moss-green winged back chair, one leg curled under her, and called Trixie onto her lap. Callum cleared a stack of sketchbooks from a beaten up leather ottoman nearby and sat down.

"How's Brian?" she asked.

"Good, I think."

"And Cade?

"No idea. I hardly ever talk to him—or he hardly talks to me, more like it. You know that."

She sighed.

"I didn't come to small talk, actually," he said. "I . . . I want your opinion on something." She looked surprised and he hurried on. "I quit my job."

"So I heard." There was no humor in her voice and Callum could imagine how his dad had ranted.

"Do you think I did the right thing, or did I make a mistake?"

Caren sipped her tea again and seemed to focus on something behind Callum, out of his view. He was about repeat himself, when she said, "Why did you quit?"

He started to shrug, then realized he was being stupid. He'd come to her for advice and it seemed like she might actually give him some, so he should talk. "A lot of reasons," he said, then proceeded to explain how he felt trapped and resentful working for Duncan, and had only just realized that was *his* fault, not

Duncan's. And he talked about Nina, as much as he didn't want to.

"I just think . . . " he finished, hardly even wanting to acknowledge the words aloud, "that maybe it wasn't all Nina's fault things were so bad between us. I always knew who she was. She was honest, at least. I started dating her because of who she *wasn't*—"

"You've done that a lot—dated women you didn't really care about because then if it ended, you wouldn't feel the kind of pain you felt over Jo."

Callum leaned forward, clenching his tea mug so tightly he worried it might break. He forced himself to loosen his grip. "You remember *Jo*?"

"I remember a lot of things," Caren said dryly. "And your father's been railing about her ever since you gave your notice. Thinks it's her fault."

"What do you think?"

She sighed heavily. "That I'm a terrible person to come to for advice. I've taught each of you, unintentional as it was, to live unhappily and to accept that as normal."

To say that Callum was shocked by this observation and admission would be a gross understatement. "I don't think—"

Caren waved his words away, silencing him. "Do you still love Jo?"

He nodded. "But I don't have a chance with her."

"So why else did you quit, if it wasn't some attempt to get a girl?"

"Because being with her again made me realize,

with her or no, I need more in my life. I want to do something I love, or at least try to. I want to create something I feel is important—even just to me."

"Then you already know the answer to your own question, don't you?"

Callum started to shake his head, but Caren reached out and stroked his cheek, stopping the motion. "I don't know how you managed it, but good for you. I think, if you'll forgive me for being so hypocritical, you should tell Nina what you just told me. It will be freeing. And don't give up on Jo either." She gently moved Trixie to the floor and got to her feet. Callum realized their visit was almost over and followed her lead.

"Thanks," he said, bending to kiss her cheek.

She tousled his hair. "No, thank *you*, little dove."

He laughed at the embarrassing nickname. "For what?"

Caren didn't answer. Leaving the crowded work-space, Callum took in the myriad of canvases big and small that lined the walls and stood stacked here and there, all beautifully rendered flowers and landscapes that she had no trouble selling. He considered the large, hidden work in progress. "So are you going to show me that one or not?"

Caren glided out of the room, Trixie at her heels, as if she hadn't heard him—and then she spoke very clearly. "Or not."

Chapter 26

JO COULDN'T BELIEVE HOW QUICKLY Ray's acreage sold. She'd been expecting it to stay on the market until spring at least. The turnaround was dizzying.

"It makes me a little bit sick," Samantha said.

Finally, Jo thought, feeling a buzz of warmth and connection toward Samantha for the first time in weeks—at least until she said, "I knew we should've asked a hundred grand more."

Jo held up her hand. "Don't. I'm so not in the mood." She shoved her first box of packed things onto the blue tarp that she'd lined the wet box of her pickup with.

Samantha perched a tiny container on the tailgate. "I have to confess something."

"Umhm?" Jo asked, hefting a second box from the porch.

"I'm surprised by how cheerful you're managing to be about all this."

"Cheerful?" Jo rubbed her hands together to warm them. "I don't know about that. Realistic maybe. The world's not over. I have money in the bank—or will, right? You know me. I like to dream, sure, but deep

221

down I'm practical. When something's done, it's done. . . ." Her voice trailed off. "But don't kid yourself, I'm really sad. And when I think about Uncle Ray, I feel even worse. He'd be sad too—and pissed." She leaned against the side of her truck, felt moisture from the cold metal seep through her jeans and pulled away again.

Sam didn't dispute her words, and Jo sighed and heaved a garbage bag of clothing into the cab's passenger seat. "You were right. Is that what you want to hear? I didn't have enough money to pull it off, and yeah, maybe it is for the best. Maybe I can't handle putting my heart into another for-the-love-of-it-operation. Maybe my next business will be something I don't care about at all, something purely for money."

"Seriously, Jo? No. . . ."

Jo shrugged. But then she scooped a tiny bit of the wet snow that lined the top of the bumper and threw it at Samantha. "Of course I'm not serious. Who do you think I am? You?"

"Ha ha," Samantha said. "Good one." She grabbed her own handful of snow and whipped it back at Jo. After a few minutes of play, they loaded the remainder of the boxes from the porch, and Samantha got into her SUV.

"I'll meet you at your new place—though I still think you're nuts to stay in town," Sam said.

Jo shrugged. "No place else to go at the moment, and at least I have a job here."

"Yeah, at a dirty little lure house—" Jo's glare cut

off whatever else Sam had been about to say about Jo's place of employment. "Well, I figure I'll stick around until January, keep you company for Christmas and New Year's—but then it's warmer places for me, baby, much warmer places."

Jo nodded and pulled a crumpled piece of notepaper out her pocket, handing it to Sam. "Here's my address and new landline. I needed an old school phone for the entry system."

The moment Samantha's SUV disappeared around the bend, Jo plunked herself down on the second stair of the porch. Her butt was already damp. What did a bit more water matter?

She wrapped her arm around one of the huge log poles that supported the porch's roof, and leaned her cheek against its cold, smooth-as-satin surface. Years of rubbing, weather, and stress had polished the wood and only made it more beautiful. If only people were as lucky.

"I'm sorry, Uncle Ray." Jo's breath made white puffs in the air. "I'm really sorry."

When her bum and fingers were numb and her nose started to drip, Jo finally got up, stiff with cold, and hobbled to her pickup. She couldn't bring herself to say good-bye to the place. She just couldn't.

Hoover whined when she climbed up and settled beside him in the cab. "I know, boy. I know."

It hit her as she drove out of the property: she was making this bumpy trip for the last time. She and Samantha had hired movers for the furniture they were keeping. A local secondhand store had a van and an employee who would pick up the rest.

Jo wondered why she'd turned her sadness over letting the place go into a joke with Samantha, instead of sharing the depths of her disappointment.

But what was the point of making Samantha feel bad? It wasn't her sister's fault. And Jo would find a new dream. She would. Despite what she'd told Callum—and despite how she hated that he was right when he spoke so patronizingly of her to Nina—she was a dreamer. She knew how important it was to find a flame and keep fueling it so it burned bright. Hope gave you a reason to keep waking up everyday, a reason to work. And besides, she also (right again, stupid Callum) just couldn't help herself. It was how her mind worked.

Chapter 27

Jo let Christmas and New Years come and go without a lot of fanfare, not her usual style at all. To Eddie's delight, she willingly worked every day and any hour he could throw at her.

"I appreciate it," he'd said gruffly. "Most normal people want days off this time of year."

"Yeah, well, I've never been all that normal," Jo had replied, making him laugh, though she was unsmilingly serious.

People who had attended her dinner party were kind and invited her and Samantha to various seasonal festivities. Dave continued to strive to be part of Jo's life, and Jo considered attempting to pawn him off on Sam—until one last Dave episode made her realize Sam didn't deserve him either.

In a moment of weakness, on New Year's Day, wanting to do something that wasn't centered on watching other people enjoy their big extended families, she'd agreed to go for a walk with Dave. When he met her at her apartment, he startled her by knocking right on her actual door.

"How'd you get in? You didn't buzz for entry."

He smiled easily. "Someone else was let in. I followed them."

Living out at Ray's had spoiled Jo. It had been so lovely and private that she'd forgotten how different town life was. Another loss and adjustment.

They got to-go drinks, a Mocha for her, a green tea for him, and headed toward the Millennium trail. Somehow the conversation turned to Callum as she'd hoped it would; she was a glutton for punishment, what could she say?

According to Dave, Callum had a quiet Christmas holed up with some friend of one of Brian's "friends."

"Doesn't really sound like Callum," was all she'd said, taking a big mouthful of whipping cream and chocolate—and almost gagging. Instead of rich and comforting, the drink was sickly sweet and cloying, like they'd doubled the syrup and forgotten the coffee.

"Oh, so it's like that still, hey?" Dave asked.

"Like what?"

"You still like him."

Jo stopped walking, set her cup on the ground, then pulled mittens out of her pocket and put them on. She picked her cup up again. "Maybe."

"I don't believe it," Dave said wonderingly. "I just don't believe it."

"Oh, don't be so dramatic," Jo snapped and re-sumed walking at a faster pace. Dave's long-legged stride quickly ate up any distance she put between them.

"Well," he said. "If you're so set on having him,

just tell him in plain language."

"What the hell, Dave? What would that do?"

Dave shrugged. "Callum feels bad for you. He told me that—said that maybe if you'd stuck around and married him back in the day, maybe your life wouldn't have been such a wash."

"My. Life. Is. Not. A. Wash."

Dave continued like she hadn't spoken. "Besides he still has feelings for you. He thinks you'd do better with a steady man in your life, someone to take care of you. I think, if you asked, he'd date you again, maybe even marry you."

"Out of pity? Are you kidding me?" Jo hurled her still-full drink at a garbage can they walked past. The lid burst on impact, the contents splattered, and the container disappeared into the rest of the garbage.

Dave sipped his tea. Shrugged again. "Nah, he's tired of being single too. Besides people get together for worse reasons."

Jo said good-bye quickly. She was done pretending that Dave had any motive other than trying to poison her against Callum in the hopes of changing her feelings toward himself.

And so life went on. She passed through the remainder of January in a grief-dazed stupor. Without Ray's house to focus on and conjure good memories—and to provide so much work that she didn't really have time to think—she had more time to dwell on the loss of the closest thing she'd had to a father figure, and even more time to think about Callum.

Always Callum. No matter what stupid Dave said.

A small-but-growing-larger part of her now worried that perhaps curiosity about what had become of Callum—or a long hidden, unacknowledged longing for what had been—had fueled her decision to return in the first place. And this worry made her realize that perhaps she wasn't as committed to staying as she'd once thought. Yes, she wanted to live in Greenridge, to make a home there, but if she was going to, it needed to feel like a place of hope and possibility. These days, it felt too much like a memorial for things she'd lost.

Chapter 28

CALLUM WALKED THE PERIMETER OF the grounds, his boots squelching in particularly boggy parts, and went over every detail of his phone call to Jo. She'd sounded shocked to hear from him—but she'd agreed to meet. She'd agreed! He surveyed the heavy evergreens that sheltered the clearing around him and took in the moisture-beaded limbs of the cottonwoods and alder that stretched up into the misty sky. Even now, in February, the gloomiest, least promising part of the year, the place was perfect. Or it would be, so long as . . . so long as he could explain what he was hoping to Jo in a way that (a) made sense, (b) made her understand he wasn't all the terrible things she believed about him, and (c) convinced her that he was worth one more scary risk.

Yes, this property—River's Sigh, a romantic name he was sure Jo would like—was smaller than Ray's acreage and would never be a lodge-style B & B—but maybe it was better? The house was detached from a ring of cabins that ranged from extremely rustic to almost habitable. They could still provide breakfasts, and people would probably love the privacy the separate accommodations provided. And true, there was no direct river frontage—but the river was close. You could hear it mumbling and moving even through the small fringe of forest where he stood, and it was a short, comfortable hike to a rocky beach if you cut across the nearest property—property that was Crown land, so realistically no one would have a problem with him, *with them*, wearing a trail down to the water. Plus, the grounds were home to a pond and a small creek—a creek with great trout fishing if the kid he'd ran into that morning could be believed. Jo had to see the potential—*their* potential. She had to.

Callum thought about the years he'd wasted holding onto his fancy house just so Nina wouldn't get it, wouldn't live in his dream. And that's what he should have told Jo—that the reason he thought, no, *the reason he knew*, she should sell and give Samantha her half and pick a new project was because he had firsthand experience with someone purely interested in money. It was hard to recognize that quality in a person you loved, so of course Jo didn't see it—and he still called bullshit to her insistence that she and Samantha were alike. He'd been an idiot not to recognize the difference and cling to it right off. It was like being with Nina had scored his eyes, left his vision impaired. He could no longer reliably see what was right in front of him. But now he had seen, or did see—*was seeing*. But had his reacquired ability come too late? He wouldn't blame Jo, couldn't blame her, if she didn't talk to him again. But he had to try.

He paused by the front porch, again undeniably smaller than Ray's, but still more than big enough for a hanging swing, and tried to imagine the house from Jo's eyes. Would she see the battered cobalt blue door as an eyesore or as whimsical? Would she like the new, yet old-fashioned looking multi-paned windows? What about the cedar shake siding? It could go either way: charming—or old and in need of replacing.

And where was she? The thought hadn't occurred to him until now, but it was possible. . . . She might not come. She might've only agreed in the first place to get him to leave her alone. He resumed pacing, hands in his pockets, one fist clenched over the object of his hopes, replaying all he wanted to say over and over again in his head.

And then, finally, tires grumbled and crunched on gravel, and she was suddenly there, pulling up in her old pickup, good old Hoover looking like he owned the passenger seat. Which made sense. He did, after all.

Jo parked by his car, undid her seatbelt, then rolled up a window. It was like she was moving in slow motion.

When she got out of the truck, Hoover sprang down too. Callum was so eager to fix everything between them that he practically bounded over to her.

"Hoover-boy, you have nothing on me," he said, and reached down to scratch the mutt's ears.

Hoover gave him a disdainful look, ducked his head, and sidled over to the other side of Jo's legs. Jo looked as confused as Hoover did about the comment.

So he wasn't off to the best start.

"Do you want to go for a walk?"

She shrugged and crossed her arms over a shirt he thought was too light for the weather. She was probably freezing. "No thanks." She turned away from him, looking left, then right. "Nice spread," she said, but her tone was indifferent—and felt like ice water dumped down his back. Callum tried not to gasp.

Breathe, he commanded himself, just breathe. You can have the mother of all anxiety attacks when she leaves. Be cool till then.

Jo arched an eyebrow. Callum smiled back—or tried to—unhappily sure he looked half-crazed.

"Come on, Callum. Out with it. Why'd you invite me here?"

He motioned toward the house's bright blue door. "Want to come in, get out of the cold? Have coffee or something?"

Jo's arms tightened around herself, and she tilted her head and studied him.

"Please," he said, voice soft. "It's like I said on the phone. I just want, *I need*, to talk with you."

Inside, Jo parked herself on one of the high stools he'd put around the granite topped kitchen island. "Nice kitchen," she said.

"Yeah, it's got amazing counter space," he answered—and wanted to punch himself in the face.

Then he noticed his reply had almost gotten a

smile out of her. What other comments could he make about the kitchen?

"I've been baking a lot since I moved in."

Jo nodded, but didn't look at him. Instead she stretched her arms out in front of her and studied her hands. He was losing her.

He poured them each coffee from the insulated carafe he'd gotten ready earlier and piled fresh cranberry-orange scones on a heavy crockery plate.

She took the proffered mug and wrapped her hands around it, but declined the baking with a small shake of her head. "It looks delicious, but I'm not hungry."

Callum pulled a stool closer to her, thinking he should've suggested they go the living room, *sit soft*. Had it really been over four months since she'd said that to him? "Callum."

He set his cup down without taking a drink. "I have so many things I want to say to you, I don't know where to start."

"Just spill," she said. "I'll wait for you to make sense of them."

He hated how calm and serene she seemed. He'd wanted her to jump around the place, flitting here and there with idea after idea.

"Most of them are apologies."

She sipped her coffee cautiously.

"Okay then—first I just need to say I'm sorry for our stupid misunderstanding, *my* stupid misunderstanding and assumptions, and for my jealousy, and the unforgivably hurtful comments I made."

"Not unforgivable—but yes, pretty stupid." She smiled slightly and it made him bold. Too bold.

"Of course you should've kissed me back. I wish you would right now."

Her hand jerked. Coffee sloshed over the side of her mug. She looked away, licking the droplets off the side of her hand.

He pushed on. "And I'm sorry about the sale, the *loss,* of your Uncle Ray's. I wish it had worked for me to go into business with you then, when you asked. And more than that . . . I wish I had let you finish before we argued—had understood what you were really asking before I jumped to the wrong conclusion, a conclusion that I should never have arrived at because I do know you, Jo. I do."

"Then?" She went silent again and stared at the mug in front of her without taking another drink.

"Yes, *then*. That's what I'm asking you. I mean this place—that's why I bought it. For you. For us."

"For *us*?" She started shaking her head and only stopped when he touched her shoulder.

"Yes, well, you see . . . I've been hoping . . ." It was corny, but he couldn't help himself. He *was* corny. He lowered himself to one knee and withdrew the velvet box he'd been carrying around in his pocket for a week.

Jo pressed her hand over her left eye, like she had a brutal headache. "Please don't do this, Callum."

"I have to. Then I'll know I did what I needed to.

Was brave when it counted."

A small tortured sound escaped her, and she bit down on her lip—but at least she was looking at him again.

"Will you marry me, Jo? I know I don't deserve it, but . . . Lord knows I want the chance to prove myself to you—for life. For our life. Together."

"I—I don't know what to say."

"Say yes."

He held out the ring case and rested his hand on her knee, thinking, nonsensically, that if he could just touch her, all the things he was feeling, all the emotions he couldn't quite put into words would somehow transfer from his heart to hers through her skin.

She slid off the stool like he'd burned her. "I can't. You don't get it at all, Callum."

"What don't I get?" he whispered. "If you just tell me, I'll get it." He didn't want to beg, but he would if that's what was needed.

"You were right. That's what you don't get—and what I finally do. What did you call me?"

He shook his head, mutely. What had he called her? Something awful obviously—or, at least, she thought he had.

"When you were oh-so-helpfully 'defending' me to Nina before our last meeting?"

He shook his head again, and her eyes flashed with the first passion she'd shown that day. Passion against him. He got up from his kneeling position, legs and heart leaden.

"You shake your head, but I can tell you remember. A dreamer who can't help herself. Who gets carried away. Who feels instead of thinks—"

"No," he said. "No."

"Yes, Callum, *yes*. Those are practically exact quotes."

He wanted to press his finger against her lips—no, he wanted to press his mouth against hers. He wanted to kiss her until she understood that he was beside himself and had been ever since she returned to town and he'd first laid eyes on her again—and since before that even, since the time she'd first left him. And then he wanted to keep on kissing her until she realized that he'd said all kinds of crap trying to escape what he felt—what he was afraid to feel. And then after that, he'd kiss her still more—until she realized that yes, he'd said the things, but while she'd heard them as insults, he'd meant them as compliments. But the time had passed since he could just kiss her like that and have it be okay. He'd wrecked all that spontaneity. Words were his only chance of redemption—but he was completely bereft of them, too.

"Do you have anything to say? Anything at all?"

He could only stare.

"It hurt to let go of Ray's, yes—but it was just a place. I can buy another *place*. I can develop interest in another business. You tore down who I am. You devalued me."

Come on, man, speak, a voice inside him implored. And how he wanted to obey, to explain that she'd twisted his words, that he hadn't meant what she inferred—but impact was the consideration these days, not intent. No defense came to him.

"I've spent a lot of years of my life—exhilarating years, Callum, but exhausting ones, too—pursuing my dreams. And, contrary to what you obviously think, I'm capable of working toward their fruition. I believed in the power of having a vision—in my work life and in my love life, and I—" Her voice broke a bit and bitter grief rose in Callum's throat at the sound of it. "I should thank you, Callum. You're right. A dream on its own is nothing. And I can't do it anymore. The risk, the pain, it's too much."

"But I'm asking you to marry me."

She blinked and looked away for a moment. When she met his eyes again, hers were dry. "I know you are, but *why*?"

He forgot he was still holding the ring case and dropped it. The delicate box landed upside down, hiding the polished white gold band from view.

"Why do you think?" he asked, stretching to recover the box.

It wasn't the right answer, and Jo reached the box first. She studied the ring shining away on its velvet bed with an inscrutable expression, then snapped the tiny case shut and placed it on the cold granite slab behind her.

"I can see myself out, Callum. I'm sorry."

Callum followed her to the door mutely, then

collapsed into one of the chairs around the big family-sized table. He didn't move for a long time. And when he finally did, he got up, walked over to the island, retrieved the ring and slipped it back into his pocket.

Chapter 29

JO STOOD ON A LOG overhanging the deep, black pool beneath her, rod in hand, hook and lure on—a tiny sparkly wedding band that caught the tenuous spring sun and promised a good catch. She didn't cast. Couldn't bring herself to break the glass-smooth water. What was she doing? Maybe Samantha was right. Maybe she should just blow this Popsicle stand. Take her money and run.

But no, a trickle of conviction dripped through her—small, but undeniable. Over the darkest months of winter, she'd contemplated running again, yet decided she wouldn't. She couldn't help it. She loved Greenridge. It had grown on her, ironically, the way her sister did—a deep love/drive-her-crazy thing. And there was something to be said about living in a place where at least some people had known her when she was young. Maybe if she had parents or other extended family that wouldn't feel so important, but it did.

And yes, it would be hard running into Callum from time to time, at least at first—but that would get better, too.

Callum.

Oh, what seeing that ring had done to her insides! Days later, her heart still pounded when she thought about it. Her stomach still tightened. Her face still warmed. She'd almost thrown pride aside. But what if it didn't work out? They'd already shown how incompetent they were at talking things out, at understanding each other, at actually being what the other person needed. She loved him—and thought he actually might love her like he said he did. But since when was love ever enough? Her mom had loved her and Samantha. She had loved her uncle Ray. And Devin too, what seemed like ages ago.

Could warm, fuzzy romantic love grow into a more consistent, enduring sort of thing that wouldn't eventually rip your heart out?

Yeah, right. That's a great plan. Get married and hope true love follows.

She swatted a mosquito. *Oh, look—I actually do think and override my feelings occasionally. Take that, Callum!*

She packed up her bag and walked out to the road. Not in the mood to fish—a new first for her. She threw her backpack into the cab and walked around to the truck's driver side. Hopefully the other firsts in store for her would be less utterly depressing.

Her cell rang just as she pulled her seatbelt across her chest. She buckled the latch, hit Talk and said hello.

"Is this Jo Kendall?" asked a pretty voice with a

slightly clipped accent.

Jo figured it was a telemarketer and tried not to be rude. "Yes, it is. Who's speaking please?"

"I'm Martha Klassen." The first name came out Mar-ta, the German variation of Martha, but it didn't really matter how it was pronounced. Jo recognized the name.

"How can I help you? If it's questions about the property, I recommend you speak with my sister Samantha. She handled the sale."

"No, nothing like that. My husband and I have been renovating the home, and as we were replacing one of the windows and insulation, we found one of your letters caught in the middle of the wall."

"Really? That's like something out of a storybook."

Martha had a pleasant laugh. "Yes, we thought so too."

"What did I say? Who was it to?" It must've been one of the copious notes she'd written in longhand and distributed to friends when bored in biology.

"I really couldn't say. The envelope's sealed. It's addressed to you."

"Addressed *to me*, really? Wow. I have no idea what it could be." A tiny thrill shivered through Jo. So fun—and weird—even if it would no doubt turn out to be nothing.

"I'm flying out tonight for a few days, but I'm in town running errands right now. May I drop it off for you shortly?"

They discussed timing and unfortunately, Jo didn't think she'd make it back to her apartment before Martha was done.

"I could deposit it in your mail box."

"Oh, that'd be perfect if you really don't mind."

"I don't mind a bit. It's not even out of my way."

"Well, thank you—and have a good trip."

"You're welcome. Perhaps if our paths cross again you can tell me what was in your mystery letter."

Jo laughed. "Well, I guess that depends."

They said good-bye and Jo pressed end, then sat for a minute or two without starting the truck. A mysterious letter? Pretty cool. It was probably just some thing she'd written to herself, like resolutions or predictions for her future, then stashed away, but even finding that would be awesome. Too bad it wouldn't be some fantastic old love letter.

It was hard not to race back to the apartment, then even more difficult to make sure she took all her things out of the truck—but it would totally suck if her stuff got stolen out the box just because she was impatient.

During the drive home, the hook had come loose from the rod's eye where she'd tucked it to prevent it from snagging anything. As she pulled the rod out, the hook caught under the edge of the metal toolbox she stored in the truck box. Jo tugged hard, the line broke, and the lure flew off. Annoying. Her line must be getting soft, still, better to discover it needed replaced now than later with a fish on.

She picked up the sparkling lure, slipped it into her pocket, and carried her gear upstairs. She'd sort it out and run it down to her storage room after she read the letter.

Her heart skipped as she unlocked the brass mail compartment labeled 308 and withdrew a yellowed envelope. It bore no stamps, no return address, and no sender's name—but "Jo Kendall" was printed in square letters across the front and underlined twice in the broad, hard strokes of an urgent—or impassioned—hand. Curiouser and curiouser! She didn't let herself open it just yet.

Excited by the intrigue and wanting to prolong it, like a kid sneaking another chapter of Nancy Drew with a flashlight under the blankets, Jo went through a set of procedures before she let herself open the letter. She changed into pajamas even though it was still early. She had nowhere to go, so why not?

Hoover, sensing something was up, shadowed her closely, almost getting himself stepped on more than once. She put on water for tea, let it steep, and poured a mug. She snuck two pieces of fudge out of a container she kept swearing she was going to put in the freezer to slow the treats' disappearance, but so far hadn't managed to. She wrapped herself in a blanket on the couch, positioned her tea and snack within easy reach on the end table—and finally, finally, *finally* let herself pick up the envelope. Watch, it would be a list of chores from her uncle or something equally anticlimatic.

"It's just another case of you making a big deal about nothing," she muttered, but her cheeks hurt with the intensity of her grin—a grin that faded the minute she unfolded a sheet of loose-leaf paper and gave it an initial once over. She blinked, hoping, ridiculously, that the contents of the page would magically rewrite themselves. They didn't, of course. She reread the letter slowly, word for word.

"No," she said when she was done. Hoover keened in sympathy. Her chin dropped to her chest. "No. No. *No*."

After ten or so minutes of sitting absolutely stock-still, tea and goodies forgotten, she got to her feet and rummaged through the jacket and jeans she'd worn earlier. Finally she found what she was looking for: her cell phone.

She tapped Samantha's name in her contact list. The phone couldn't connect fast enough.

"Samantha?" she blurted the minute it sounded like Sam picked up.

"Pardon? Yes, hello—who is this? Jo?"

"Yes, it's me. Can you come over?"

"Right now?"

"If you can, please. Martha found a letter in one of the walls they're fixing."

"Martha?"

"The woman who bought Uncle Ray's—"

"A letter?"

"Yes, and it changes everything, *everything*."

"What kind of letter?" Samantha's tone had a

hard, suspicious note. "You're not trying to pretend there's some more recent will are you? It's too late."

"I can't talk about this over the phone—"

"I'll be there in five minutes."

"Perfect."

While Jo waited for Samantha, she alternated between pacing the apartment and pausing to reread the letter. She practically had the thing memorized by the time Samantha rang.

Her door was open and she was waiting in the hallway for Samantha before the elevator even reached her floor. Samantha took one look at Jo's face and started to run.

"What is it? What?"

Jo shook her head, motioned Samantha in, and slammed the door.

"If you don't tell me exactly what's going on right now without another second's delay, I'm going to smack you!"

Jo handed her the letter, crossed the room and wilted into a chair.

It took all of thirty seconds for Samantha to shriek. "Are you kidding me? This is for real?"

Jo shrugged miserably and scratched Hoover's ears. Poor guy seemed to be taking it as hard as she was.

"Aw, Jo . . . " Samantha was uncharacteristically speechless. She strode over to Jo and put an arm around her in an equally rare show of physical comfort. "You had no idea?"

Jo shook her head. The letter stared up at her from where Samantha tossed it.

Dear Jo,

(Jo, Jo, Jo! Just writing your name makes me happy. ☺)

If you're reading this it means I'm a bigger loser than you already know I am. (Ha ha, that was a joke. Relax!) For real it means I've tried and tried to call your house, but the phone isn't in service or something. I can't make it tonight. I'M SO SORRY. I do want to marry you, more than anything, but I don't want to have to sneak away like we're doing something wrong.

My dad was being worse than usual tonight, and I didn't want to leave my mom alone with him for too long. He was, again per usual, ranting on and on about how I'll never amount to anything, that you and I are just kids and it will never work out, and a bunch of other crap about you and me (and Cade and Brian and Mom and pretty much the whole world) not worth repeating.

He's wrong. What we have is real. The kind of love that lasts forever and only gets better with time. I will never love anyone the way I love you—and I'll never want to. You are the sexiest, hottest, funniest girl I've ever met, and the only person who has shown me you can go through shit in your life but still be HAPPY. We're going to be so happy, Jo! Years from now we'll tell our grandkids about how we had this plan to elope, but that I messed it all up—but that in the end it didn't matter because our love was meant to be, we held out, and in the end got something way better.

I know it's lame and I know you're right that we can make it without my dad's help—but I don't want to just "make it." I want to give you everything you deserve that you don't have now, a home, stability, whatever you want.

That's the only thing he's right about. I do want a career so I can make enough money to take care of you and any kids we ever have—and he was pretty clear that if we get married right now, I'm cut off, he won't loan me money for school, etc., etc. One day I'll cook or bake or do something I WANT to do, but for now . . . I think getting an education is best. Don't hate me! He won't keep us from seeing each other though because he's an idiot and thinks we'll "outgrow" each other. I know and you know, though—one year, five years, fifty years, we'll still be as in love as we are now.

Please don't be too mad for too long. Just think of how big I'll owe you. ☺☺ I'll make it up to you any way you want, hint, hint. ☺ (Ha *ha again, but not joking!) Try to call me tonight or come see me at work tomorrow.*

Yours forever, baby. XOXO,
Callum

Hoover yawned and stretched at Jo's feet, pulling her attention away from the letter again. Sam was talking. "If it's any consolation, I'm sure it would never have worked out long term. If he couldn't stand up to his beast of a father then, he would've caved over something else later."

Jo glowered.

Samantha bit her lip and nodded. "But it would've been nice to find that out for yourself, hey? To have been able to give it a shot, or at least choose whether to give it a shot or not?"

"You said it."

"So go to him now and say it's stupid you guys have had all these misunderstandings and hey, what a coincidence, the funniest, sweetest thing happened. The person who bought Ray's discovered a letter he wrote that you never got."

"No"—it came out a gulp—"that won't work. We're not really ignoring each other anymore. We talked yesterday."

Samantha's arm dropped and she stood up. "See? That's great."

"No, you don't get it—" The similarity between her comment to Samantha now and the one she'd made to Callum struck her painfully. "He asked me to marry him."

"So why the heck are you whining?"

"I told him no."

"You what?"

"And worse."

"Worse than no?"

"Yeah. I told him he'd killed all the best parts of me—the dreaming parts. That I can't, or won't, take risks anymore."

"That is bad."

"Thanks a lot!"

Samantha walked to the glass patio doors and peered out at the small iron-fenced sundeck. "Did you mean it?" she asked, without looking Jo's way.

"No, yes . . . I don't know."

"Well, which is it?"

"Of course I can still dream, you idiot."

Samantha grinned. "Yeah, I didn't figure you were cured that easily."

Jo threw a cushion at Samantha. She deflected it. "So tell him the truth, that you're scared, but you're willing to try—and for crying out loud, you have to explain that you never got this letter. The poor guy. How it must've felt when you didn't call—just left town without even bothering to respond or explain."

Jo thought she knew exactly how it felt and sighed heavily.

"Oh, stop being such a wuss. It's not like you."

A smile curved Jo's mouth, but disappeared as quickly as it had come. "I want this to be a big win, too—a huge happily-ever-after-moment, not just another reason for my ridiculous insecurity and lack of confidence to take over."

"So let it be—the big win, I mean."

Jo shook her head. "I just have so many doubts."

"Of course you do because you're not insane. But based on what exactly?"

"Some stupid stuff Dave said."

"So Callum writes you the most romantic letter ever written to a kid, promising his love for eternity, then good to his word, asks you to marry him when you meet again years later—yet you take something Dave says over what Callum does?"

"It's not that simple." Jo relayed the humiliating conversation she'd had with Dave about Callum feeling sorry for her, then added, "Callum wrote that letter when we were both so young. Feelings change. Or maybe his feelings haven't, but his motives for—"

"*Dave* said all that? Implied Callum might date you, might even marry you, out of *pity?*"

Jo twitched like something slimy brushed against her. "Yeah, it sucks—wait, where are you going?"

Samantha only paused when she reached the door. "I just remembered something I have to do," she said grimly.

"It can't wait?"

"No, it can't. Sit tight. I'll be back in a bit."

Jo couldn't sit idle or she'd go insane. She fed and brushed Hoover, then decided to have a shower, hoping Samantha would be back from whatever was so important by the time she was done.

The hot water pounded the knot in the back of her neck and she took deep, steam-filled breaths. She used a body scrub that she'd been meaning to try and wished past relationships were as easy to shed as dead skin.

Oh, Callum. He'd looked so hurt—no, devastated was a better word—when she said she wouldn't marry him . . . but what did he expect? She wasn't some pathetic emotional charity case. Feeling badly for someone, for how their life had turned out, was nothing to base a relationship on. Why couldn't he want her the way she wanted him? There was a time when she would've settled—when they were teenagers, for example. She would've taken whatever he was able to give her. But now? No, she'd tried that once already, thank you very much.

She took her time shaving her legs—and still Samantha didn't buzz to get let in. Finally, feeling pretty sure she'd drained every bit of hot water the apartment building had to offer, she stepped out of the tub and spent even more time moisturizing.

As she slid her hands up the outside of her thighs and buttocks, she wondered if she was the only person who was going to touch her that way anymore. Shrugging off the thought, she trekked naked into her bedroom, slid into fresh underthings, and a soft long-sleeved cotton shirt, then grabbed the jeans she'd worn earlier. As she pulled them up over her hips, something sharp pricked though the denim pocket and into her skin.

What the—oh, right. The lure.

She gently unhooked it from her flesh, went into the bathroom and swabbed the spot with rubbing alcohol just in case, after resting the hook and its glittering beads and sparkly wedding band on the vanity.

The hook, she noticed, was bent—probably from when she pulled it loose from the toolbox. She grabbed a pair of scissors, cut the hook free and deposited it in the trash, then separated the lure from the wedding band and returned them to her pocket for safe keeping until she was near her tackle box again.

The door system buzzed. Samantha. Finally!

She pressed enter, then wondered if she should put the kettle on for more tea. Would having Samantha around for the evening be comforting or not? She didn't get to think on the question for too long. Samantha was knocking in record time.

Jo opened the door and her mouth fell open. If there was anyone she wanted to see less at the moment than Callum, Samantha had managed to find him.

"Dave? What are you doing here?"

Samantha stood slightly behind him, and didn't look remotely apologetic.

Jo considered shutting the door on them both, and perhaps the thought showed in her face. Samantha pushed Dave forward, almost bowling Jo over.

"Get talking, Dave," Samantha commanded, shoving herself in after him. "Now. And don't leave a single word out."

Chapter 30

JO TURNED OFF ALL THE lights after Samantha and Dave left and sat in the dark for a long time. Finally, unable to bear being alone in her head a moment longer—and knowing what she wanted, *needed*, to do, she dug her phone out and entered Callum's number. It rang and rang and rang. After six rings and still no voicemail, she was about to hang up. Then he answered.

"Hello?" he asked huskily, like he'd been sleeping and run for the phone, or maybe like he was angry and had considered not taking the call at all.

"It's me."

"Yes, what's up?" Not the warmest reception, but not the coldest either—and at least he hadn't pretended not to know who "me" was.

"We need to talk," she paused, then added, "I mean, I'd like to talk. Can we?"

"Of course," he said smoothly, but there was an off note beneath the calm in his voice that she didn't quite understand. "Do you want to meet for coffee?"

She was quiet. Was tomorrow good enough? Now that she knew, knew for sure what she wanted to say, knew she wanted them to at least try, she'd really been hoping—

"Or . . ." Callum hesitated and when he spoke next, he didn't seem quite as composed. "Or did you mean tonight?"

"Yes . . . *please*," Jo said, hope heavy in her voice. She'd been so harsh. He certainly didn't owe her any favors.

"That's . . . fine, no, good. Where do you want to meet? The Zoo's open till nine—oh, wait . . ." Jo knew he'd just glanced at a clock and realized that that it was ten to already.

"Actually, I was hoping you could come by my place. And that maybe you'd bring me baking one more time . . . and that maybe this time I'd accept it?"

Dead silence met her ears. For far too long. "Callum? Hello?"

"Yeah, I'm still here," he answered—and there was another long pause. A flush of heat throbbed in Jo's cheeks and thundered in her ears. She'd waited too long. He'd taken what she'd said to heart and she'd lost her chance.

"Sure, I can come by, I guess," he said eventually, at a volume she had to strain to hear.

"Great! See you in fifteen minutes or so?"

"Okay," he said, then mumbled something that sounded like, "Just go easy on me, okay?" Before she could ask him to repeat himself or to clarify what he'd meant, he broke the connection.

Jo lit candles all over the small living room, put

the kettle on, then also put out wine glasses and a bottle of red, just in case. Then she spent a few minutes on her face and dabbed a soft citrusy fragrance Sam had given her for Christmas just below her earlobes and on the inside of her wrists.

It felt like he'd never arrive—and then he did. The phone on her wall rang and she answered it, smiling into the receiver.

"Hello, Callum. I'm in 308."

"What a coincidence. I'll be in 308 shortly, too."

She laughed and let him up.

"Hey," he said softly as she opened her door to him. "What's up?"

"Nothing, everything. Just come in, come in."

Callum obliged and as he stood in her entrance-way and passed her his coat, Jo was hyper-conscious of his physical presence.

"I didn't bring baking," he said.

"No, no, of course not."

"Of course not? Why of course not?"

Jo laughed and they stood a moment longer and for some reason, maybe because they were so close they should've touched or something, but didn't, it grew awkward.

She shook her head. "Uh, come in, like I said. Sorry." She moved deeper into her small home, leading the way to the living room. "I thought we could sit soft? And what would you like to drink, tea—the water's hot already—wine? Or, if you're hungry, I could make you something to eat?"

"Jo." The tone of Callum's voice stopped her.

She reached out and put her hand on his arm without thinking. "What?"

Callum looked down at her hand—then moved his gaze up to her face. "I thought I could do this, but I can't," he said, sounding like he'd been stabbed. "What are you playing at, Jo? We're not really friends anymore and since the other night—just tell me. Why did you call me? Why did you want me to come over in such a hurry?"

Jo nodded. Fair questions. And he was right. They weren't friends these days—and if she'd hoped for something sweet and easy like candlelight and toasts for this moment, she also knew, after everything he'd said, she'd said, and they'd *not said* . . . well, that was too much to hope for.

"Please sit down. I have a lot of things I need to say. *We* have a lot of things, I think."

Callum's brow creased, but he settled beside her on the couch—close. She hoped it was a good sign.

Jo took a deep breath and opened her mouth—but no words came immediately. She had all this hope, too much of it really, and it was choking her. She held up one finger to motion she needed a second, then stretched toward the coffee table and retrieved the fateful envelope Callum had addressed to her all those long, long years ago. She handed it to him without comment.

"What's this?" he asked—and then flipped the envelope over, revealing her name in his hand. His face paled and his blue eyes burned impossibly bluer.

"I never got it, Callum. I didn't know you'd even written it until today. I sat at the damn bus station, waiting and waiting, and hoping." She closed her eyes against the pain. Callum was silent. "I called your house, I called Ray. . . . I thought, I mean I was sure, you'd changed your mind, thought of course you had, actually—"

"No—*no*." The simple word, repeated, made Jo open her eyes again. Callum was shaking his head, staring at her like he'd never seen her before in his life.

She bit her lip and nodded, then fumbled for more words. "I know. It's awful. I, it, us. . . . Everything would've been different."

Callum lifted his hand and she held her breath as his fingers traced her cheek. "You really . . . you really never got my letter?" His voice was a mixture of wounded disbelief and wonder.

She shook her head.

"Unbelievable." He chuckled dryly, a bitter sound that hurt her. "Do you know how I felt?" he asked. "How angry? How hurt?"

His questions seemed hypothetical, but she answered anyway. "I imagine," she whispered, "you felt much the same as I did."

He dropped his hand, looked furious. "So much wasted time!"

"No." Jo touched his jaw, bringing his eyes to hers once more. "Look at the mistakes you and I made—

writing a letter instead of saying what you needed to say face-to-face, my taking off instead of staying to confront what the truth actually was—then later in our personal lives, too. If we were capable of such poor choices, we weren't ready for each other. It's better this way."

"You actually believe that?"

She half-grinned, half-winced. "Well, I have to, don't I? And what choice do we have, really, but to go on from here? Like I always say, we can't undo the past."

Callum laced his fingers through hers. Her stomach tightened at even that small touch, and he smiled just a little. "You do always say that—yes. But I'm so sorry. You must've felt so, so . . ."

"Absolutely devastated for years? Yep."

With the hand that wasn't holding hers, Callum gently pushed a curl off of Jo's face and tucked it behind her ear. "I meant every single word and promise I said to you back then. I never should've written that damn letter. I should've come, made sure I found you in person, not let my dad—"

Jo pressed her finger to Callum's mouth. "Shh, no. I should've trusted you, trusted us—should've known that what we had was real and stayed around to fight for it, or at least to find out what had happened—but I was too insecure, too full of wounded pride, too sure no one could ever really love me."

"Oh, Jo," Callum whispered against her hair, pulling her close. "Jo."

They were quiet for a long moment, and Jo's heart hammered in her chest. Where would they go from here? Just a few more things to share, then time would tell.

"There's more, Callum," she said quietly.

"More?"

"Yes . . ." Speaking quickly, and trying not to smear Dave more than his actions and words did themselves, Jo told Callum about all the misunderstandings she'd had about Callum, about who he was, what he wanted, and what he didn't want, fuelled by Dave. At one point, Callum dropped her hand and raked his fingers through his hair.

"I'm so sorry," she said. "But it's true. He—"

"No, no—I believe you. I just can't believe I didn't see it." Callum went on to share the ways Dave had meddled in Callum's opinion of Jo, and how he'd set him up to be an ass. "Not that I need much help in that department," he finished.

"I should have trusted my gut about you, seen through him. . . ." Her heartbeat was still going crazy. She wondered if Callum could hear it.

Callum nodded. "Me too." His thumb rubbed slow circles in the heel of her palm.

"So," she said a little breathlessly.

"So," he echoed. "This is unexpected. And a little mind-blowing."

She nodded and laughed a little. "I'll say."

"And that's it now, right? Everything's out in the open. No secrets."

"Everything," Jo confirmed. "Not one hidden. So where does this leave us?"

"A very good question indeed—and one I want to explore, but I need to do something first."

"What?"

Callum shifted on the couch, pulled Jo onto his lap, then nudged her to straddle him. He stared up into her face, smiling.

"Is this what you wanted?" she asked, leaning in.

"Absolutely," he whispered against her mouth. "For forever."

His tongue met hers and heat surged through her. Callum moaned lightly and kissed her deeper.

She was so distracted that at first the knocking sound didn't register—

And then it did. She pulled back, every nerve conscious of his grip on her hips and the warmth pooling within her. . . .

"Don't answer it," he said, voice rough. "They'll leave."

And the sound suddenly made sense to her ears. Someone was at her door.

"I . . . I should see who it is. Maybe it's a neighbor with a problem. No one can get up here unless I buzz them in. And in any case, they're not going away." As if to prove the truth of her statement, three more raps issued forth.

Callum groaned.

By the time Jo got to the door and opened it, a curly-haired blonde had just turned away and started down the hall.

"Hello," Jo called. "Are you looking for someone?"

The girl turned back, and all warm heat and happiness dancing through Jo limped away. What on earth? It was like looking in a mirror at a younger version of herself. Jo's gaze fell to the girl's considerable midriff—okay, make that a pregnant mirror.

Behind her, still in the entranceway of her apartment, Callum cleared his throat—then stepped into the hall to join her. She heard his sharp inhale, recognized it as shock. So it wasn't just her. He saw the resemblance as well.

"Can I help you?" Jo asked.

The girl's voice was clear and well modulated—and also familiar. "Are you Jo Kendall?

Later Jo would wonder, what if she hadn't answered the door? Or what if she hadn't called out and caught the girl's attention? How would things have been different? But she had answered. And she had called out. What ifs were pointless.

Chapter 31

CALLUM'S LUNGS CONSTRICTED THE INSTANT he laid
eyes on the girl. He leaned against one of the hallway's stucco walls, a heartburn cocktail of curiosity
and dread hammering in his chest. He knew what was
coming. *He knew it*—after all, you'd have to be deaf
and blind—and intentionally dumb—to not see the
undeniable similarity of Jo and this . . . other, younger
Jo. It was hard to breath, but somehow he managed.
Until the stranger spoke again.

"Well, it's nice to meet you, *Mother*."

"What?" Jo asked, then did a 360-degree turn
without addressing the girl's comment further. "Are
you all right, Callum?"

"Callum, like Callum *Archer*, as in my biological
father?" The girl sounded as shocked as Callum felt—
like a spear of white-sharp electricity had just cut
through him.

"It's not what you're thinking," Jo blurted.
"You've got it wrong."

It wasn't what he thought? How could she know
what he thought? Callum didn't even know. That he'd
not only lost the only woman he'd ever loved, he'd

262

lost the child he always wanted to have—and had never even known existed? A wave of questions crashed over him but he was powerless to breath, let alone attempt to articulate one. He let out a scraping bark of a sound.

The girl answered like Jo had been talking to her, not to Callum. "What do I have wrong—and what on earth's wrong with him?"

"Nothing's wrong with him. Nothing at all. Callum?"

Jo's voice poured over him, calming, refreshing—awakening.

Okay, man, pull it together. You can do this. *Breathe.* It's not a big deal if you don't though. You'll just pass out. Jo will take you to the hospital. You'll live. The tiniest breath of air ever taken moved through his pain-wracked throat. He stood straighter. A little more oxygen wheezed through.

"Callum?"

He held up a hand. "I'm fine, Jo . . . Just, just deal with . . . whatever this is."

"Pardon me?" said the young stranger. "*Whatever this is?*"

Oh, no . . . he'd worded that badly. He opened his eyes. The similarity between the young woman and Jo was still unbelievable. "That's not what, I didn't mean—oh, crap."

"Excellent," said the girl. "Just what I expected." Her voice had lost its confidence though and her face turned a mottled pink. "Anyway, don't worry about it.

I have a real dad already. I didn't even know you'd be here. So what, are you two, like, still together?"

Callum shot a look at Jo who had staggered back against the wall, too—apparently battling her own anxiety. Yep, they really were a fantastic pair. But were they a couple now, "still together" as the kid said? They'd left off talking at the where-does-this-leave-us part of the conversation. He raised his eyebrows at Jo. She shook her head and some conflicted emotion he couldn't interpret darkened her eyes. For the first time since they'd reunited, he saw her thirty-three years in her face—and maybe more. The comfort in her voice that he'd clung to just minutes ago drained away. So they weren't a couple again? What was that back in her apartment then?

It felt like his brain was bleeding. She'd had his baby without even bothering to tell him they'd conceived a child, then come back, made overtures toward getting back together—and now, what? She was breaking up with him because her kid—their kid, apparently—was back in the picture? She wasn't even going to give him a chance to hear her side?

Really, you still want her, even after this? You are a fucking numbskull, Duncan Archer's voice boomed through Callum's psyche like a blow to the kidneys. The impact almost made him crumple.

She took everything from you, everything—if you had anything remotely worthwhile in you to begin with. And your child! You always wanted a child, Callum, because you are a child. This new assault bulleted through his brain in Nina's shrill nails-on-a-chalkboard soprano.

But then some inner core of steel formed within him. He'd wimped out once with Jo and regretted it all of his life. He was going to see this through. Yes, it hurt like hell that she'd trusted him so little, that she'd believed he just didn't show, and left, never looking back, carrying his child—but it also explained, that much more, maybe, why she'd fled in the first place. She hadn't gotten his letter. She'd only known his dad was dead set against their match and that Callum had stood her up. It wasn't like he'd ever been good at defending her. Of course she took his silence and failure to arrive as him bailing on her. And really, even if she'd gotten the letter. . . . It had still been him ducking out, just in a different way, hadn't it?

"Jo," he said softly. She'd been saying something to the girl sotto voce, but now she looked over at him. "What do you want me to do?"

She bit her lip, looking as if she might cry. "Aisha here"—she motioned at the girl who had, consciously or unconsciously, rested her hands on her swollen paunch as if to cradle her unborn baby—"is going to come in and stay the night and we're going to chat, but you, well, maybe it would be best for now, if you just go?"

Callum wished he could be hit with the biggest anxiety attack ever known to man just to have the pain of this conversation mitigated—but, Murphy's law, though an ocean of confusion, hurt, and thwarted desire and hope was raging through him, physically he was fine now, his breathing even, his stomach calm, his muscles relaxed. "Is that . . . that's what you want, then?"

Jo's nose scrunched. "'Want' isn't the right word, but I think it's for the best."

Callum tried to force speech. The girl was staring at him with piercing eyes so like his own, just green instead of blue. He failed to find words. He nodded lamely and turned to leave.

"I'll call soon, I promise. Trust me," Jo said from behind him.

"I do," he said, but he didn't know if Jo even heard him. She was already through her door, clicking it locked behind her and Aisha.

Chapter 32

JO SETTLED THE GIRL—SETTLED *AISHA*—on the couch. Hoover wandered out of the bedroom to say hello, a politeness he hadn't extended to Callum earlier, and hopped up to join her.

"I'm sorry," Jo said. "Do you mind?" But Aisha was already scratching his ears and crooning to him, so obviously it was fine.

Jo made a fresh pot of tea while Aisha called her dad to let him know she'd arrived and all was fine. Then they got down to the nitty-gritty. Aisha took the news pretty well, though she was skeptical at first.

"But I look just like you."

Jo studied her. It really was uncanny—except for the eye color, of course. "I know. But when you meet Sam, I mean Samantha, your . . . birth mom . . . you'll see you look a lot like her too, though she straightens her hair. You have her green eyes."

"I don't understand. Why would she put your name down as the birth mother? How'd she get away with it?"

"I can only imagine. She always has reasons for the things she does though."

"Yeah, but will they be reasons a normal person gets?"

Jo nearly spit out her mouthful of tea as a surprised laugh burst out of her. Genes were strong things, apparently—and not just for physical traits.

"Isn't it some kind of crime to fake someone else's identity and pretend your kid is theirs on, like, legal documents and everything?"

"No idea, sorry."

"Well, it should be."

The direction the conversation was heading was so far over Jo's head she didn't even try to go there. She offered her guest cheese and crackers instead, and while she was adding apple slices to the plate, a question of her own hit her.

"How on earth did you come up with Callum's name as the biological father? Samantha didn't even know him then—or not enough that'd she'd have thought to link his name to mine as a parent."

Aisha took the plate Jo handed her and wolfed down a piece of cheddar immediately. "Mm, thanks—and no, the records said 'Father unknown,' but that cousin of yours I tracked down, the one who said she'd heard you were in back in Greenridge—she mentioned him, said he was the only guy you'd went with in high school."

Throughout the evening, Jo tried calling Sam repeatedly, but got no answer each time. She left a couple messages asking her to call back, but giving no other details. "Hey, Sam, you had a baby, it's a girl—

who's a woman with her own kid on the way. Surprise!" didn't seem like a voicemail appropriate subject.

Jo didn't ask about Aisha's pregnancy and the girl didn't volunteer any information. When she finished eating, she started yawning and the evening wound up quickly from there. Jo made up the couch for her to sleep on and that was that. She was an aunt—well, an aunt who was now on her way to actually knowing her niece. Bizarre!

She said a quick prayer in her head for Sam—and for Aisha, and for herself—having less than no idea how her big sister would take the news that the child she'd put up for adoption had tracked her down and had questions.

It hit Jo sometime in the wee hours of the morning, pulling her from restless sleep, making her bolt upright in bed. *She hadn't specifically told Callum he wasn't Aisha's father and she wasn't her mother.* The last thing he'd heard about the parentage of Aisha Baily-Brown was Jo being called "Mom" and his name being given as her biological father's. What a shit show. She'd been so shocked to see Aisha, knowing immediately who she must be—and so concerned for the girl with her huge to the point of painful-looking belly that she'd just wanted to get Callum calmed down and the girl inside so that everything could get sorted out. . . .

It hadn't even occurred to her that she hadn't corrected Aisha's mistaken declaration in front of

Callum. So . . . now, what? He thought, correctly, that she'd flaked off at the first sign everything might not be easy and left town—and now he probably thought she'd done so bearing his baby, lacking the decency to let him know about it.

She wracked her brain, trying to recall how he'd seemed as he left but not a lot of details came to her. She'd been so distracted by their visitor—but maybe resigned, calm? Yes, those things. But those things, good or bad? Peaceful because he was confident in their relationship now, knew they'd work things out again? Or resigned because it was the straw that broke the camel's back and he'd decided it was time to say good-bye forever?

She couldn't bear for their new fledgling relationship to be derailed so soon—but if he didn't give her a chance to explain, if he jumped to the worst conclusions about her and was angry? She didn't know if she'd be able to bear that either.

She tried multiple times to call him on his cell phone, but kept getting the same message: "The mobile customer you are calling is unavailable at this time."

She wanted to pull on clothes and drive over to his house, but the girl sleeping on the couch stopped her. She couldn't just leave a pregnant teenager alone her first day in a new town. And what if Sam didn't call, just showed up at the apartment without warning? Apparently everyone and their dog ignored the buzzer rule and let anybody into the building who showed up.

Jo couldn't spring a surprise visit on Aisha or Sam.

Heart heavy with fears that she'd wrecked everything again, Jo said yet another quick prayer, for Callum this time, for *them*, and got out of bed. She retrieved her favorite jeans from the floor where she'd pulled them off the other day—they were still clean—and put her nervous energy to work. She made a hearty breakfast, so hearty—eggs, bacon, pancakes, fruit salad, plus toast and three kind of jam—that Aisha was a little overwhelmed when she woke up. She was up to the challenge though.

"This is awesome," she said enthusiastically. "Mmm, have you ever tried being pregnant? I don't necessarily recommend it, but it does make food a.maze.ing."

Jo laughed. Aisha really did remind her of Sam, almost eerily in fact. "No, I haven't 'tried' pregnancy yet, but if I ever do, I'll let you know my thoughts."

"Sounds good." Aisha crunched down a piece of bacon and tossed one to Hoover. It seemed to be their game, one for her, one for him. Hoover had never been happier. "Also, what should I call you?"

"Er . . . Jo? Or maybe Auntie Jo? Whatever you're comfortable with. Not aunt."

"I don't know." Aisha lifted her chin and spoke with a crusty, snooty accent. "Aunt Jo has a certain ring to it."

Jo laughed, then looked down at her hands.

"What?"

"Nothing."

"*What?*"

Jo shook her head. "I was just thinking about that guy who was here last night—Callum. I forgot to cue him in that he's not actually your birth dad."

"So . . . " A look of understanding spread across Aisha's face, but didn't prevent her from taking another large bite of blackberry jam covered sourdough toast. "You mean," she said, after she swallowed and sipped her milk. "You mean he thinks you had his kid and didn't tell him."

Jo shrugged.

"And you guys were together, *are* together."

Jo swayed her head side-to-side indecisively. She felt about twelve talking about this with her niece. "*Were* together when we were about your age. It ended—well, it just ended, but—"

"But after all these years you got back together."

"We were thinking about it."

"But he'll think you lied about . . . well, a pretty big thing, actually."

Jo lifted her tea mug in a mock cheers. "Yep."

"You need to go to him right now and explain. If you have the remotest chance to be with someone you love, you need to go for it. Life's short."

There was an urgency in Aisha's simple, almost cliché words that struck Jo. She studied her niece's face. What was her story anyway? What brought her here, so heavily pregnant, when it sounded, from the bits of the phone call she'd unintentionally overheard, like she had a family who loved and supported her?

"I will—but I can't right now."

"Because I'm here?"

"Yeah, but please don't worry. I just think it would be best for everyone if I'm here when you and Sam meet for the first time."

Aisha had made a huge dent in the meal, but even she was finally done. She pushed her plate away. "She won't be happy to see me?"

"I . . . well, I don't know." Jo twisted her tea mug in her hands. "Let's just say . . . Sam doesn't do things half way. I knew she had you, though not that she pretended to be me. And I knew she decided—a difficult decision for her—to put you up for adoption, but after it was official and you were in your new home, we never spoke about it."

"Never? As in . . . *never*, not even once?"

Jo contemplated her tea again, wishing for leaves at the bottom of the cup or something that would tell her how to proceed. "Okay, so perhaps more like, very, very, very rarely—and then only in generalities. I know she has thought of you from time to time, if only because of how adamant she is about not having other children."

"Because I was such a mistake." Aisha's tone was bitter.

Jo wasn't surprised, but she was quick to correct. "No, maybe the opposite. The one thing she feels she did right. She really liked your parents—always said, 'Finally, one Kendall girl will get raised right.'"

"What does that mean?"

Jo shook her head, feeling a bit sick, like she'd said too much, given too much away, already. These were Sam's things to share, if she wanted to, not hers.

Aisha's eyes—so like Sam's they made Jo's breath hitch—held hers for a long time. "I guess that's for me to learn from her maybe."

"Maybe."

"Okay, so here's how it will work."

Jo raised her eyebrows.

"You will go to Callum. I will do the dishes, shower, watch TV and eat. I will eat *a lot*, just saying. I will not answer the door or the phone. I'll give you my cell number though, in case you need me or don't trust me—"

"I trust you," Jo said, getting a bigger kick out of Aisha—and feeling her affection for her growing—every time the kid spoke practically.

"You have twenty-four hours. Tomorrow morning at the latest, we'll—"

"Don't be silly. I'm not going to need *twenty-four* hours."

"Never say never. You know how it goes, a little of this leads to a little of that." Aisha waggled her eyebrows suggestively.

"You, my dear," Jo said, getting up from the table, "are going to get along with your birth mom like a house on fire."

"Or not."

Damn, the kid had better be careful or Jo would just start calling her Mini-Sam.

Chapter 33

EVERY LIGHT WAS OFF IN the house, save one: a small lamp or something in what Jo thought she remembered as the study, though really, if she was honest, she hardly had eyes for the house when she'd been there, what, just a few days ago? *Crazy.* Was it really possible that the emotional roller coaster she'd been on for what seemed like forever was mere days?

Callum must've heard her truck roll in because the house and yard lit up suddenly—including tiny sparkling white lights that were woven through a mature grapevine that wound around the beams and trusses of the porch—so pretty. She parked and climbed out, sans Hoover. She'd left him with Aisha who was apparently his new best friend, bacon being the undisputed way to his heart.

As she walked the flagstone path to the porch, she continued to admire the twinkling lights and how they made the home's cedar shingle-siding glow a warm, welcoming russet color in the foggy morning light. It was like a little fairyland. She paused in front of the cheerful door and took a deep breath for courage.

"It's going to be okay," she murmured. "More

than okay, in fact. You and Callum love each other and you'll figure it out. No more misunderstandings. No more unsaid things."

A circus of happy butterflies pirouetted in her stomach as she recognized the truth of her words deep in her very core—and she grinned like a mad woman as she rang the doorbell.

"Hey," Callum said softly behind her.

She jumped about a mile high and turned. "You almost gave me a heart attack!"

Callum took the rest of the stairs at an easy pace, stopping beside her at the door. "Sorry about that," he said, but looked like he wanted to laugh.

"Is it a bad time?"

"Not at all. Why?"

"Oh, it's just the lights came on as I drove up. If you were outside . . . is there someone else here?"

Callum shook his head. "I was out in the shed, playing with a timer—long story. I'll tell you about it later, maybe." He opened the door and Jo followed after him, swallowing against the lump that suddenly formed in her throat. The only reason she could see for a timer system for lights was if you were planning to go away for an extended time.

"So," Callum said once they were both inside and had slipped their shoes off. "What's up?"

Jo hoped against hope that his casual tone meant all was good between them. He took her coat and his smile faded a bit. So then again, maybe all *wasn't* good? Nervous snakes warred with her happy butterflies—but she didn't let them win.

"Let's sit soft," Jo said. "And can we have wine?"

Callum gave her a long searing look, and his brow furrowed. "Wine? Yeah, sure—but you do know it's like nine in the morning?"

She laughed. "Yeah, but we might want it."

"Okay, but then I have another question. . . ." His smile was tentative, but at least it was there. "Cheese?"

She grinned and her heart raced. "Please." She started in the direction of the living room.

Callum nodded, but didn't move toward the kitchen. Instead he reached out and caught her arm.

The house was utterly quiet. Under different circumstances the stillness might have felt peaceful but right now it was unnerving.

"C'mon, Jo. Out with whatever it is. I'm not angry. I was sad, hurt maybe, shocked definitely, but I think I understand—"

He was right. They should tackle it right now. "Actually, Callum, I don't know if you do—"

He reached out and touched her face. "You're right, maybe I don't. But I want to. And I want to be in your life. No matter what. Months ago, when you said we were just stupid kids, I took it as you dismissing what we had, saying it wasn't as intense, as deep, as true as I always felt our relationship was . . . but now I get it. You were just saying we needed to let each other off the hook for the ways we hurt each other and let each other—and ourselves—down. We *were* really young and pretty banged up by our childhoods. It makes sense we were gun shy. But I'm not a kid anymore and I won't run. And I'm sorry I was the kind of guy that made you feel like you had to bear everything yourself and go through everything alone—"

"Callum." Jo put her arms around his neck, and he lowered his forehead to hers.

"What?" His voice was so was quiet it was little more than breath. "Please don't tell me we're done—and please, if there's another secret you haven't told me, *you can tell me.* It won't chase me off."

Jo's heart wrenched. "See, that's the thing. Your words are so sweet I can hardly stand it, but—"

"But what?"

"Aisha isn't yours."

Callum inhaled sharply. Surprised again. Maybe hurt. "Okay—" he started to say.

"No, no," Jo hurried on. "I mean, she's not mine either. She's not ours."

"What?" Callum stepped back, an I-don't-get-the-joke smile lifting the corner of his mouth. "What do you mean? How's that possible?"

"Well, if I've never been pregnant, ever, yet the young adult in question looks a freakish amount like me. . . ."

Callum continued to stare at her blankly.

"So much like me in fact, she could be a younger me, or my *sister,* or—"

"Sam! She's Sam's." Callum laughed out loud.

"Ding, ding, we have a winner. *Finally*."

Callum laughed again. "That explains it," he said.

"Explains what?"

"She seems identical to you, except for her voice. It was familiar but not *you*. She has Sam's voice."

"And her eyes," Jo agreed.

Callum caught her hand, pressed it to his mouth and kissed it.

Jo looked up at him. "Is it really this easy, Callum? Are we good?"

"We're so good," he said seriously.

All Jo wanted was to pull him down to the couch and start up where they'd left off the night before, but she, *they*, needed everything out on the table. "And if Aisha had been yours and mine, and I hadn't told her about you? Would we still be having this conversation, still be okay?"

"Yeah. I made up my mind last night—no, way before that, even. I trust you, Jo. Always have. I just didn't trust that I was worthy—or lucky enough—to have you in my life. Even when you left all those years ago, I thought it was me, something I did. I didn't know what, but I knew you had a reason."

She cleared her throat softly. He hadn't let go of her hand and was tracing lazy circles back and forth over her palm. The soft but persistent pressure of his thumb was doing crazy things to her insides and making it hard to think. "I've loved you my whole life, Callum—and it's made me feel bad."

His thumb stopped moving, but he didn't break

contact. "What?"

"It wasn't fair to other people—well, to Devin specifically. He was a douche, yes, but at the same time, right from day one he was competing for something I no longer had to give."

"Your heart?" Callum asked.

She nodded.

"You're so corny," he teased, then sobered almost the same instant. "I feel exactly the same way, Jo. And I put a lot of stuff on Nina that really wasn't about her at all. It was about me, and/or my screwed up relationship with my dad. Some day I'd like to apologize to her for that."

"Callum—"

"No, wait—before you say another word, I have to get something."

He was back seconds later with a bottle of bubbly and two fluted glasses.

He set the wine and glasses down, but kept his eyes—those ever-intense eyes—focused on her.

"It's funny that you came by this morning," he said.

Funny? She could think of a hundred adjectives that she'd prefer. She eased into the deep, plush couch and tried not to purr aloud with pleasure when he sat down beside her and pulled her close.

"Before you called me last night, I'd spent the week going over everything you said the day you came here, the day I asked you to marry me and you said no. I thought I'd go insane with it—and then I made a decision."

Here it comes, she thought and the knowledge of what her answer was and would always be made her dizzy.

"I hate to look foolish, to reveal how weak I am . . . "

Jo started to protest, but he shushed her. "But I am foolish and weak when it comes to you. Always have been. Always will be."

Jo's breath caught in her throat.

"So I figured, what the hell? Before you called yesterday, I'd already decided to see if you could meet me for coffee and ask you to consider me one more time."

Heat and joy coursed through Jo. She tried not to bounce in her seat.

"And if you said no again, I'd honor it, leave town for a while to lick my wounds and decide what to do."

Jo smacked him. "Come on, fellah. Hurry up. You're killing me here."

Callum grinned and rummaged for something in his pocket. "And then, you called. I was sure I was arriving at your place to receive a final crushing blow—news that you were leaving, but couldn't go without making one more thing absolutely clear."

"You were kind of right," she said in a stuffed up voice.

"And then last night turned to out to be everything I hoped for—or was gearing up to be until the brat showed up anyway."

Jo laughed, but her mirth was cut short when Callum revealed what he'd pulled out of his pocket.

The ring—without its pretty velvet box this time—winked up at Jo. And even though she'd been expecting it, her eyes misted.

"Last night, when you said if I offered you baking this time, you wouldn't refuse me. Did you mean it, or were you just being cruel?"

"Um? I don't get it."

"I was hoping you were speaking symbolically."

"I hope I was too—if that would've been a good thing?"

Callum looked shy. "If I ask you to marry me one more time, will you say yes?"

"Well, they say three times is the charm. Try it and see."

He laughed. "C'mon, Jo. Don't torture me. Marry me, please. For better or worse, the whole shebang."

"Yes." Jo nodded. "Yes, I will marry you—and yes, I would love to be your partner in every way you can think of."

"Mmm, in every way, eh?"

Jo winked. "And then some."

Callum's eyebrow rose and his mouth quirked. He looked her up and down, not bothering—and no longer needing—to hide his desire. "I like the sounds of that." His voice was so low it was almost a growl. Then he leaned in and kissed her—her collarbone, her neck, her jaw—and as her back arched toward him, her mouth again. . . .

She was breathless when he took her hand and slipped the warm gold band onto her finger. It fit snugly and felt just right. Jo got a little light-headed looking at it.

"I wish I had something. . . . Oh, wait!" She dug into her jeans' pocket. "I don't think it'll fit your finger—but have it until I can get you something better."

Callum took the rhinestone-studded wedding band she'd cut off her hook earlier. "Is this a wedding band for catching *trout*?"

Jo sniffed. "You shouldn't mock. In fact, you should be flattered. That's from my favorite lure."

Callum slid his fingers through the belt loop of her jeans and pulled her against him. "And you're *my* favorite lure," he whispered.

"Oh, pretty talk—" but whatever she was going to say next was cut off by Callum's warm mouth on hers.

Chapter 34

JO SAT IN THE CAR outside her apartment, cursing herself for her mistake. Buzzing with happiness and ideas and dreams for the future—so many ideas and dreams!—she, like a ninny, hadn't thought things through. Earlier she'd known full well she needed to break the news about Aisha in person. Now, distracted and wishing with every fiber of her being that she and Callum hadn't had to separate after a lovely kiss or two, she'd not only answered the phone when Samantha called just now—she'd naively caved to Sam's pressure to "spill it already." Now listening to her sister, having heard her shocked silence and then an odd, sharp gasp, she realized too late she definitely, one hundred percent, should have relayed the news in person.

"I don't care if she's the nicest kid in the whole world—and why wouldn't she be with my genetics?" Jo didn't smile at Sam's usual attempt to joke, just waited for her to rave on. "I'm not interested in meeting her. Just tell her . . ." Sam's voice softened to a volume that was difficult to hear. "I can't."

Jo rubbed the steering wheel back and forth under

her hand. "I didn't say she was the 'nicest,' just *nice*. And I don't think it's as simple as just deciding not to meet her. I think she needs to meet you. Has questions only you can answer. She's pregnant and—"

"She's what? Oh, great. How on earth did that happen?"

"Well, I suspect the usual way, but if you need some education, I'd be happy to buy you a how babies are made book."

"Hilarious, Jo—but I'm the one who attempts to diffuse awkward situations with lame jokes."

"True."

"Look, just tell the kid, tell Aisha—such a beautiful name, hey?—that I'm sorry if things haven't worked out for her. I'm a screw up and that's really all she needs to know. I did the best for her I could—and the best I could was giving her a chance by giving her away."

"I don't think she's looking for an apology or a reason or anything. She seems to like her family, and you're not a screw up. Just talk to her."

"What part of *can't*, can't you get, Jo?"

"Sam, I don't ask a lot from you."

"Yeah, right."

"I don't—Ray's property mess aside. And I never meddled or brought this up before. We've never even really talked about it."

"I'm sorry, Jo. I really am. Tell her I've left town—that's why you couldn't get me yesterday."

"*Have* you left town?" It actually would be like

Sam. Exactly like her, in fact.

Sam sighed. "Not yet, no—but I have given notice and started packing."

"So rescind your notice and stay another month. Just one, and not just for Aisha. For me. I want to show you River's Sigh B & B."

"What?"

"You heard me."

"So it's game on between you and my lawyer, then? Things are all hunky-dory?"

Jo laughed. "He was my boyfriend before he was your lawyer, and yes"—Jo glanced down at her ring shining in the sunlight—"things are great."

"How wonderful for you."

"Oh come on, don't be like that."

"I'm not—or, well, I don't mean to be. I'm sorry. I am happy for you guys. I know you've always wanted this, it, him. . . ." Jo could practically see Sam's hands waving about as she spoke.

"Stay, Sam. *Stay.*"

There was a long, long pause. Finally, sounding sad but resolute, Sam answered. "No. And hey . . . I'll contact you in a few days and let you know where I am."

"But—" It was no use. Jo was talking to dead air.

Chapter 35

THE INCREDIBLY TINY CHURCH HAD seating, literally, for a max of nine people, and it still wasn't filled to capacity.

"It's like a doll church or something," Aisha said, turning her head to take in the petite pews, small stain-glassed windows, and aisle that was all of ten feet long.

"Yeah, I know. Isn't it lovely? It's always amazed me that the early settlers even built it. It's like it was created for one family or something. Callum and I used to sneak in here, back in the day. We even pretended to get married once, went through the vows everything—"

"Were you drunk?" And there it was again: Sam's sentimentality and rosy outlook on life alive and thriving in the flesh of her biological daughter.

"Well, maybe," Jo admitted grudgingly. "But even then, we really felt we were meant to be together."

Aisha squeezed her hand. "That's so nice—and anyway, you're not drunk now."

Jo looked over at her niece and squeezed her hand back. One day Samantha would realize, hopefully, that yes, loving and letting yourself be loved opened you up for potential hurt and pain—but also for incredible joy and fun and, well, everything that made life worth living. "I'm glad you're here, Aisha."

"And I'm so glad you and Callum have that little cabin that's in decent enough shape for me to stay. I'll be a big help around the place. You'll see."

Jo nodded. She wasn't sure how much help her growing-larger-by-the-day niece would really be—or even why Aisha was so determined to stay in Greenridge to have her child, especially when it seemed to be breaking her father's heart. Still, she was happy to get to know Aisha better, regardless of what work she might or might not do, and she was willing to wait for Aisha to open up—

And suddenly her mind wasn't on Aisha or on her sadness that Sam wasn't there. Callum bounded through the door at the back of the small church, and he was all she could see. His eyes sought hers, only hers, and she couldn't breath. This was actually happening. She was marrying Callum Archer! She stood up and together they approached the simple pulpit. The minister appeared from a side door, followed by their witnesses, Callum's brother Brian and his date, and the ceremony proceeded. They had written their own vows and Jo was sure they each spoke their hearts—but she was glad they'd put them on paper to treasure later because she was hardly aware of what they said. Her heart pounded and her blood thrummed.

"Do you Callum Archer, take this woman, to love, honor and cherish till death do you part?"

All she could hear, all she wanted for the rest of her life, was his simple, low-voiced promise. "I do."

Epilogue

JO RETRIEVED THE LIGHT BLUE envelope from where it was wedged between the window frame and the wall in her office and opened it. She smiled as she read the note—then shook her head, cheeks warm, as her insides tightened and heated in delightful, if slightly torturous, anticipation.

Callum—what a weirdo! Her business partner. Her chief cook and bottle washer. *Her husband.* Would any of it ever get old? She hoped not.

Meanwhile she picked up her cell phone, hit reply, and—after a moment's thought—sent a few lines that would hopefully bring him as much immediate discomfort as his letter had brought her. And then she got to work. Their first guests were arriving in two days, and Aisha, though only weeks away from being "ready to pop" in her own oh-so-eloquent words, had proven worth her now considerable weight in gold. The cabins were in beautiful shape. Jo just needed to plan breakfasts to wow their company and make sure the finishing touches were just right. And then, she was sure she'd have time, she might sneak away. She had a new lure to try—a flashy yellow and black thing called a Hornet. She suspected she'd still add a wedding band though. Wedding bands, after all, were precious things.

Dear Reader,

I loved getting to know Jo and Callum and seeing the birth of River's Sigh B & B, my own dream getaway. If you enjoyed it too, you'll be happy to know their story—and the stories of so many other people living in or visiting Greenridge—continues in *Hooked*, Book 2 of the River's Sigh B & B series.

Feel very welcome to visit www.evbishop.com, sign up for my newsletter, find me on Facebook, follow my Tweets, or drop me a line at evbishop@evbishop.com. I'd love to hear from you! And on a similar note, reviews really, really help authors. ☺ Please consider leaving a rating and a few kind words on Amazon, GoodReads, your blog, Facebook, or anywhere else you like to hang out when your nose isn't in a book. Thank you so much for reading.

Warm regards and best wishes,

EvBishop

For a sneak preview of HOOKED read on. . . .

Chapter 1

FRESH FROM THE SHOWER, BAREFOOT and dressed only in a robe, Sam wrapped her arms around herself and turned in a slow circle. Five stars or not, a hotel room was always just a hotel room, wasn't it? It was beautiful with its teak four-poster bed, matching highboy and desk, and snow-white linens, but generic nonetheless.

She settled into the leather wingback chair, the room's best feature in her opinion—a lovely, comfortable thing that felt like it hugged you—and put her feet up. A niggle of surprise tickled her as she uncapped a pen and reached for the spiral bound notebook on the table beside her. Who'd have thought? Samantha Kendall using a *diary*. But she couldn't help it. The movement of her hand across page, the scent of the paper, the process of filling the sheet with the mess in her head—slowly at first, then so fast her hand cramped—soothed her and helped her see more clearly than she had in a long time. Her life, once so beautiful and busy, felt empty. Come to think of it maybe that was the appeal of the journaling. She filled something. Created a tangible mark that she was here. That she lived.

The coffee pot on the desk across the room sighed and sputtered.

"Ah, my faithful friend," she whispered, then got up, doctored herself a mug of the dark espresso blend, and settled down again.

She sipped her hot drink and drummed her fingers on her notebook. What to say, what to say?

She paused, drank more coffee, and ran her fingers through her damp hair. Finally she began to write.

Sheesh, three pages minimum is going to take forever today.

But it didn't. By the time she had two cups of caffeine in her, she'd churned out her minimum, plus another three pages—yet she wasn't calmed down any. She was edgier than ever. She scanned the last bit of the page, biting her lip and barely resisting the urge to tear the sheets loose and throw them away.

There's nothing I hate more than my sister being right about anything, but I have to hand it to Jo. She is right about this, and the pro and cons I wrote yesterday only confirm it.

I always figured Aisha would reenter my life at some point, if only, like seems to be the case, for medical information and "closure." (How I hate that damn word!). I just thought I'd be at a spot in time, personally and professionally, that I could be proud of-or at least not a bloody embarrassment. But at the same time, I guess it's not about me, is it? (Ha ha, quick, someone tell Jo I actually said that!) I would've done anything to have someone to talk to, when I was stuck in the same boat Aisha's in, so how can I refuse her request to meet?

My two biggest fears: that she'll ask about the asshole who fathered her and I'll break down (No, I won't-but what can I say about him that won't just be this huge ugly shadow over her?), or that she'll hate me- which is pretty hilarious because I definitely don't want her in my life permanently.

That was the line that stopped her. She shook her head, bit deeper into her lip, then crossed the last line out, drew an arrow, and scribbled furiously.

That she'll hate me, which I'll totally under-stand, or worse, want something I don't have to give her. All of my love for her went out the door with her the day I gave her a chance for a better life. (Don't even get me started on how I feel about her idiot parents letting her get knocked up. Her life was supposed to be better than what I could give *her!) What if she wants a relationship? I have no frigging clue what I'll do.*

Samantha closed the book, tucked her pen into its coil binding, and stashed them in her suitcase.

She paid special attention to her outfit and did her makeup and hair just so, but it wasn't until she sprayed a light mist of perfume in front of her and walked through it that she admitted she'd made up her mind.

Yeah, yeah, yeah. She'd return to Greenridge. She'd see if she could be of any help to Aisha and answer any awkward questions her biological daughter had.

And then, so long as Jo and Callum were willing to let her monopolize one of their B & B cabins—and why wouldn't they? Her cash was as good as anyone's—she'd spend some concentrated time figuring out what exactly she herself wanted next and why her life, which she'd always enjoyed, wasn't enough for her these days.

She cocked her head, smiled at her reflection in the mirror, and nodded approval—both at the image she projected and the new thoughts in her head. She was an excellent planner and there was no reason she couldn't get herself back on track. And once she had a new direction in mind, she'd leave Greenridge in the dust and never return. The place was a black hole. In lieu of a welcome sign at the beginning of town, there should be a plaque that read, "Abandon all hopes of having a life, ye who enter here."

And if Jo wanted to visit now and again? Well, she'd have to sojourn out of her hobbit village and head for the city. Sam was done with the ghost town of bad memories. She was sick of the family-focused "great place to raise kids" motto that everyone in town seemed to spout. Not everyone had kids—or wanted them. And she was beyond weary of how the place reminded her that except for her one solitary sibling, Jo, she had no family. Everyone was dead. There'd be no TV movie worthy reunion or redemption scene. Greenridge was like one big beer commercial for all the things she didn't have. And didn't want, she reminded herself.

CHARLES STUBBED HIS TOE ON the stuffed-to-bursting rucksack he'd stowed by his office door and stared at the ringing phone like it might bite. The call display showed T.C.O. Literary Management all too clearly—and unfortunately his agent Theresa, the "T" in T.C.O., knew he was home. After all, he'd just sent an e-mail seconds ago admitting it. He sighed heavily and picked up.

"Theresa, hi. Good to hear from you."

"Don't bullshit a bullshitter, and get real. You knew that e-mail wasn't going to fly."

"But—"

"And no buts." Her voice softened. "I feel for you. You know I do—and I'm on your side even if it doesn't feel like it, but it's time, Charlie. Past time. And if you can't see that, maybe it's time to rethink your career."

Charles sank into his office chair and rolled back and forth across the room. He didn't want to "rethink" his work. He loved what he did, what he wrote. Or he used to. And anyway, it wasn't like he hadn't considered doing something else. Just absolutely nothing came to him that didn't sink him even more deeply into the mire of apathy and disillusionment he seemed unable to pull himself from—and now, with his daughter, Aisha, living God knew where and insisting she was staying there to have her baby, he didn't even have the occasional bright spot of her presence.

"You've used up all your reserve books—even your earliest ones that were previously unpublished for pretty good reasons. It's just a good thing some loyal readers don't care what you write as long as the story says Jax Bailey on the cover."

"Thanks a lot."

"Oh, you know what I mean. Don't get pissy. I love your books. You've earned reader loyalty—but even diehard fans are starting to grumble on the Interwebs. You can only play the dead wife card for so long before people start to think you need to get over it."

Charles managed to not throw the phone across the room, but only just.

Theresa seemed to sense she'd crossed a line.

"Sorry, that was crass. Obviously, healing to a place where you can write again isn't an easy one, two, three process. I know you're doing the best you can, just barely hanging on, and I know it will take time— but I'd hate to see you lose everything you worked so hard to build."

Too late. Everything he'd worked for died when Maureen did. Still, Theresa wasn't the enemy and she was on his side. He knew this. He also knew he'd probably exhausted every extension possible on his contract. And he made a decent living—and Maureen's life insurance had paid off the mortgage and left a little besides, but not enough to see him through life—and definitely not enough to provide ongoing stability to Aisha and her little one, should she decide to keep it. And he was a young(ish) man. Forty-four was nowhere near the time to retire even if it felt closer to eighty these days.

"They need a new book, or, and it's pretty nice of them, almost human in fact, they'll forgive the contract without penalty, but if you ever want to write for them again, it'll be like starting new."

Perish the thought—and no, that wasn't melodrama. "How long?" he asked.

"I got you six months, but that's it, final offer, last extension."

"Okay," he said.

"Okay?" Even though their connection was a little static-filled, the surprise in Theresa's voice was loud and clear. "Just like that you say *okay?*"

"Do I have a choice?"

"No, but I still thought you'd be a harder sell."

They wrapped the conversation up quickly from there, and Charles was careful to sound more positive than he felt. Six months, if he was his old self, was more than enough time to get a solid book to his publisher. But he wasn't his old self—and didn't think he ever would be again. Maureen had been gone three years, yet in some ways it was like she'd passed away yesterday, the grief would hit so fresh and raw. In other ways, however, it was like she'd left a lifetime ago, which, hard as it was, was sort of the truth. Neither his nor Aisha's lives were the same. They had new existences altogether, as if their time on earth had been divided into separate realities: Life with Mo. Life without her.

He stood up, scooted his chair under his desk and turned off his computer, then grabbed his laptop. He was sick of himself and the endless woe-to-me pool he wallowed in. Even his self-pitying thought, "Everything he'd worked for died when Maureen did," wasn't fully honest. Only half of what he worked for and lived for had passed on when she did. He still had their daughter, and who knows, maybe a grandbaby too.

He hit the lights and hefted his rucksack. Soon, with any luck, he'd be in a better writing space *and* headspace. For a moment he wondered if he should've told Theresa his plan, then shook his head. Where he spent his time wasn't her business and she'd just worry. Besides, though she'd be skeptical, he could write—or not write, heh heh—just as easily in the boonies as he could at home.

And if Aisha was intent on setting up a temporary home in Greenridge, wherever that was, with this aunt whoever she was, in the hopes of connecting with her birth mom—who back in the day had seemed level-headed, but now he worried was a callous flake . . . well, he wasn't going to just abandon her to the wolves and wilds. He'd take up residence in one of the cabins that were "so far beyond cool that he couldn't possibly imagine how cool they were," to quote Aisha, and support her in whatever ways he could. His daughter was the only family he had left and if anything came between them, damaged their relationship, or hurt her it would be over his dead body.

What's ahead for Charles and Sam? Find out in HOOKED, Book 2 in the River's Sigh B & B series, coming Spring 2015!

About Ev Bishop

 **Ev Bishop** is a longtime columnist with the *Terrace Standard,* and her other non-fiction articles and essays have been published across North America. Her true love, however, is fiction, and she writes in a variety of lengths and genres. If you're a short story lover or read other genres alongside Romance, visit www.evbishop.com to learn more.

Some short story publications include: "Not All Magic is Nice," *Pulp Literature* (forthcoming), "The Picture Book," *Every Day Fiction Magazine*, "Riddles," *100 Stories for Queensland,* "On the Wall," *Every Day Fiction Magazine,* "My Mom is a Freak," *Cleavage: Breakaway Fiction for Real Girls*, "HVS," "Red Bird," and "Wishful," (available through Ether Books).

Women's Fiction novels include *Bigger Things* (Winding Path Books 2014), which is available in digital or paperback wherever books are sold, and *Mosaic* (forthcoming). She also writes romance under the pen name Toni Sheridan (*The Present*, Pelican Book Group, 2012, and *Drummer Boy*, Pelican Book Group, 2014).